Diamond Geezers

Greg Williams was born and lives in North London. He is the editor of *The Esquire Book of Sports Writing* (Penguin, 1995). Formerly Senior Editor of *Esquire*, he is now the Deputy Editor of *Arena* and is currently working on his second novel.

Diamond Geezers

*

Greg Williams

FOURTH ESTATE • *London*

First published in Great Britain in 1997 by
Fourth Estate Limited
6 Salem Road
London W2 4BU

5 7 9 10 8 6

A catalogue record for this book is available from
the British Library.

ISBN 1-85702-749-3

Typeset by MATS, Southend-on-Sea, Essex
Printed in Great Britain by Clays Ltd., St. Ives plc, Bungay, Suffolk

For Lisa

Acknowledgements

Thanks to:
MA, DB, RB, MD, SH, TH, AH, JI, MM,
GM, DM, EP, NKR, AS, JS, TS
and my family for all their
support and encouragement.
Special thanks to
JG and CU
for sorting me out.

Chapter One

It was just a job. Nothing personal.

On occasion Trevor would chase the slags for months – tune into the pub sub-babble, visit a string of poxy flats and broken-down bedsits, kick in doors at dawn, scare blubbering, grief-stricken girlfriends and their sticky kids, listen to everyday hard-luck stories worn smooth as pebbles from years of overuse.

No one understood. They didn't look at it from his point of view. He had a job to do, money to collect.

And catching the mugs was the easy bit. What really got on his tits was the bit after he'd netted them. Having to listen to the inept excuses and the pleas for clemency, witnessing the exodus of dignity and smelling the fear upon them.

It ruined his day. Worked its way into his clothes, clung to his skin. But the worst were the tossers who couldn't take a bit of stick with some honour, especially with family watching. No self-respect. That's what got them in the situation in the first place. It was a fucking embarrassment.

He was only doing his job. It weren't personal.

Take the other week. A bit of bother with some geezer who owed Ron a ton. It weren't a lot of money, but it was business. It was over on this estate in Euston, and he'd had trouble over there before, so he put a rounders bat (easier to conceal and better in confined spaces – like hallways – than a baseball bat, which stays in the boot for straightening out motoring altercations) inside his jacket, just in case. A little bit of insurance. Never can be too careful. *KnowotImean?*

Trevor rings the doorbell and this young bird answers the door. He storms in giving it the large, getting his foot inside the door, baying for her old man. It turns out the geezer he's after is some fucking war veteran, eighty years old if he's a day.

He's the bird's fucking *grandfather*. He's sitting in the lounge watching TV and shits himself when he hears the commotion. But he ain't concerned about getting a slap from Trevor, he's more worried about catching it from his granddaughter who's standing there in a white-bra-gone-grey doing her nut because he's been pissing away his readies on the gee gees while some stop-at-nothing Ralphed up hard case comes knocking on the door asking for money that's marked for rent.

Once she's got a dressing-gown on she only makes the geezer fucking limp over to the front door, apologise, and turn over half his week's pension. The old git can barely fucking speak he's so decrepit. And Trevor's feeling a right nonce standing there holding an offensive weapon inside his jacket while an eighty-year-old war veteran tries to work out terms for repayment.

Silly old cunt.

Other times they'd come just by chance. Like tonight.

He was footing it along a mutilated walkway on some estate off Manor Park when he heard the buzz-fart of a scooter pulling into the courtyard below. The driver came to a halt, jumped off and opened up a container on the back marked with a sticker saying 'Driver carries no cash'. He balanced a greasy cardboard box on the seat of the scooter and reached into his pocket for a piece of paper. He looked at it closely, couldn't find the address, so took off his helmet.

Sometimes you get lucky.

Trevor recognised him immediately. The cheeky Paki kid. Zaffir something. Into Ron for a K, more with the fucking juice. He'd stopped his payments three weeks ago and disappeared. Trevor had been looking for him all over, but the kid had done a bunk. That was the kind of shit that Trevor couldn't bear, the kind of shit that really got on his nerves. Bang out of order.

The kid was taking a fucking liberty.

Zaffir folded away the piece of paper and began to make his way up the piss-reeky stairwell. Trevor hid himself at the top listening to Zaffir's carpet-quiet Nike footsteps. Copped himself a nice pair of Footscapes with that money, thought

Trevor. A broken light flickered above him, seemingly in sync with the gusts of icy wind that blasted up the stairwell. Zaffir was getting closer. Trevor could make out the sound of a nylon jacket as the surfaces brushed together. He waited until Zaffir was close enough to smell the beer on his breath before he stepped from the shadows.

'And where the *fuck* do you think you're going?' he asked. Zaffir stopped still.

'Speak up, son. Where the fuck are you going?'

'Second floor. Pizza.'

'*Pizza?*' Trevor sounded like Zaffir had said Uganda.

'Yeah.' Something passed across Zaffir's face. *He knew the score.* He was blinking too often. He was trying to swallow the fear.

'You getting paid for this?' continued Trevor.

''Course.'

'And what are you doing with the money?'

'Nothing.'

'Wrong answer. I'll tell you what you're doing with it – you're mugging me off. That's what you're doing. You're vexing me.'

'Look, I'm gonna get you your money,' said Zaffir, trying to be conciliatory. Trevor cut him off.

'I've been chasing all over fucking London looking for you.'

Zaffir shook his head. 'Look, I ain't got nothing to give you at the moment, all right? Why do you think I've got this job? I ain't got no money.' Trevor remained impassive. Acted like Zaffir didn't exist. 'There's a few things I've got to sort.'

'A little habit?'

'No. No habit. Cashflow, innit.' The boy was pale. Could have passed as an Itie or a spic. Thick black hair tied in a ponytail. He was perhaps an inch taller than Trevor but didn't fill the space as well. Younger than his stubble suggested. There were no lines around his eyes, marks on his skin. He was seventeen, tops.

Trevor stepped close. Zaffir tensed, his eyes closed as if he didn't want to see what was coming, his mind doubting his legs and heart in what was to come.

'I don't think I'm making myself clear, son,' said Trevor. 'I don't think we're on the same bus. *KnowotImean?*' He squared his body, grabbed the pizza box and frisbeed it down the rank steps.

'For fuck's sake!' yelled Zaffir and took off, bouncing down the stairs. Trevor headed after him, thinking the kid was making a run for it, but touched down at the bottom of the steps right next to his quarry who was crouched over the steaming food.

'What the fuck did you do that for?' shouted Zaffir. The mist of fear had evaporated from his voice. 'I'll have to go all the way back now.'

Trevor shook his head, as if in sympathy. 'You don't get it, do you?' he said. 'You're in above your neck, son. You owe me folding, plus the juice. When you're on the cuff you speak to me. You hide, you only make it worse. Excuses. All day long I have to listen to fucking excuses from slags like you.'

'Then why don't you go fuck yourself?' said Zaffir, getting to his feet.

That's when Trevor hit him.

He punched Zaffir so hard on the chin that he heard the kid's neck snap back. But it was the following noise that was more sinister – the heavy, hollow, low sound of the kid's head smashing against a raw brick window ledge. Trevor stood there for a few moments listening to his racing heart, his chest rising and falling rapidly. The fingers of his right hand opened very slowly, like some flower in bloom captured by time-lapse photography. Zaffir didn't move. Trevor turned him over. Claret all over the place. There was a gash on the back of his head so deep he could fuck it. If he wasn't already brown bread he was on the way out.

Feeling in his jacket pocket for his car keys Trevor looked down at the pizza which was crumpled on the floor like a wino's jacket. Ham and pineapple.

He hated fucking pineapple.

Zaffir was late. He was pissed off and he was late. Not only that, he'd been driving round the wrong estate for the last fifteen looking for an address that was only a couple of minutes down the road. When he pulled into Burlingham Court on the Merrivale Estate he glanced up at the dimly lit walkways, looking for movement. After a spate of attacks and robberies Frank, the Pizza Shack manager, had decided that the delivery boys should be accompanied by a minder. No one too heavy, you understand, just another pair of eyes, another body.

That's when he hooked up with this black kid, Marshall, a right fucking nutter, who got a perverse pleasure from hacking sputum, snorting discharge and spluttering phlegm all over the floppy-boxed tomato and mozzarella. He'd always say the same thing as he flicked the moist secretion on to the oily surface, 'Probably makes it taste better anyway, innit.'

Other times Marshall would go quiet, plant his enormous Sony earphones – the size of two fruitbowls – either side of his head and crank up his Walkman with enough volume to put his central nervous system into shock. Marshall was into drum and bass. Zaffir thought it was still called Jungle, but Gerald said that nobody called it that any more. *Nobody.* So, rather than engage in hostilities over it, neither ever fed a cassette into the car stereo. As Zaffir followed the fanned sweep of his Escort's headlights from one deserted street to another, machine-gun beats and the heartbeat of the bass leaked from the Walkman, accompanying the bronchitic rattle of the car's ropy exhaust. Given that he could still hear the drum and bass, even when he had the car radio locked into FREAK FM, Zaffir considered it a miracle Marshall had not gone deaf.

One Wednesday night Marshall didn't turn up for work. No warning, no farewell. He just didn't show up, disappeared into London, the way people do. Zaffir didn't suppose that it made much difference: Frank had already decided that security was a waste of time anyway. Too expensive. So Zaffir was working on his Jack Jones again, back on the fucking moped, waking up half of London with its mosquito wheeze.

The dosh was a little bit better now though, but not much. Every little counts, he'd say to himself as he loaded another American Pepperoni or Neptune's Treasure into the crusty carrier on the back of his scooter. Every penny mattered now that he had this debt hanging over him like an executioner's axe.

It had been against his better instincts to borrow money from strangers. But where the fuck else was he supposed to get it? The bank didn't take him seriously when he asked for a loan. *And how are you proposing to repay us, Mr Khan?* some girl with a silk scarf round her neck scoffed through the bullet-proof glass. *And what is it for? Is it necessary?* How was some *harami* in a BHS cotton–rayon mix blouse meant to understand about Mecca? He'd have more chance of getting the money by saying that he wanted to deal crack in Dalston than by telling them that he wanted to send his mum on a pilgrimage. There wasn't enough space on the application form to explain that she was worried about not going to heaven.

That's why he'd gone to Ron Chisholm. Well, not to Ron directly, of course, but to Trevor, Ron's brother who took care of things for Ron on the Taylforth Estate where Zaffir lived. Trevor – who Zaffir supposed was in his mid thirties, always wore a navy Ralph Lauren cotton jacket and white trainers and kept wiping his nose with the heel of his hand, even when he didn't need to – had focused his grey eyes on Zaffir and explained the terms and conditions. Before he peeled off twenty second-hand bull's-eyes Trevor said that he was going to ask him to offer his word that he'd brass up. And if his word wasn't good enough Trevor knew where Zaffir and his mum lived, Trevor added, pointing a bony finger at him.

Not any longer he didn't. Zaffir's mum was out of the country for four months: a trip to Saudi Arabia followed by some time with the family in Pakistan to dry her arthritis out. Meanwhile Zaffir was staying round at his mate Warren's. The plan was to do a bunk on the money for a few months, then suddenly appear with all the cash, plus interest. Profuse apologies, no hard feelings and all that. With a bit of luck he would escape a kicking.

So what he didn't need was a slow week. He'd had a couple of days off with the flu that had been doing the rounds; felt like someone had pumped his head full of dirty bathwater. The rest of the week had been a scramble to try and make up the lost time. If he could stash a hundred a week for the next three months it should see him clear, keep Trevor off his back. Worse than that he'd had Mandy, his girlfriend, on his case all last week, calling him up, playing stupid games. Phoning him and then getting all arsey.

'What's the matter?' he'd ask her.

'I'm all right,' she'd reply sulkily.

'Mandy, tell me what's the matter.'

'Nothing.'

'Is it something I've done?'

'Maybe.'

'What have I done?'

'*Nothing.*'

'Is it something I've said?'

'No.'

'It's something I've said, ain't it?'

'Maybe.'

And on and on. It seemed to Zaffir she only ever belled him for a whinge. It was getting beyond a joke, really titting him off.

So all he needed was to get a turning wrong this evening and end up in the wrong courtyard on the wrong estate trying to decipher Frank's illegible handwriting on a delivery form saturated with cooking grease. He only realised he was on the wrong estate after knocking up some terrified old granny who wouldn't open the door to him. She said she had a dog. Told him to go away before she called the filth.

Funny thing was the right place looked exactly the same as the wrong place. Same difference. The pizza was probably cold by now anyway. Never mind, they can heat it up in the microwave. Good as new.

He locked his helmet on to the scooter and started heading up the stairs towards the third floor.

Talk about bad luck.

It took Zaffir a few moments to work out who it was standing at the top of the stairs. The light was behind him, so his face was shrouded in darkness . . . *Trevor Chisholm.* It was the spite in his voice that finally made the penny drop. Zaffir couldn't believe it. *Of all the fucking people.*

He'd rehearsed this meeting in his head dozens of times but the script went out the window as the fear kicked in and his stomach tightened and his ribcage struggled to hang on to his exploding heart. He was pissing in the wind with someone like Trevor, someone who made a living from scenting the funky blue hash of fear. Fuck the Pepsi taste challenge, geezers like Trevor could suss the taste of fear faster than a dog can find a turd lolling in a playground.

But he was surprised how angry he became when Trevor knocked the Hawaiian Special out of his hands. His shitty week oozed up into his throat, crystallised in that one feat of malevolence. Balling his fists into tight, nutty rocks he swore at Trevor with a boiling, ruinous hatred.

It was the last thing he knew before a kind of hush settled over his world.

Chapter Two

Some days he got out of bed and he felt fine. Others he didn't.

It was a cheap trick. He knew that much, but he still had faith in it. Since childhood Russell Fisher had believed that getting out of bed could be made easier by keeping his eyes closed for the first five minutes after abandoning the sheets. It was a gimmick employed mainly during the cold winter months. And this was February, maybe not the coldest, but certainly the bleakest month of the year: the month when the sky was so low across London that it looked like it had fallen from above and settled on the rooftops, the month street people huddled on Tube platforms, their hair turned wiry by dust and the vestiges of last summer's warmth.

At six in the morning, it was still inky outside.

He swung his legs from the jumbled bed and padded over to turn the gas fire on. The machine hissed to life and Russell stood in his boxer shorts with his eyes closed, his breathing still set for deep sleep. He stood feeling the warmth of the bed rising from his body and the heat of the fire stinging his calves. The bathroom was a flight of stairs down from his two-room bedsit, so he would have to summon the energy to get there. His bed was next to the fire, which was next to the cooker which was next to the ceramic sink, which was above the tiny battered fridge that kept him awake at night with its uneven humming. He'd put a curtain over the entrance to the other room; it would be too cold to go in there until spring.

He turned his body slightly so that he thought he was facing the sink. He opened his eyes and there she was, staring right at him; Cindy C wearing nothing but a pink fuck-me swimsuit, still wet from the ocean, her hair slicked back and dripping. Russell gave her a wink, but she didn't smile back.

Taking the key to his room Russell trotted down the stairs to the bathroom. It was used by the upstairs tenant – Mr Abache, a Nigerian who worked nights as a security guard and studied for a business diploma during the day – and by Russell's landlord, Mr Oza, and the staff of his grocery shop below.

As he relieved himself, his feet warm on the glutinous linoleum, Russell looked out at the muddle of crumbling Victoriana that was Illingford. Most of the buildings had been constructed well over a century ago during a time of optimism and progress, when the wealth of the empire had jammed the docks of east London. That was before half of it was flattened by German bombs. Now concrete and glass interrupted the even flow of red Victorian brick like milky white caps in a row of ancient teeth. Nothing stirred outside, not even a cat patrolling its nocturnal beat. In the distance the lights of the City glimmered like sunlight striking a fish in a pool of water. Russell yawned and thought of his Uncle Vic, who worked in the motor trade. 'Time enough to sleep when I'm dead,' he would say, necking a quick cup of rosie before shooting off to Penge to bicker over the price of another uninsurable death-trap. (His other favourite, always uttered in a tone of unimaginable persecution, was: 'That is *fucking* highway robbery.')

Although he'd managed to keep it up for years, Russell was still always quietly satisfied by his ability to get to the gym most mornings. Once his stomach had finished bubbling with early morning nausea he liked to feel the blood rolling through his veins. A creature of order and habit, and knowing that he needed every bit of help he could get, he laid out his clothes on a chair by the bed the night before. His shirt, jacket and jeans hung empty, their silhouette fleshing out the lines of a two-dimensional man.

As he gunned his Renault 5 GT Turbo down the rain-slicked streets towards the gym he was slowed only by a couple of tinkling milk trucks from Lord Rayleigh's dairy. Waiting at a red light he watched a sleepy-eyed Asian newsagent fussing with his brown wool scarf in between laying out the day's news and cracking open fresh cigarette cartons, his hands still ringing from the astringent bite of the bare steel shutters that enshrined his shop through the darkness.

There was only one person Russell knew who would be up at this time; the caretaker at the gym, John Skinner, who was known mostly as 'Skin' but to some as 'the troll', on account of his squalid basement home beneath the gym. It was only last year that he'd agreed to stop cooking on his primus stove after gym regulars had had a whip-round to buy him a microwave. He'd told Russell that he 'still couldn't see the fuckin' point of the thing,' and was now convinced that it would cause a tumour 'the size of a bull's bollock' to swell inside his stomach.

Russell thudded his fist on the sooty door. Inside, Skin's uneven fat man's footsteps could be heard trailing across the floor. 'That you, Russ?' he asked, not waiting for a reply before the door swung open.

'Silly old sod,' said Russell. 'Could have been anyone. You could be fucking brown bread.'

'But you ain't anyone.' Skin leaned against the door frame, his bulk blocking Russell's view inside the flat. It smelled of cooking oil and damp. 'You want the key or what?'

'Yeah.'

'Just made a brew,' said Skin. His head ballooned from the scooped neck of his shirt like a pink bubble. White tufts of hair poked out from under his thick underarm flab.

'I'm all right, mate,' said Russell. 'I'll pop by after.'

'Yeah, well turn the fucking lights off when you're done and clean up after yourself,' warned Skin with mock seriousness.

Pinching Skin's right cheek Russell blew the fat man a mock kiss. 'It's all right, mate. I don't sweat.'

'On your bike, you silly cunt.'

It started as distant thunder rising up from deep beneath the streets, like some subterranean explosion. The vibration of the Central Line pulsed through the clogged London soil and shook the bench Russell was perched on. A plastic bottle of Diet Pepsi bounced on the floor, its contents effervescent against the washed-out red of the linoleum.

As superstitious as an old Cypriot lady at the altar Russell followed a routine when getting himself ready to work out: stripping his upper body and pulling on his old claret sweatshirt first, he then pulled on his green cotton Lonsdale shorts, his socks (left foot first) and trainers (right foot first).

Russell could tell that Skin had shined the mirrors which lined the walls of the gym the night before from the smell of cleaning fluid that had settled over the underlying odour of stale sweat. Often his reflection would be obscured by the dried drops of salt water that had flown from the boiling brows of the wretched and exhausted. Since his teens Russ had liked to come to the gym, pump up his chest, whittle away at his stomach, stretch out his hamstrings. Maybe even rattle the speedball and thud the heavy hanging bags.

At this time in the morning, as long as there were no trains passing beneath, the gym was the stillest place that Russell could imagine. It reminded him of a pond he used to visit when he was a kid, up near the reservoir, a place where there was never any wind. He would crouch by the water and feel calm; here it felt as if the problems of the world could be smoothed over like a patch of disrupted sand.

For a place where so much energy was expended the gym possessed a serenity rarely found in the city. Sometimes, as he hunched over, his hands on his knees, pulling deep draughts of oxygen into his aching lungs, Russell was sure that he could hear the blood rushing around his body as loud as water crashing from a dam, such was the silence in the room.

During the day the place was largely frequented by the kind of men who have worked with their hands all their lives: tough, thirsty men with ears like old wallets and lungs the size of Hoover bags. The nature of their work left them no need to visit a gym. They came only because it was there. They came because they liked to box even though they skipped like they were wearing army boots and wore athletic supports to stop their knees from splintering.

Russell stretched out and did fifteen minutes' skipping to warm his muscles before doing half an hour of bench presses and some bicep supersets with the tarnished barbells. The smell of the iron would stay on his hands all day, a reminder, along with the dull ache in the rest of his upper body, of his morning exertions. Ten minutes with the speedball, another ten shadow boxing, and then three hundred crunching sit-ups took him up to seven thirty.

Rolling his shoulders and neck Russell lurched towards the changing room, his mouth feeling sulphurous and dry. Sticking his head in the clammy grey basin he turned the tap on and lapped the cold, sharp water which made his teeth ache.

After collecting his towel he twisted the creaky faucet in the shower. It was bordered by a run-off channel laid in the tiles which had become coated with a blanket of algae. A soap dish hung lamely to his left, a hole where it had been fastened leaking tributaries of rust on the wall.

He cursed Skin as he walked back to the benches through the dust and grime. It seemed that no matter how thoroughly he washed his feet they would always be caked with filth, suspicious-looking stains and human hair before he got back to the bench. On his way the temptation to look in the mirror was one he could not resist. When others were getting changed and he didn't want to appear vain his technique was to pretend to have something in his eye and go to the mirror to remove it; that way he could sneak a peek at his reddened skin. Beneath it he was as hard-bodied as a bee.

A quick Italian shower, another look in the mirror and Russell was off; remembering Skin's words he switched off the electricity and the room was cast in a blue half-light. Hazy sunshine battled to squeeze through the blackened windows at the top of the hall. Further along the wall the windows had been blacked out with old copies of *Boxing News*. Russell treble-locked the door and lugged his old Adidas sports bag back over to Skin's gaff.

The door was slightly ajar, so Russell went straight in. The old man was slouched in an armchair having fallen asleep watching breakfast TV. Crusty foam bulged from the wool weave that had split long ago under its owner's weight. The chair was not so much an object of repose, more part of its owner, like some fabric goitre.

Russell turned off the TV. There was traffic on the roads now, a low murmur that made the walls shake slightly. He looked through to Skin's kitchen at the back of the flat. A knife was plunged deep into a tub of canary yellow marge and a bag of sliced white sat on a sea of crumbs next to a calcified kettle and bag of Red Label. It reminded him of the dark kitchen where, as a boy, if there was nothing on the telly, he would eat a doleful Sunday lunch with his parents and sister. Between jumbo mouthfuls his father, Eric, a sprawling, voluble warehouseman, would berate his son for his lack of ambition and bemoan his inertia and absence of enterprise, before regaling Russell with stories of his own triumphant youth, turned sour by an accidental pregnancy and unwanted marriage.

No one deserved that, his father would say. And once it has happened nothing can ever be the same.

Russell's silence would fill every recess of the solemn, tidy house as loud as a scream. His mother, who spent her days clipping money-off vouchers from newspapers, dusting china ornaments and reading *Woman's Realm* (before the invention of daytime TV), would shuffle back and forth in her pink nylon slippers, carrying dishes to and from the worktop saying nothing, lest her husband should tire of lamenting his misfortune and look for a fresh target. Occasionally she would look at her silent son and say impatiently, 'Oh, *stop it*, Russell.'

It was only later Russell would realise that the well-stocked medicine cabinet, with its rainbow of prescribed orbs, ovals and capsules, was the reason for her silence. She had always been a fragile woman; the strained smile on her face in the photo that hung in the front room – the photo of a newly married couple – bore witness to the fear that ruled her heart and paralysed her in the face of her tyrant husband. From his early teens Russell could have used his bulk to silence his father but had always resisted dishing out a beating solely because it would shatter the fanciful notion of family that his mother cradled to her breast like a winning lottery ticket.

The family took a drubbing in the early eighties when Russell's older sister, Claire, left home to have a baby with a

Trinidadian in Harlesden. Claire was resourceful in her independence and still managed to keep a comfortable home despite her relative poverty. Her father had refused to go and visit. He had never seen his grandson and would not have his daughter's name mentioned in the house. He was aware that his wife made clandestine excursions across London lugging cakes fondly baked in her own oven and that she kept a shoe-box full of pictures of her grandson stuffed deep in her bedside cabinet. Once, after leaving home (and when he knew his father would not be around), Russell went to visit his mother and found her in the living-room with the photos spread around her like some melancholic picnicker, gently sobbing.

There were things he wanted to say to his parents, but he never knew how, so in the long years that followed his sister's departure Russell took his concerns out of the house and to school. *Guardian*-reading teachers at the comprehensive he irregularly attended looked upon him with frustrated optimism. Here, they thought, is a young man with great potential who has been alienated by life; if only he could give a little, make some sign, we could open up to him the vast possibilities that would liberate his imprisoned spirit.

They never got very far, although in fact Russell had not minded school much. Indifferent towards academic life – he abandoned formal education as early as he legally could – he distinguished himself at games (a canny midfield hustler in the Paul Ince mould) as well as liking history (First World War, the Rise of the Nazis) and English literature, for which he received his one and only 'O'-level pass (grade A) after an original and spirited interpretation of Graham Greene's 'The Destroyers'. 'That,' he would tell his mates on the bus, brandishing the flaky paperback, 'is a fucking good read.'

This was years after he had grasped that his existence in this mean, dispiriting family would pass with time. As an adolescent he would shut himself off from the arguments, the silent dinners, his father's beatings, and sit patiently, just waiting for life to begin. Much of the time he roamed the neighbourhood with his friends, smashing milk bottles and playing football, returning home scratched and smoky long after dark.

Where his father was loud-mouthed and indiscreet – when Russell thought of his father he always pictured him sitting watching TV, scratching his crotch and cursing the football results – Russell was reticent and watchful. For Eric Fisher the world was a bag of shite. The Prime Minister was an inadequate, his family a disappointing liability, and his football team, West Ham, a constant source of embarrassment. 'You're just a bunch of cunts,' he'd shout at his wife and son, and strangers, late at night, when the pubs had turned out.

He'd even shouted it at Russell and his first steady girlfriend, Jane, after one particularly vitriolic lunch tagged on to a Sunday drinking binge. Russell had suffered this kind of thing so many times before that he was immune to the stinging words, the heat of bitterness. But Jane had been upset by the experience and soon afterwards found a way of extricating herself from the relationship.

Jane had been the first girl he'd ever brought home to meet the family. He'd done it, albeit reluctantly, for his mother, to give her something to think about when the house was empty. Jane was good at getting on with people, had been working at Boots peddling Max Factor and No 7. She was a couple of years older than him and had lived away from home for a while. There was something grown-up that he'd liked about her. She liked his quietness, his backbone. But one night soon after the incident with his father she took him out to a Mexican restaurant and, over a jug of sangria and two orders of chicken enchiladas, broke the bad news. She didn't want to see him any longer. Russell had felt stupid, had got dressed up for the occasion in his only jacket and tie, but it wasn't much of a thing, wasn't anything that hadn't happened in the past or wouldn't happen again. That's what he told himself. Inside he was hurt like never before. Even his father had never inflicted that much damage. He still felt her absence like an amputee senses a missing limb.

There had been plenty of girls after Jane. Disco dollies and gummy one-night stands, plump pub girls and pram-pushing school dropouts. Russell put himself about, though never with any false promises. But after Jane his liaisons had no teeth, no intent. They were plain and honest and simple and girls knew that. He'd never slammed a door to impede a flying shoe from some disappointed lover, never avoided phone calls from someone who expected his company on a Saturday night. He walked away without any remonstrations or tearful admonishments. He never expected an invitation to stay and he was never offered one.

With Jane it had been different: he took her to Brighton a month after they'd met and sent her flowers at work on Monday. He'd never done that before and she belled him on the mobile. 'People never usually send me flowers unless I've slept with them,' she whispered. Shielding his mobile from another trainee sparky who was fitting a light switch on the other side of the room, Russell pointed out that he *had* slept with her. 'Yes,' she said. 'But it's different.'

Russell never knew what she meant by that but, in the way that men don't allow the unanswered questions in their lives to become obstacles to contentment, he chose not to ask whether his life could be improved by pursuing it.

They went to Brighton a lot after that, ploughing through distant tracts of suburbia where a settled man might choose to raise a family – Norbury, Norwood, Purley – down the A23 late at night. And when they finally silenced the engine of Russell's belligerent RS 2000 and their bags were stowed in their room they would eat scampi and chips on the lunar beach before returning to the intimacy of their spongy B&B bed. It was all that Mr Hargreaves, the balding owner of the hotel could do when they returned, red-cheeked and oily mouthed, not to offer Russell a genial little wink.

It was ten years since Jane, ten years of treading water, plodding along, getting by. Ten years of wondering what might have been. He knew that he wouldn't be an electrician all his life; couldn't wait to move out of that shitty bedsit, maybe even leave London, get some sunshine on his back and a hand slipped lovingly inside his own. Looking at the tub of margarine on Skin's kitchen counter Russell knew that he was ready for change and that somehow, if he willed it hard enough, it would come as surely as fireworks in November.

In the living room Skin started breathing heavily in his sleep, hazy nasal sounds, like a hibernating grizzly. Russell thought it best not to wake him and slipped quietly out the front door, making sure that it was locked behind him, and into the London babble.

Chapter Three

Councillor Malcolm Goodge stood behind his desk and waved the newspaper in the air before flinging it into the centre of the room. It settled on the worn beige carpet forming an awkward, ugly shape.

'I don't *believe* it,' Hedge bellowed, clenching his fists with frustration. 'I just don't fucking believe it. What the hell are we supposed to do? Can someone tell me? Please? I mean just what the fuck are we supposed to do? How the fuck am *I* supposed to prevent race attacks? And now this shit.' He gestured with his thumb through a large PVC-framed window behind him.

Three floors below, on the street, a couple of hundred people were milling around chanting slogans. Dotted among the crowd were the usual suspects: three-year radicals, their rucksacks stuffed with copies of *Socialist Worker* and university essays. But the majority of the crowd were not the usual demo rentamob. It was mainly made up of Asians, of all ages and backgrounds – predominantly Pakistani, but some Indians as well – concern and anger buried deep in their brows.

Goodge ran his hand forward from the crown of his head, flattening his hair. It was a repetitive gesture he made when troubled, and he'd been doing it a lot recently. Despite his pugnacious nature Goodge didn't enjoy being in tight corners. It made him feel smaller than his five foot six, slightly more overweight than his plump midriff might suggest. And then there was the question of his hair – which had gone from a well-groomed raven black to a thinning lattice-work of flecked grey during his five years as leader of Illingford council.

'I get hung, drawn and quartered by the press because this guy happens to be living in a council house and claiming benefit as well as working for some fucking pizza joint. I mean what the fuck am I supposed to do?'

Lesley Dare waited for him to come to the end of his spiel and left a little pause just to let him absorb the empty bluster of his speech. Her manner was cool, professional, with a hint of patronisation; her voice possessed the clipped disengagement of the southern upper middle class.

'What are they calling you this time?' she asked.

'What do you mean?'

'In the paper.'

'Oh, Gormless Goodge.'

'Makes a change from Comrade Malcolm though,' laughed Dare.

Goodge turned to the window.

'Don't go too close, they could see you,' said Dare, stretching her arm along the back of the sofa. 'Might incite them. You don't want to have to spend your life under police protection do you?'

Goodge sat on the edge of his desk and leaned back. Fingers intertwined behind his head. 'Sometimes, Lesley, death threats seem as good as a blowjob compared to the shit that gets flung at me down in the chamber.'

Lesley raised her eyebrows. Crow's feet showed up faintly at the sides of her eyes like tributaries of a major river. Inanimate, she looked thirty. Animate she was pushing her age: forty. Malcolm had always liked the way she dressed. Fashionable without ever being too effortful. Businesslike but flirty enough for her to be able to take advantage of the men who were susceptible to that kind of thing. Like him. Sometimes she tied her auburn hair back, but for the last couple of months she'd grown the fringe long and swept it to the side, like the models in the fashion magazines. He liked that – the fact she cared, looked after herself. There was a part of Goodge that thought it might be for his benefit.

Lesley lit a cigarette and re-crossed her legs. 'I don't know what you're getting so worked up about,' she said, waving her hand to disperse the smoke. 'These things always blow over. They'll shout things outside the town hall for a couple of hours. Throw things at a few policemen, get bored and then go home for their tea and watch themselves on the local news. Maybe video it to send to their relatives in Birmingham. It's really no big deal, Malcolm. It's too bloody cold to stand around demonstrating. What we have to worry about is finding the money to deal with Hillacre before the press get hold of that damn report.'

Hillacre was a large council-run 'multi-dwelling unit', as some parts of the social services called it. It was one of half a dozen last-chance saloons for single mothers to grab a quick gin and lime before their children were taken into care. Mess up here and your kids were placed in children's homes and you were on the street. A recent council-commissioned report, which Goodge had suppressed, had denounced Hillacre as unfit for human habitation. The sanitary conditions were described as 'grossly inadequate', the heating system hadn't worked for two of the previous three winters and the residents' attitude towards the home was 'blasé to the point of anarchy'.

The last criticism was the one that could cause the council the most embarrassment. The report had discovered that Paul Copping, Hillacre's forty-year-old odd-job man, had been on the job himself. After impregnating a young mother of twenty-three he turned his attention to her eight-year-old daughter whom he terrorised, with the mother's knowledge, for a period estimated at six months. The mother, it was later discovered, had been paid in crack cocaine by Copping, who had three previous convictions for paedophilia.

Another resident, Belinda 'Tabby' Stevens, was running a call-girl service from her flat. She'd brought in two girls she'd known from her days on the streets and encouraged Hillacre residents to supplement their giros by servicing the salesmen who called in on the way home to their wives in suburban Essex.

Goodge kneaded the muscles in the back of his neck, his knuckles showing white. 'Hillacre can wait,' he said. 'I'm not worried about Hillacre at the moment. We can do the necessary work and move the girls. By the time the press find out the whole thing'll be over. Nothing for them to get their teeth into. It's that guy Rasheed that worries me. The man's a menace. He's managed to convince half of the Asian community that I'm the one running around committing racist beatings. He's got their ears. He's powerful. He makes me nervous.'

Lesley smiled. She was the kind of woman who gave up her smiles easily, a big white slash that seemed to blot out half her face. A colleague had once commented that her smile had become her erogenous zone to such an extent that she could probably conceive through her mouth.

'Malcolm, you've got to relax,' she said, eyeing a 'Solidarity with the ANC' poster pinned to the back of the door, its edges curling like a stale sandwich. 'This isn't a big deal. What you do is very simple: you arrange to meet Rasheed. Have a big showdown with the police, get your picture taken shaking hands with Rasheed and give them the "offering security to all residents of the borough whatever their race, creed or colour" bit. It's kid's stuff and you know it.'

Goodge stopped twirling his Biro round his index finger. 'What time is it?' he asked.

Lesley checked her watch. 'Half five.'

Goodge picked up a TV remote from behind his in-tray and zapped the TV. He flicked through the channels until he found the local news. A smartly dressed young black man was holding a microphone to a shorter Asian man of about fifty who spoke rapidly and confidently from beneath a thick moustache. Beneath him a caption read 'Councillor Abdul Rasheed'. Goodge groaned and turned the sound up.

'. . . further to that many within the community are asking questions about the leadership of the council. If Malcolm Goodge cannot guarantee our safety, if he is unable to find those who attacked and brutally beat Zaffir Khan, if he cannot motivate the police force to provide adequate patrols within the borough, then very clearly he is not the man we elected. He is failing to represent the community – many of whom voted for his promises of a borough free from racial harassment – and we shall see what the community feels about this at the next council election.' The camera panned to the presenter, but before he could open his mouth the television flashed black.

'What the fuck did I tell you?' Goodge mumbled his words while trimming a loose bit of skin on his thumb with his teeth. 'Did I not say that man was a fucking menace?'

'So we have a rough couple of council meetings. So what?' asked Lesley. 'He's trying to threaten you. Trying to make out that if you don't come a courtin' he won't deliver the Asian vote. So what do you do? You take him aside and agree to do whatever he wants. Make him feel like the big man, get him on your side and then dump him when the thing blows over.'

'He'll be all over the papers tomorrow,' said Goodge. 'We really don't need all this shit right now . . .'

'Like there's ever a good time for adverse publicity . . .'

'There's no need to be facetious, Lesley. I just have a feeling that this shit is all getting out of hand.'

Lesley sighed theatrically and stood up. 'I've got to get on with a couple of things – got to be out of here early tonight, going to the theatre.'

Goodge was sliding along the wall, trying to peek out of the window. Outside a man with a bullhorn was trying to whip up the dwindling crowd.

'I wouldn't worry, Malcolm,' said Lesley. 'They're not going to lynch you. I doubt they'd even recognise you.'

'Reminds me of that saying,' said Malcolm, 'that there'll never be a revolution in this country because the royal family are such good shots. You know, we'd all be running up the Mall with scythes and machetes and they'd just pick us off like pheasants.'

'Or peasants. Anyway, Malcolm,' said Lesley, sashaying towards the door, 'looks like you'll be working late. Do use the back door on your way out. Buy you lunch tomorrow?'

'Yeah,' said Malcolm, watching her wiggle out of his office. He was starting to feel hungry already.

Chapter Four

Friday night at the Black Prince. Russell was surrounded by noise. A bass thumped from the stereo, a barman was shouting to a customer who had forgotten his change, a group of girls ridiculed a chicken-costumed man collecting money for needy kids – 'tortured tots' as he put it. Two great-gutted beer monsters in acrylic jumpers sat on tall stools chanting at each other. Older men with bellies like someone had stuffed basketballs down their trousers seemed perpetually to be passing pints out from the bar. A few teenagers with angular faces, mean expressions and ugly moods leaned against the wall sipping bottled lager. Broadened by snappy Stone Island jackets, baggy jeans and box-fresh trainers they ran restless hands through short hair and twiddled with huge sovereign rings that adorned their hands like golden plates. They monitored the bar; watching, laughing, learning.

Russell was going for broke on the *EastEnders* fruit machine. He'd pulled the old scam of turning the machine off once he'd won, to erase its memory of the payout, but the landlord had started whining, so he was now playing by legal means. The downside of winning was that during the payout the machine played a dismal digital version of the *EastEnders* theme tune.

'There you go,' he said as three cherries plopped into view and the coins rattled into the tray below. The landlord cast an eye over Russell as the machine started cranking out the theme tune again. 'Tell you what,' he said, shovelling out the coins, 'bite into a cherry and you'd hit something about the size of Mick's brain.'

'The only thing between your ears is your fucking nose,' said Mick.

'The only thing between your bird's tits is her belly button,' laughed Russell, slapping Mick on the back. They returned to their sticky table and picked among the sudsy Hofmeister glasses, ripped beer mats and brimming ashtrays for their drinks. Steve and Russell found themselves sitting on their own as Mick and Curtis were stalking a couple of birds who had been making eyes at them over the rim of their Bacardi and Cokes.

'Look at them two,' said Steve, nodding towards Mick and Curtis. 'On bush patrol again.'

Russell clocked the girls and gave them a not-even-with-yours-mate look. 'Where have Terry and Eamonn got to?' he asked Steve.

'Terry's brother's car's fucked,' said Steve, rubbing his eye. Steve hated smoky places. 'I told him not to buy that Jag, man. They've gone over to his yard to recharge the battery. *Chaa.* Ever since he got that motor he ain't had *nothing* but aggravation, man.'

Steve was Russell's oldest friend. The two had been knocking about with each other so long that nowadays they didn't even have to talk to be comfortable. Steve had had all his hair shaved off completely for several years now, which had earned him the nickname Marvin, after the boxer Marvin Hagler.

He was a powerful man, but tinged with a slight sadness, the result of a promising football career being ended at the age of twenty by some shitkicker (or 'quashie' as Steve preferred it) Millwall reserves stopper lumping him in the knee and rupturing his cruciate ligament. He was still sometimes recognised in the street, but this, as he pointed out to Russell, was little use to him as it was only ever men who came up to him and began conversations with the words, 'Didn't you used to play for West Ham reserves?' His argument was that had he played for Man United reserves he could still use it as a passport to getting laid.

Steve toyed with the gold hoop that pierced his left ear, listening to Russell's chat. Behind them Curtis had his tongue down a lip-gloss girl's throat. Russell noticed that the girl had an enormous cold sore at the side of her mouth.

'You heard Norman Grant got cancer?' asked Steve. Norman Grant was the former landlord of The Black Prince.

'You're joking aren'tcha?' said Russell, startled. 'Norman Grant? Must only be in his forties.'

'Don't matter how old you are, mate,' said Steve, finishing a pint. 'If they find out you've got cancer of the nerves and that, you're buying the farm and your family are going down the fucking coffin shop sharpish.'

'But how do you know when you've got it?' asked Russell, suddenly feeling lumps beneath his skin.

'It's all in the fucking detection, man,' said Steve, warming to his subject. 'You can live a righteous life, eat Bran Flakes every morning and run round the park, and it don't matter. You don't catch the Big C early enough then it's curtains. Might as well have spent all your folding on fags, chips, pizza and lager. My Uncle Clevie, right, he died of cancer of the colon, innit. Poor bastard couldn't even take a shit, had to wear one of them fucking colostomy bags like what the Queen Mum wears.'

'God bless her.' said Russell.

'They said to him that if he'd come in just two weeks earlier they could have saved him. But he'd been visiting family in Jamaica and by the time he got back the stuff had spread throughout him. Poor bastard just shrivelled up and died in front of us.'

Mick and Curtis interrupted Steve with a display of truly oafish belching. Every time one outdid the other a huge primeval bawl exuded from a number of people in the pub – AAAAAAAAAHHHHH – their mouths agape, tongues wagging, faces contorted like gargoyles. Curtis ran out of steam and gave up, informing the group the result would have been different if he'd been allowed to use his arse – AAAAAAAAAHHHHHHHH. The lip-gloss girls, unimpressed, moved around to the other side of the bar.

Wobbling unsteadily, Keith, an older regular of the pub, came over. His curly red hair fell in livid stripes across a pockmarked face which had a junky's beaten quality. His skin was so thin you could see the fluid moving beneath the surface. He waved a cast around to show everyone that his puny right arm was broken. Pushing his chin against his chest he belched from the waist, like an opera singer projecting into an auditorium. 'Fell over on the kerb on me way back from the pub last night,' he said. 'Woke up in hospital with this thing on.' He paused theatrically for the punchline. '*Well plastered!*'

AAAAAAAAAHHHHHHHHH.

Russell laughed. Keith was someone he'd known since school, someone who had been written off many times yet, like some psychotic jack-in-the-box, he always bounced back. His body seemed to have resources of strength that defied the normal rules of physiology. The tear tattooed at the corner of his eye was a legacy of his time spent in a 'youth offender unit'. Back then it was known simply as Borstal; a legalised prison camp where twitching, institutionalised, ex-army prison officers played out the twilight of their working lives executing Mrs Thatcher's Short Sharp Shock. In between the slopping out, square bashing and ritual beatings Keith had picked up a habit during the early eighties' heroin boom.

After a brief period of freedom he found himself back inside on two counts of burglary and one of TDA. This time he moved up a division into the major league, doing a stretch in Wormwood Scrubs. A skinny eighteen-year-old with a habit, he descended into prostitution; a prison slag who dispensed blowjobs and peddled his arse in return for gear. Once paroled he was diagnosed as having the virus and returned to thieving to support his raging habit. He kept his prison experiences quiet, knowing there are some stories that should not be told. Russell watched him, saw the doom in his eyes, the knowledge that his life was a series of calamities, that his time was limited.

While he smiled at Keith's antics Russell kept an eye on the rest of the room. For much of the evening a geezer had been standing alone by the bar downing bottles of Beck's. Every now and then his mobile would chirrup and he would have a short muttered conversation before placing the black plastic back in the pocket of his Polo blouson jacket. He was medium build, but hard-boned and wiry. Unshaven and with short, messy dark hair he had thick eyebrows and a long nose that dropped straight from his forehead at an acute angle to his face, like a beak. Russell could see that it was skewed, had been broken a couple of times. Geezer looked a bit tasty.

He had spent a lot of time glancing over towards the corner where Russell and his friends had congregated. Other punters in the bar had clocked him but pretended not to see. It was that kind of place. No one saw anything. Russell had given him the once-over soon as he'd walked in. Too much conspicuous wealth – pressed Polo shirt, Armani jeans, box-fresh Reebok, Rolex wrist-snapper (kosher). Normal but noticeable.

Russell had been aware that he was being watched. Skimming his eyes across the room he made eye contact with the man again. This was bang out of order. He strode over to the bar and stood as close to the man as he could.

'Five pints of lager, please, love,' he asked the barmaid. He turned to face a pair of dull grey eyes looking through him.

'You got enough of an eyeful yet?' Russell spoke calmly, showing that he wasn't intimidated. 'You fancy me or something?' The geezer didn't flinch. ''Cos you've been fuck-ing staring at me ever since you came in.' The man picked up his chaser glass, put an ice cube in his mouth and crunched it.

'You Russell Fisher?'

'Who wants to know?'

'Civil question, son.' The 'son' was meant to let him know who was boss. The two of them must have been around the same age.

'What if I am?'

'Got some business I need to talk with Russell.' Maintaining a deadpan stare Russell cranked his alcohol-drenched mind into dredging up any information that could help him nail the outsider's angle.

'You used to get involved at the football, didn't you?' said the man, stroking his stubble with the back side of his hand. Russell remained silent. There was no way the geezer was old bill, but he had this level of authority about him, a sombreness possessed by the older coppers who'd seen it all before. The barmaid slopped five pints of frothing lager on the sodden beer towel.

'Nine pahnd, love.'

Russell handed over a crisp Friday night tenner to the barmaid without taking his eyes from the man next to him. Suddenly he connected. Maybe this geezer was something to do with the old days – maybe he's been sent over the water from Bermondsey to settle some old score between him and Millwall. But, no. No one would have the front to come in here and try that shit. Not round here. Russell felt he was being tested. For fuck's sake, he was on home ground here. Who was this wanker who thought he could come in here and try and take the piss? Russell nodded.

'Yeah.'

'Heard a couple of years ago you were the top boy round here. Heard you was a trader.'

'What about it?'

'Nothing. I'm an Iron myself. Never got into any trouble though. Nah.' He screwed his face up like he'd just bitten into something bitter. 'Mug's game, all that.' Russell was stumped.

'You see I can understand a man liking a good ruck now and again, but that's all schoolboy stuff, innit? I mean, why risk your neck for a fucking football team?'

Russell conspicuously looked into the corner of the room momentarily before returning his gaze to the stranger. He wondered what on God's earth had washed up on his shores this evening.

'You working, Russell?'

'Yeah, sparky.'

'Nice. Working boy, then. Spend your time wiring up Barratt homes and helping old grannies with dodgy doorbells? Do a lot of smoke alarms, do you?'

'Keep taking the tablets, mate,' said Russell, picking up some of the drinks. 'No offence, but I didn't come here tonight to tell me life story to some geezer I ain't never clocked before who keeps asking me stupid questions.'

'I wouldn't go.' The geezer put his hand on Russell's arm. Russell brushed him off, bristling now. 'I know you're running out of drinking time but it might just be worth your while. Name's Trevor Chisholm.' He didn't offer his hand after the introduction. 'There's a thing we've got to talk about.'

'What fucking "thing"?' said Russell.

'A job.'

Russell picked up three pint glasses. 'I've already got a fucking job.'

'What are you making? One hundred and fifty, two hundred pound a week?' asked Trevor. Russell kept shtoom. If only.

'I'm doing all right. I get by.'

'You get by,' said Trevor, shaking his head. 'What kind of fucking talk is that? You're what, twenty-eight? Thirty? You're already sounding like an old man.' He lit a cigarette. 'It's bollocks, mate. But I don't really give a shit. All I know is someone put a good word in for you with my brother, that's why he asked me to come down here when I've got better fucking things to do on a Friday night. So I'm going to give you the information and if you've got any fucking sense you'll come down and have a talk with him. Thursday. You know Merlin's Cave, Essex Street? Come down Thursday night, eight o'clock, and say Ron Chisholm is expecting you. All right? Now don't be a fucking fool.' And with that the man chugged the rest of his vodka and tonic, smacked his lips, hiked up his belt and strode out the door.

Russell picked up the pints and headed back to the table. He knew about Ron Chisholm. Knew about his loansharking and gambling operations. Another lowlife who'd managed to scramble his way to the top of the pile by stomping on other people. He was good at what he did. Chisholm had got it all – the suburban mansion, the flash car, the gold jewellery. And there was something else he'd got as well. Something Russell wanted. He made a mental note to keep Thursday night free.

Chapter Five

Tucked away behind a warehouse down a narrow Victorian street, Merlin's Cave did not endeavour to solicit much passing trade. Nightclubs in Illingford were, as a rule, brash, boastful places demanding attention, drawing people in with flashing lights, red carpets and plastic canopies that sheltered punters while they were roughly searched by pumped-up bouncers who teetered only moments from 'roid rage. Dolled-up Page Three princesses poured into lycra and mini-Ts romped through the thick red cord that separated the queue from the explosion of neon into which they disappeared followed by Polo geezers with cropped hair, gold earrings and sovereign rings.

Merlin's Cave wasn't that kind of place. The owner, Ron Chisholm, had a few big earners every month which filled the place with teenage ravers, and he made sure the door was kept tight to ward off other dealers who might try and muscle a slice of the Ecstasy trade. It kept the staff on their toes and helped the accountants to make the ledgers appear kosher. Ron used Merlin's more as the centre of his 'entertainment and leisure' empire, which consisted of four wine bars, a snooker club and two arcades. Most of the time Merlin's Cave was empty bar half a dozen men who drifted in and out throughout the day and took care of Ron's other equally lucrative business, money lending. Frankie, the manager, kept visitors in beer and bacon and eggs, made sure the ashtrays were empty and, when Ron was around, ensured that Phil Collins' doleful croon purred from the speakers.

Russell glanced at his watch. Quarter past eight. Didn't want to appear too keen. He parked round the corner by a bookie's and listened to the soles of his new trainers squeaking all the way to the entrance of Merlin's. Hearing voices on the other side he banged on the door. He could tell that the climax of a joke had just been reached. Laughter echoed behind the door. Russell rapped again. A gap appeared and the smell of marijuana swept out of the club. A squat man, about thirty years old with a shaved head and acne-scarred face, cupped a roll-up in his right hand. He wore a Ministry of Sound MA1 jacket.

'Yeah?'

'I'm here to see Ron Chisholm.'

'Name?'

'Russell Fisher.'

'In you come.'

Russell stepped through the doorway to see another, younger man with straight blond hair tied back in a ponytail. He had no upper lip, which gave him a feline appearance. He raised his chin to acknowledge Russell.

'Ron's downstairs,' said the acne-scarred one, leading the way. A red carpet patterned with grey martini glasses stretched before them. They went down one flight of stairs, turned a corner and headed into a huge room which was centred round a wooden dance floor. To the right a bar occupied the whole wall. On the three other sides shell-backed settees of purple velveteen surrounded fixed circular tables. James Cagney, Marilyn Monroe, James Dean, Joan Crawford, John Wayne and other Hollywood stars stared out from the enlarged publicity stills that adorned the mirrored walls.

Acne Scars halted before crossing the dance floor. Russell stared through the darkness and saw three men sitting at a table. One was clearly in charge, as the other two were leaning towards him deferentially. His voice was barely audible, soft enough to make the others listen hard. Trevor sat in the next booth smoking a cigarette, an empty plate, slicked with ketchup, pushed away from him. He stared at Russell. Russell looked back at him but was offered no form of recognition.

Russell and Acne Scars waited a couple of minutes for the other men to finish talking and move to another booth, Trevor scratching his face with the back of his hand, staring, dull-eyed, beyond Russell. The big man beckoned Russell over. He didn't offer Russell his hand, remaining seated at the table.

'It's all right, Craig,' he said, dismissing Acne Scars. 'Russell, ain't it? Sit down, Russell. Ron Chisholm, glad you came. My brother tells me you're a busy man. Want a drink, son?'

'Lager.'

Ron turned round and shouted, 'Frankie! Bring us over a couple of Red Stripes, will you? I'm spitting feathers over here. And make sure they're fucking cold, all right?' Russell glanced at him. He was probably about forty and heavy for his height, which was around five eleven, but looked comfortable with it. His hair had receded and turned grey, and was cut short. His sharp blue eyes turned slowly in their sockets, the rims were pink as uncooked pig's liver. There was a tiredness about him that was heightened by his heavy jowls, which he pulled at occasionally.

Russell lit a cigarette.

'Yeah, you can smoke,' said Ron. Feeling a little light in the stomach Russell nodded, acknowledging his mistake without being too deferential. He put his cigarette in the black plastic Carling ashtray that sat in the middle of the table. The two men in the next booth conversed quietly while keeping a discreet watch on what was going on behind them.

'Ever heard the expression "downsizing", Russell?' asked Ron. Thinking it might have something to do with matching boxers of different weights Russell shook his head. He noticed that Ron had grey hairs sprouting from his nose like tendrils and tried not to stare.

'Frankly,' said Ron, 'I ain't surprised. It's an American expression. Basically it means sacking people, chucking them out of work. So it's got all kinds of, er, bad associations. So they thought they'd replace it. KnowotImean? So they invented the word 'rightsizing'. 'Course it's a con because it's exactly the same thing. Same fucking thing – people being told they ain't needed no longer, that they're surplus to requirements.'

Russell nodded. He had no idea where this was going. Frankie came over and plonked two bottles of lager on the table. He was a thin man with his shirt unbuttoned to his chest. He brought with him a smell of shoe polish and frying. The way he plastered his thinning jet black hair back on his head with grease reminded Russell of his father.

'You see, Russell, I run a business,' continued Ron. 'So I like to stay in touch with the latest changes in the world of management and commerce. KnowotImean?'

Russell didn't want to be flushed out. He nodded and pulled on his cigarette.

'The situation that I've recently had in my own business has been one which I would describe as restructuring. Americans might call it "rightsizing" but I don't give a dog's bollock about that. KnowotImean? Anyway, I've cut away some of the dead wood within the organisation in order to streamline it. That caused me to look at the rest of the company to try and work out what it was exactly that we were missing. And that's why I'm talking to you.'

Russell nodded, baffled. The geezer sounded like something off the telly, some kind of government economics lackey.

Ron folded his arms and levelled his eyes at Russell with patience, as if he were a maths teacher explaining a particularly difficult equation. His voice was quiet and even. 'I hear that you can handle yourself. Box a little. Take care of yourself,' he said. 'I think it's important for a young man to do that. Everything in moderation, that's my motto. Now I've heard that you used to run a little firm of your own down the football.' Ron didn't offer Russell an opportunity to confirm or deny this. 'Don't agree with it myself. Bunch of fucking degenerates. No respect. Spell in the army would do them some good – that's what my old man used to say. And, you know, I'm inclined to agree with him. But I hear that's all behind you now and that you keep your nose clean. I like that. I don't like a fuss. Don't like no bother.'

'I've got a job,' said Russell a little too bluntly.

Without missing a beat Ron continued in exactly the same, flat tone. 'Yeah, I heard about that. You're a sparky. Good job. Good prospects. You got your own business?'

'No,' said Russell.

'So you sit around waiting for someone to call you out the Yellow Pages, let their fingers do the walking, so to speak. Am I right?'

'Well, it's a bit different . . .'

'*Yeravinalaugharent'cha?*' Ron cut him off, his mood changing. 'Listen, Russell. You ain't fooling me, you ain't fooling yourself. Being a sparky is a nice, safe job. Sure. Unless you've got your own business you ain't never gonna do much more than keep your head above water. Believe me.'

'I'm thinking maybe . . .'

'Hear me out before you jump in,' said Ron. 'Just you try and grasp what it is that I'm fucking saying here: what I'm offering you is a leap into another league.' Ron slipped back into his teach-yourself-business text. 'Plus a rather attractive range of perks and benefits.'

'Doing what?' asked Russell.

'Good,' said Ron as if Russell had said something he agreed with. 'In my organisation I don't really have job titles. I suppose the job I have in mind for you is a troubleshooter. KnowotImean? Sometimes I'll want you in the club keeping an eye on things, other times I'll want you to drive me around on appointments, meet clients for me and suchlike. Russell, I've got plenty of muscle around. Look at Barry and Mark there. Tweedledumb and Tweedle fuckin' dumber. Geezers like that are ten a penny round here. But someone who can handle himself and can use his head is what I'm after. Someone who's going to weigh up all the options rather than just steam in smacking people about.'

Russell chugged on his bottle of beer, his Adam's apple bouncing up and down four times.

'I'll pay you five hundred a week,' said Ron.

Russell's heart missed a beat. Riches beyond the dreams of avarice. He wasn't clearing much more than £500 a month at the moment. It was silly money. Cash money. A result. He'd be a mug to turn it down.

The fact was he couldn't turn it down.

'Wotcha say, Russell?' asked Ron. He put his hands on the table revealing several slabs of gold in the form of sovereigns.

'I'll have a go,' said Russell after a few moments. 'For a month. Give us both a chance to see whether it's going to work out. If I don't like it I go back to being a sparky. You don't like me you tell me to piss off.'

Ron looked at him with contempt, his eyes thinning ominously. 'Areyoushaw? *Areyoushaw?*' Russell froze inside, convinced that he'd misjudged the moment. He watched as Ron's face melted and he chuckled to himself.

'I like that, "I'll have a go". Russell, I'm going to agree for two reasons: firstly it's a fair deal, can't argue with that. Secondly, the successful businessman's greatest asset. Know what that is?'

Russell shook his head and Ron slipped a sly smile across his chops.

'Instinct, son, instinct. Without instinct you ain't nobody. Whether you're the heavyweight champion of the fucking world or you're a Paki in a corner shop flogging dirty mags and fags, you've gotta use your instinct. Follow your nose. KnowotImean?'

Russell knew what he meant. He wouldn't describe it as a sixth sense, or even foresight. The only way he could explain it was after he'd read this article in a magazine about the kind of chemicals that animals secrete when they're afraid. His cousin Paul, who bred Staffordshire bull terriers, said the same thing. 'Dogs,' he had explained earnestly, 'smell fear like you smell shit.'

'I think it's going to work out,' said Ron, lifting his bottle of beer by its neck with two fingers. 'A toast.' Russell picked up his bottle. 'To taking care of business,' said Ron. Russell leaned over towards his new employer.

'To taking care of business,' he said. The two men clinked bottles. Ron sloped back in the scalloped chair and smacked his lips. 'I think this is going to work out, you know,' he said, looking directly at Russell.

'When do you want me to start?' asked Russell.

'Tell you what,' said Ron 'Let's just think of this as an induction, shall we?' Russell took a swig from his beer. He didn't want to drink it too fast, didn't want another one, but wanted to look busy, like he was up to something. Ron was testing him. Seeing how cool he could be. That didn't bother Russell. He could be like fucking ice.

Craig appeared at the bottom of the stairs. He was with a tall wiry man with a pink face and messy black hair who kept tugging at the sleeves of his jacket. Motionless, Craig looked across the room. He said something to the other man but not loud enough for him to hear, so he had to lean right in to make the words audible. Speaking in little more than a murmur was clearly the way they did things round here.

'I don't mean to dump you right in it, Russell, but you might want to sit and watch what's going to happen here,' said Ron. 'See this tart?' He pointed to the tall man. 'That slag has been hassling me for a fucking job for months. Now I've asked around a bit, done me research like, and he's a slag of the first order. He's got form for mugging an old granny outside her own home, year later he robbed a young girl who was out walking her tot in the park. Those are just the fucking convictions. He calls himself Pikey, but he should have chosen Cunt. The man's a slag. He's been fucking pestering me and fucking asking me for work for so long now that it just ain't right. Something's got to be done.'

Ron nodded at Craig who, instead of shoving Pikey over and trotting back up the stairs, accompanied him across the room. The men stopped short of the table. Silence. Ron let it go, enjoying the power of the space. Eventually he spoke. He looked at Pikey as if he were a racehorse he was going to nobble. Shoulders back, fists clenched, Pikey stared back; not aggressive, just posing.

'Why the fuck are you back?' demanded Ron.

'I'm after work,' said Pikey. Russell could see a thin film of sweat accumulating above his upper lip. He wore a cheap leather jacket that was too warm inside the club.

'For work,' said Ron, unimpressed. 'What you going to do for me?'

'Pikey shrugged. 'What do you want?'

'Why do you want to work for me?' snapped Ron impatiently.

'Because I want to be on the firm,' said Pikey.

'Why's that then?' asked Ron.

'The rewards would be good.' Pikey's voice was thin, dry. There was a slightly musical quality to it, a faint trace of an Irish accent.

Ron raised his chin sharply. 'Good rewards? Areyoushaw?' Craig and Mark started to laugh. 'Good rewards? What's that fucking mean?'

Some job interview, thought Russell.

Pikey was trying to be conciliatory. 'I just mean that you're the top boys round here and I wanted to try and get in on whatever's going.'

'You are having a laugh,' said Ron shaking his head. 'Listen, when you came here what the fuck did you expect? Some balding old geezer in need of some muscle to take care of business for him? Some old duffer who needs a helping hand to wipe his own arse? Some cushy number looking after the door on clubs and getting sucked off by barmaids?'

'I, er . . .' Pikey raised his palms but couldn't cut in fast enough.

''Cos my name's not Cunt and no one's going to tell me otherwise, understand?' said Ron, sitting up straighter now. 'If you want to get on the firm then you've got a long fucking way to go.' He leaned back in the booth, changing pace. 'How much do you want this job?'

'At the moment, more than anything,' said Pikey sincerely.

Ron curled an oily lip. 'Oh dear. You – are – having – a – laugh, aren't ya?' he sang. 'Sort him out, boys.' Stepping from the shadows, Terry and Mark snapped a pair of handcuffs on Pikey, tied the struggling man to a chair and placed a mail bag over his head. The room was silent except for Pikey's epileptic struggling and trembling voice. Terry disappeared and came back with a large jug of water and a tin of lighter fluid. He emptied the water over Pikey and then sprayed the fluid all over the hood. Pikey gasped for breath, his sobs becoming desperate.

'Right, you cunt, Mark has given you a bit of a petrol shower,' shouted Ron. 'Nasty stuff.' He flashed a grin at Terry. 'Terrence, have you packed in smoking yet?'

'No, guv,' said Terry. 'Matter of fact I'm gasping for one right now.' Terry produced a Zippo lighter from his pocket and conspicuously fired it up.

Pikey screamed. 'Please no. Oh, *please*. Fuck. No.'

'I'd be careful with that naked flame, Terry,' said Ron. 'There's petrol all over Pikey there. There could be a nasty incident if you accidentally dropped the lighter.'

'Please. Let me go,' squealed Pikey. 'Just let me go. *Don't do it. Fucking don't do it.* Please.'

Ron stood up in the booth and pointed at Terry. A cigarette smouldered between his stubby fingers. 'Terry! Terry! Put that fucking lighter away. Pikey is covered in petrol. If you drop that lighter we'll be having an indoor barbecue and I don't know what the fuck the council health and safety officer would have to say about that.'

Pikey slumped in his chair whimpering to himself. Ron nodded to Terry who whipped the bag off. Pikey slumped against the ropes that held him. His face was purple with strain, the whites of his eyes popping from his thyroid grimace like a pair of fried eggs.

Ron had a little trouble sliding his bulk from the booth, but then he liked to take his time in these situations. Straightening his jacket he approached Pikey. He shoved his face close to his victim, jabbing his cigarette under his captive's nose. Pikey strained to keep away from its glowing tip. Ron spat his words.

'When you want to work for me as much as you just wanted to live, come back and see me,' said Ron. 'Until then stick to chain snatching and dipping in Oxford Street.'

Pikey just snivelled. 'Yeah, yeah, OK, OK. Thanks, Ron. Thanks.'

'Now fuck off,' said Ron, pushing the chair over. 'You ain't even worthy to smell my shit.'

Terry and Mark untied Pikey and shoved him up the stairs, kicking and slapping him like a couple of tyrannical school bullies. Ron turned to Russell, grinning expansively. 'You see, Russell,' he smiled, 'you see what a laugh we're going to have?' He expanded his arms out from his chest to encompass the room. 'We're diamond geezers, Russ. Diamonds.'

Chapter Six

Russell shrugged his shoulders, trying to loosen the dull laziness that had settled upon his frame. He'd been driving all morning, Ron lording it over him in the back, asking him to stop here ('Got a token out of the *Sun*, pizza for a penny') and there ('gotta pick up the dry cleaning'). His back was giving him hell. Squirming around in the heated front seat of the Jag Russell had adjusted the back rest so many times that Ron had raised his nose from a Walker's Grab Bag.

'What's wrong with you?' he asked, his teeth – stained old piano keys – speckled with morsels of beef and onion. 'You got piles or something? Arse grapes? Getting rid of it soon. Loan, innit. We'll get something else sorted next week.'

It was an interesting use of the word 'loan'. The vehicle belonged to a second-hand dealer by the name of Cheesy Macree who had borrowed some money from Ron a couple of years ago when an incident of Jewish lightning took out his ailing plant-hire business. After the usual stalling the insurers had dug in and decided they weren't going to cough up. 'The Cheese', as he was known to his associates, had backed off, not wanting to push a point too far, and borrowed a wedge from Ron to get a leg up in the car trade.

The Cheese had in fact payed Ron off long ago, but the fat man kept grumbling about 'interest accrued' and struck a deal with the luckless Cheese to keep one of his cars on permanent loan. Hence the silver P-reg Jag that Russell was edging up Goods Way with Ron sitting in the back like some dictatorial potentate.

'Tell you what, Russ,' said Ron, his voice absorbed by the smooth, silent interior of the car, 'the Cheese has got a nice 8 Series coming in Wednesday. Pukka interior. Calves' leather.

Think we should give it a spin. Ascertain whether it's in working order.' Russell was concentrating on avoiding a brace of black teenage gangsters playing chicken across the the road, doing their odd stepping-on-coals pimp shuffle, hands straying to their crotches as if checking some talisman.

'Eh?' said Ron. 'Check if it's in working order, eh, Russ?' Russell looked in the rear-view mirror. Ron was staring out of the rain-smeared window chuckling to himself. It was a strange thing; Ron would never laugh at his own jokes in company – Russell supposed that that was a job for Terry and Mark – but when it was just the two of them in the car he would spread across the back seat, legs akimbo, his arms snaking across the upholstery, a smirk worked across his rough features. Ghosting through the builders, wage slaves, pavement princesses and needle freaks of King's Cross Ron gazed smugly from his executive limo as if it were some imperial yacht unbesmirched by the filthy waters around it.

'Bust a left, Russ,' instructed Ron, leaning forward and tapping the younger man on the shoulder.

'What, here?' questioned Russell.

'Handsome.'

They turned into the Atlantic Estate, passing a sickly teenage girl who walked grimly behind a pushchair, which contained a mixed-race baby wrapped tightly in a wool blanket. She was hunched slightly because of the rain, a cigarette plunged hungrily into her pale, white rat's countenance.

The Jag pulled past a couple of cars perched on stacks of bricks. Only the basic body and chassis remained; the rest had been picked clean, left like the skeleton of some prehistoric creature stripped of carrion. The psychology of driving a Jag to an area like this was very simple: if you had the front to bring it in then you probably had the large to back it up.

'Park up just over there,' said Ron pointing, still captaining from the back seat.

Russell pulled up facing a raw brick wall. 'Body and Soul Sound' was scrawled in a child-like lower case script in red spray paint among a confusion of elaborately bombed tags.

The two men jumped from the car. Russell felt a tinge of pleasure as the central locking thunked solidly within the door casing. Ron turned the collar of his camel coat up against the rain which was now so fine that you couldn't see it, enveloping both men like a gas. Russell reached up and felt his face warm beneath the cool liquid.

Ron set off across a small patch of waste ground towards some flats. The path they trod was a short-cut to an overpriced convenience store run by twitchy Sikhs who conspicuously kept baseball bats under the counter and a dismal, forlorn pub notorious for its Friday lunchtime strip show. Discarded fast-food wrappings, empty beer cans and empty cigarette packets – limp in the rain – lined the cocoa-coloured trail.

The leather soles of Russell's shoes – he'd started dressing up a little for work now – caused him to slip, his legs working hard in short, shuffling motions. Ahead of him Ron walked with his head down, his hands stuffed deep in his pockets, leaping from grassy clump to gnarled greeny-yellow patch, circumnavigating the mud.

The buildings looming over them had been built in the mid 1970s, a time when the council had the cash to build houses courtesy of a sympathetic central government. The years since had been leaner. The council could barely find the cash to maintain basic essential services. Russell remembered that his own grandfather had been found a home on an estate similar to this a couple of miles away. It had been a month before the sanitation department came to remove his body, and this was after a week of bitter complaints from neighbours about an unseasonal plague of bluebottles.

A concrete stairway led up to a paved concourse area. Each split-level flat had its own front door and next to it a slatted kitchen window which looked out on to the concourse. Some people tried to give the place an air of cheerfulness – plants, dolls and trinkets were put on window display. Most kept thick curtains permanently drawn, promoting an atmosphere of abandonment. The original doors had consisted of wooden frames with upper and lower panels of glass with wire running through it. Some remained, but most residents had purchased sturdier replacements with elaborate locks and sinister spy holes. Russell noticed a couple of places where windows had been replaced by slabs of chipboard nailed crudely in place; the result of a break-in or a drunken kick during a domestic.

Ron strode purposefully ahead, occasionally taking the odd swipe at a discarded cigarette packet on the walkway. A pudgy white woman in a red Umbro track-suit and slip-on shoes eyed him with suspicion when he wished her a good afternoon. He stopped at the end of the walkway, waiting for Russell, and pulled a face. 'I thought you were fit,' he jibed. 'Come on, we've got business to take care of.'

The pair stopped outside number 63. The bell echoed shrilly inside the flat. A young man with messy short blond hair, as if he'd just got out of bed, came to the door clutching a mobile phone.

'All right, Ron,' he said, opening the door for the two men.

'Nice one, Glenn,' said Ron, striding in. Russell nodded at Glenn but received no reply. The flat showed no sign of habitation. Greasy marks remained on the kitchen linoleum where a cooker and fridge had once stood, but since then the purpose of the place had changed. Walking through the flat into the living room Russell saw dozens of baths packaged in plastic and cardboard stacked up on top of each other. At the back of the room, in front of the windows, there were a number of toilets.

'How's business?' asked Ron.

'Can't complain, Ron. Can't complain,' said Glenn. 'You?'

'Getting by,' said Ron sarcastically.

'Showers, taps, faucets, pedestals, accessories all upstairs in the bedrooms,' said Glenn. 'Nearly broke our fucking backs getting them up here though, I tell you, Ron.'

'Is this all from the same source then, Glenn?' asked Ron.

'All council approved,' said Glenn, a shit-eating smirk on his face. 'Supposed to be going into some flats they were going to build a while back. Been sitting in a fucking warehouse for a couple of years. No money, innit.'

'It's a crying shame.' Ron looked Glenn up and down disapprovingly. 'Well ain't you going to offer us a cup of tea or nothing?'

'Well, it ain't exactly . . .' started Glenn.

'Joking, son. Joking,' said Ron, slapping Glenn on the shoulder and grinning at Russell. 'All right, Glenn. I've seen the gear, and I'm a man of my word. I'll take the lot. Every fucking washer. Price we agreed earlier, yeah?' said Ron reaching into his pocket. 'It's all in scores.' He waved a stack of twenties around in Glenn's face before handing it over. Glenn thumbed through the notes, distracted, wanting to check they were kosher but not wanting to upset Ron.

'This ain't the amount we agreed, Ron.' He sounded tired, jaded by the inevitability of Ron trying to shaft him and the effort of finding the energy required for his own counter-shaft. The older man reached over and clutched Glenn's shoulder.

'You know the score, son,' said Ron, like he was telling a child why he couldn't stay up watching TV on a school night. 'Like last time. Half now, half on delivery of merchandise. I'll get you the address tomorrow. Like 'em by the weekend. Got a bunch of Paddy plumbers just desperate for a bit of knockdown gear.'

'Don't know if we can, Ron, it ain't long . . .' Glenn followed Ron back towards the front door waving the money in one hand, his mobile in the other. 'I mean there's a lot to sort out, Ron . . .'

'You're killing me here, Glenn,' said Ron firmly. 'Tell you what, I'll give you a twoer on top.'

'A monkey,' said Glenn, 'for delivery, like.'

'Most irregular,' said Ron, his jaw setting hard. 'A twoer it is, then.'

Ron swung the door open. 'Saturday, son, otherwise I'm sending my bogtrotting mates over to see you.' He reached over and pinched Glenn's cheek. 'Stop worrying, son, you're too young for all that. Wait until you grow up and get some proper worries. Come on, Russell, let's give it the off.'

Russell squeezed past the silent Glenn who stood contemplating how he was going to transport the knock-off stash across London before the weekend. Russell knew that he'd find a way somehow.

*

'He'll go far, that kid,' said Ron settling himself into the back seat. 'Dare say if I hadn't got in first he'd have tried some funny business. Knows a lot of people down the council. Always got good moody gear. And no one ain't ever going to come looking for them. KnowotImean? Nice arrangement. 'Course he tries it on, what with the delivery and all that, but I like to see that.'

'Where to?' asked Russell, trying to get comfortable.

'Back to the club, Russell. Home, James.'

After a couple of minutes Ron started to whistle, a low reedy sound that strayed off-key during even the least challenging parts of 'Strangers in the Night'.

'You like Sinatra, Russell?'

'My old man likes him. Used to play him and Frankie Vaughan when we were kids.'

'Well, Russell,' said Ron, leaning forward, 'I ain't got no intention of insulting a member of your family, but in my opinion Frankie Vaughan ain't in the same league as Frank Sinatra. No offence. I'd say Frankie Vaughan ain't fit to suck Sinatra's dick. That's like saying you listen to Elvis Presley and Tommy Steele, Genesis and Herman's Hermits, Elton John and Barry Manilow. In this world, Russell, there is genius and there is bollocks. Sinatra, Presley, Genesis, John – genius. Vaughan, Steele, Hermits, Manilow – bollocks. Can't argue with that.'

'I'd put Marvin Gaye in the genius camp. And Anita Baker,' said Russell.

'Ah, but you have to put someone in the bollocks camp as well. Who? *Who?*'

Russell pulled up at a traffic light, puffed out his cheeks and thought. 'Frank Sinatra,' he said, turning round to meet Ron's gaze. 'Wind up.'

'I'm glad about that, Russell, I really am,' said Ron flatly.

They drove along in silence for a while before the thought struck Russell. 'You know who really is bollocks,' said Russell. 'Paul McCartney.'

'You're right there, son,' said Ron, but Russell didn't really feel that his heart was in the conversation any longer.

Chapter Seven

'He's shit. He's fucking shit!' shouted Terry at Frankie, who was building a pyramid of playing cards along the bar when Ron and Russell trooped down the stairs at Merlin's Cave.

'Who's fucking shit, Terry? Who's fucking shit?' asked Ron, overhearing the conversation. 'V and T, Frankie, and a lager for Russell.' Terry went quiet. Russell slung his jacket in one of the booths and settled on a stool next to Ron.

'Chris Armstrong,' muttered Terry.

'Compared to?' asked Ron as a bottle of tonic whispered into a tall glass next to him. Russell nodded at Frankie and pulled on his lager.

'Go on, Terry. Tell him,' said Frankie, buoyed by his new ally.

'I was just saying he ain't as good as everyone makes out,' said Terry.

'Wrong answer,' said Ron. 'Truth is it don't matter how many goals Armstrong scores. He will always be crap. So the correct answer is that Chris Armstrong is utter shit compared to *anyone* else in the Premier League. For real.'

'Except Dion Dublin,' said Russell.

'Except Dion Dublin,' said Ron, raising his glass.

'Anyone peckish?' asked Frankie, gesturing towards the kitchen. 'I went out this morning.' Russell didn't know what this could possibly mean. He had never seen Frankie cook anything other than burgers, bacon, chips, beans and eggs. 'We've got burgers, chips, beans, bacon and eggs,' said Frankie. 'Anyone peckish?'

'That all you cook?' asked Russell.

'Yeah,' said Frankie in a what-of-it tone. He slung a tea towel over his left shoulder and put his hands on his hips.

Russell noticed his wiriness, how the vinyl belt on his Stapress hipsters bulged from his navel like an Adam's apple.

'Just wondered.' Russell shrugged.

'What you fancy then?'

'Chips, burger, beans, bacon and egg. Two slices.'

'Coming right up.' Satisfied, Frankie went into the kitchen and started pulling things from the fridge.

Ron slid off his stool. 'Russell, got to make some calls. Check on the ball and chain, have a word with the Cheese and – I'll ask him about that BMW. We've got a couple of errands to run this afternoon. If you want to pop off for a while make sure you're back about two, all right?' Ron hitched his trousers and headed through a door marked 'Private'.

Russell looked along the bar at Terry who was sulking, pretending to be reading the sports pages of the paper. Russell didn't buy it – he didn't know anyone who hadn't read the sports pages by lunchtime – but couldn't be bothered to start a conversation with the bulked-up, sullen man.

'Listen, Frankie, I'm going out to eat, OK?' he shouted.

'You're joking, aintcha? It'll be ready in a couple of minutes.'

'Tell Ron I'll be back by two, all right?' said Russell, disappearing up the stairs.

Frankie appeared from the back room, spatula in hand. 'I'll keep it warm for you, if you like.'

Russell slogged up Market Lane towards Ivy's caff. The traffic inched past in the drizzle, some children in the back of a Mondeo pressed their faces against the window where they hadn't drawn patterns in the condensation. A desperate mum dragged a pit bull, a kid and shopping basket through the rain, blinking as the drops fell on her eyelashes, the kid hitting the dog on the back of the head with a rolled-up comic. A sign in a butcher's shop read 'Keep the flu out. Eat more mince.' Further up the road the street's gutter harshness was sweetened by the warming blanket of frying bacon that surrounded the caff.

The heat was just about bearable inside. Russell noticed that

Ivy, the owner, had put some stickers advertising a new soft drink in the window. Already the steam inside the caff had caused them to bubble like the skin of a squash.

Behind the counter a poster of the Italian team Torino was faring little better. The players had lost the glossy Mediterranean health of a few months ago, the combined forces of heat, moisture and light turning them to anaemic, dough-faced London ghosts. The poster belonged to Sandro, the sandwich maker, his homage to his former life in Turin. Every August he disappeared for a month, spending much of the time watching his team train in their mountain retreat. Russell had never understood how he could be so devoted that he gave up his annual break to watch them train, yet was unable to see them throughout the rest of the year except on TV. He'd asked him once: Sandro shrugged as he squirted salad cream on a floury bap and told Russell that training was all he could bear. When he was living in Turin he would leave games early, even if Torino were winning, because he couldn't cope with the possibility of defeat.

Ivy and Sandro were as good a team as Torino: Sandro with his barely concealed pain, his nervy fatalism; Ivy with a good word for everyone, making customers feel like they were in her front room, not a public place. The effect was assisted by Ivy's liking for moccasins, which she bought every six months from Marks & Spencer. It gave her a homely appearance, as if she was pottering around her own kitchen. Her father had been a merchant seaman who arrived in London after the war with a Singaporean bride. A year later Ivy was born and grew up to be a dancer in West End shows. A good run in a chorus brought her a tidy lump sum with which she bought the café, originally juggling her dancing with overseeing her business. As her limbs stiffened and her muscles began to ache more than they used to Ivy went to fewer auditions and, even though she was offered a job as a movement teacher at a local college, devoted herself full-time to the café, occasionally disappearing up west on quiet afternoons to catch a matinée with her cousin Glenda.

Rummaging around in a box on the counter looking for a

bag of cheese and onion Russell shouted his order – corned beef and tomato in a crusty roll – over to Sandro who wiped down his knife and set about his task with practised speed. At the till Ivy was totting up the bill for a couple of builders, big fuckers with barrel chests, wiry cropped hair and jovial manners. 'Six seventy-five, please, love,' she said, peering over the frames of her big pink glasses. Most of the time they swung on a chain between her breasts. Ivy perched them on her nose only to read the notes she wrote herself to keep track of customer's orders.

'Hello, Russell.' She smiled. 'Keeping well, love?'

'Keeping well,' said Russell. 'You all right?'

Ivy put a hand to her collarbone. 'I don't want to sound like some old granny, Russell, but my varicose veins are giving me hell. I'm a martyr to 'em.' She gave the builders their change. 'Thanks, boys. I suppose it's all those years dancing, and now standing up all day feeding the waifs and strays. Still, better on me feet all day than on me back. I don't think I could do that if they paid me.'

'That's the idea.'

'I'm too old for all that,' laughed Ivy, crossing herself. 'Cuppa rosie, love? White, two sugars innit?'

She disappeared into a milky cloud of steam. 'You sit down, love, I'll bring your roll over as well, all right?'

Wolfing down his lunch, Russell thought about the last few days he'd spent with Ron. It was all very strange. It wasn't that he hadn't enjoyed the job, it was more that he wasn't quite sure what was wanted from him. It was as if he'd been sucked on to some fairground ride: fun in short doses, but the point of it all was obscure. If he was Ron's minder then that was one thing. Ron was bound to upset a few people, considering the line of business he was in. But Russell couldn't figure the angle, couldn't work out why it was him; he wasn't the only tasty geezer in Illingford and Ron could rustle up a goon squad within minutes if he really needed it.

Draining his mug he decided that as far as Ron was concerned he was a trophy, like one of those blonde girls with tits and tans you see with businessmen old enough to be their fathers, the ones who play with their salads in posh restaurants and look bored all the time. But there was one difference: Russell wasn't bored. Yet. There was something he needed first of all. He had a job to do.

Best not to question the arrangement. It suited Russell fine for the moment. He was pleased to be around Ron, but not for the fat man's company, nor even the money. Ron had something that Russell wanted, something that had been Russell's all along. And Ron didn't know it yet, but Russell was planning on taking it back.

Chapter Eight

'So do you want it or what?' asked Frankie, his right eyelid flickering with anger.

'I'm sorry, mate,' replied Russell climbing on to a bar stool and picking up the *Sun*. 'Needed to get some air. Grabbed a bite while I was out.'

Frankie disappeared back into the kitchen and noisily scraped the food into the bin. He might as well have been banging a drum. 'There's people fucking starving in the world,' he shouted. He came back to the bar, slipped Simply Red into the cassette player and turned the volume up loud.

Lotto potto, tits, tories, ops, tots, football and sexual calamity. The usual stuff in the paper. 'Where's Ron and Terry?' shouted Russell.

Frankie pretended not to notice.

'Oi! Frankie! I know you've got the hump. Where are Ron and Terry?' persisted Russell.

'In the office with a couple of geezers,' said Frankie. 'Some deal. Say they can can get beer piss cheap. Bring it back from France duty-free on a lorry. Ain't even knocked off.'

'Well, it's gone two o'clock,' said Russell, checking his watch. 'Ron said he wanted me back sharpish.'

Frankie stuck out his bottom lip. Not his problem.

Russell at least wanted Ron to know that he was ready to rumble whenever needed. He walked across the dance floor and knocked on the office door. There was no answer, only a pregnant silence He made to walk away but stopped. They couldn't have heard. He tried again. Still no answer. He opened the door.

Before he could comprehend why, his world dissolved around him.

*

The pain seemed to be behind his eyes, like his eyeballs had been bathed in bleach and rolled around the sockets. The haze began to rise but Russell didn't understand why he couldn't move his arms.

'You cunt,' came a hoarse, wild voice. 'Move and you're dead.' A boot struck him in the groin and he rolled over. Opening his eyes he saw two men in black leather jackets, jeans and white trainers. They could have been twins except the taller one was black, the other white. The white one was pointing a handgun nervously round the room. The black one was working over Terry who was tied up and slumped in a chair. His nose looked like a canned tomato, his eyes had virtually closed up – two slits in a rump steak. There was a cut over his eye the size of a baby's mouth.

'You make any noise,' said the black one to Terry, 'We get really nasty.' Low-rent gangsters who'd learned all their lines from the movies. Vicious little thugs enjoying their moment as top dog, mouthing off to mask the fear. The black one kicked Ron in the back twice, and Chisholm's flabby body shook like a tree thick with foliage in a strong wind.

'Tell us where you've got the fucking money,' said the white one. 'You tell us, we leave, no one gets hurt.' He was extraordinarily ugly. His face was almost completely flat, his eyes the kind normally only seen on fishmongers' slabs. He had a small star tattooed on his left earlobe; 'Wayne' in blue ink across the back of his livid neck. He kept licking his lips and pointing the gun between Ron and Terry. Occasionally he would turn and check on Russell, who was playing dead, trying fully to recover his senses.

'You two have made a big fucking mistake,' said Ron, his voice flat and disarmingly calm. He was looking at no one, facing a corner, his shirt and tie scarlet with blood from his crushed nose.

'We know you've got the fucking money,' screamed the white one. There was no control in his voice. 'There's ten grand in this shitty office. Now fucking give us the fucking ten Gs, you old cunt.' The white one had lost it. There were chalky white marks at the corners of his mouth where his saliva had dried. He was screaming at Ron and Terry. He wanted to be there less than they did. He was distracted and frustrated, he couldn't believe how badly they'd fucked this up. 'Something Got Me Started' thudded through the door.

Russell felt round his wrists. They'd been wrapped with insulating tape. If he strained he could rub his right thumb nail against the tape and make an incision. The black man reached into a sports bag they'd left on the floor.

'Give us the fucking money! Give us the fucking money!' the white one shouted.

'Just keep the fucking noise down, will you?' said his partner. 'Fucking calm down.' He was in his mid-twenties. He had a shaved head and goatee. Probably a raver. Needed the money to pay off some debts, maybe start a venture of his own. Get a drugs franchise at a friendly nightclub. From the bag he pulled a small blowtorch. He turned a dial and the gas rushed from the canister. With a flick of his wrist he sparked a lighter and the heat flared with a whoosh like a jet plane. He stuffed a rag into Terry's mouth bent down and spoke to Ron holding the flame near his face. He spoke intimately, as if he and Ron were the only men in the room.

'We're about ready to go now, and we ain't keen on waiting around, so I'll make this really simple.' He blinked twice with the tension. 'Unless you tell us where the money is hidden your ugly friend over there is going to get even uglier. *Now where is the fucking money?*'

Ron shook his head. 'How about this? Your mother fucked a pig and the pig died of shame.'

Without another word the black one jumped to his feet, approached Terry and tore his shirt down the front, baring his chest.

'You cunts have asked for this,' hissed the white one.

Terry, his feet tied to the chair legs, his arms fastened behind him bucked like electricity was being passed through him. His eyes were enormous, spread across his face, his brow drenched with sweat. His skin looked as moist as a freshly landed fish.

The black man passed the blowtorch over Terry's chest, holding the flame on his right nipple.

The white one didn't feel a thing.

Russell connected a left hook to the left side of his head, right at the point where his ear met his jawbone. He heard the shattering of bone and knew the weaselly shit would be on a liquid diet for a month. Before he'd even hit the floor Russell had reached his partner, kicking the man's knee joint apart from the left side so that it splintered like a lolly stick. He would walk with a limp for the rest of his life. Russell reached over, picked up the gun then turned and freed Terry. The weapon felt strange in his hand and he was worried that he might accidentally discharge it. The smell of burnt flesh was nauseating. It was a stifling, dreadful odour seemingly out of all proportion to the three-inch bubbled, glossy patch of purple that now occupied the place where Terry's right nipple should be.

'Yes, my son! Yes!' Ron shouted. 'You fucking little bastards, you cunts!' Russell bent down to free his boss and help him to his feet. As he was unfastening the binding a thudding noise, like heavy mail sacks being thrown in the back of a lorry, made him turn round. Behind him Terry, his yellow YSL shirt flapping from either side, was kicking the black man in the back and legs. His bottom lip curled in, he looked as if he was either on the brink of tears or murder. The man shouted, 'No! Stop! Stop!' Terry jumped on his knee joint. The man sat up as if the floor were on fire, but was knocked back down by a kick to his face. It was a couple of moments before Russell registered that the patter of noise on the floor was two of the man's teeth. He tried to fend off the kicks to his head and abdomen with his forearms crossed in front of him. Terry worked silently but frantically, his body jerking inelegantly every time he delivered a kick.

Ron took no more than a couple of livid, equalising kicks at his former captors before stepping over the body of the white one lying unconscious on the floor, his legs skewed at awkward angles. Ron opened the office door and bellowed, 'Frankie! Frankie, where the fuck are you?' There was no answer, only Mick Hucknall's white soulboy wail coming from the kitchen. Ron walked round the back of the bar and yelled, 'Frankie!'

The volume dropped.

'What the fuck happened to you? It looks like . . .'

'Bollocks to what it looks like. Call Trevor, Mick, Tizer and Gal. I don't care what the fuck they're doing, where they are, they're to be here immediately. Tell them we've got a situation.'

'What kind of situation?' asked Frankie.

'We can't decide whether to have Johnny Walker Black Label or Glenfiddich in the bar,' shouted Ron. 'What do you fucking think? Now get on the fucking dog.'

As his penultimate act of revenge Terry jumped on his assailant's head so hard that the noise echoed in the bar. When Ron returned to the office Terry delivered a final kick, almost as an afterthought, tearing the scalp away from his skull and exposing a sliver of shining ivory skull.

'Fuck's sake, Tel,' said Russell. 'Give it a rest.'

'Yeah, pack it in, Tel,' added Ron. 'You're making him bleed all over the fucking gaff. I'll have to replace the fucking carpet.'

His fists clenched, eyes empty, Terry stumbled from the office as if he'd had his shoelaces tied together. 'Get some ice and wrap it in a towel – for the burn,' shouted Russell after him.

The white one was still lying face down on the carpet, his body as flimsy as an empty glove. A small puddle of drool was collecting by the side of his face. His accomplice kept up a low moaning noise. Ron rubbed the back of his neck and surveyed his office.

'Close one, eh, Russ?' said Ron. 'Fucking little bastards bit off more than they could chew.'

Russell nodded. His left hand was throbbing from the punch he'd delivered to the white one. His breathing was shallow, his stomach ached.

'How'd they get in?' he asked.

'Through the fucking front door,' said Ron. 'Wanted to talk something over about cheap booze. Said they'd worked with Carl Miller. Carl told me they were kosher. Either he told me a porky or they've changed their operation somewhat since Carl last came across them.'

'What you going to do with them?' asked Russell.

'Don't you worry about that, son, they'll be taken care of.' Ron pulled a face. It was rueful and careworn, the smile of an old doctor watching another cancer victim fade out. 'I'm getting too old for this shit, you know. It's too fucking exhausting. Believe me. Especially when you've got to deal with fucking amateurs like these jokers. No wonder they got a kicking. Couple of queers. Did you see? Before they came in here they still had all their own teeth?' He pointed to his own mouth. 'See that? There's more bridgework in there than over the fucking Thames.'

There was a coughing behind them. 'What's going on, Ron?'

'Trevor. Where the fuck have you been?' asked Ron.

'What are you talking about? I was only round the corner. Came right round. Can't have taken more than a coupla minutes.' Trevor glanced at Russell but made no effort to acknowledge him.

'We've got a situation here,' said Ron as breezily as if he were showing Trevor to the toilet. 'Two mugs came and tried it on, but they didn't count on Russell here.' Trevor wiped his mouth with the back of his hand. Looked unimpressed.

'Trev, keep an eye on these two for a second, will you?' Ron steered Russell out of the office and reached into his trouser pocket, pulling out a wad of bull's eyes as thick as his wrist. He peeled off a lump.

'Stick this monkey on your hip, Russ, that's your wages.' He peeled off another £200. 'And there's another twoer, a little bit on top. Let's call it a productivity bonus, eh? Go on, fuck off. Dare say I won't need you now until Monday. Best keep this family only.'

He gazed over Russell's shoulder for a moment before turning and walking solemnly back into the office. The door was shut and Russell heard muffled voices inside. Seconds later it was silent except for the clunking of the lock as it swung into place.

Chapter Nine

Sometimes you needed to give them a little jolly up, something to focus their minds on the task in hand. Trevor didn't consider himself to be some heartless cunt, but some people tried to take the piss and he wasn't having that.

Old Street. Fucking bombed-out, built-up Old Street. Row upon row of breeze-block canyons where thousands lived, but never a soul seemed to stir after dark. Trevor noted the quietness of the street as he closed the car door. The glare of a late-night discount off-licence was the only sign of life. But he was under no illusions, he was being watched. He could feel craving eyes flickering between him and the car. Better make this quick, don't want to leave it exposed to the street for long.

He was in luck, he only had to go to the ground floor, one of the flats that bordered the street from behind a metal railing and an unhealthy slick of grass. As he approached the place he noted a crack in the crescent of glass above the door that had been plastered with insulating tape. Gaff was falling apart. Trevor pressed the grimy buzzer, white-turned-grey from years of probing digits. It was so decrepit he could feel the current flowing beneath his finger.

The noise of a television set grew louder as a door swung open inside the flat. Some fucking game show, one of them you got cards for in the *Sun* or the *Mirror*. Country had gone lottery fucking mad, coffin dodgers blowing a week's pension on a handful of scratchcards.

A figure appeared on the other side of the door, wheezing gently.

'Who is it?' the voice asked.

'Open up, you old cunt, it's Trevor.'

A stifled curse came from the other side. 'I thought you was comin' tomorrow, after I got me Giro.'

'It's Wednesday,' said Trevor. 'I collect from you on Wednesday. Now open the fuckin' door.'

'Ain't got no money, Trevor. I ain't being funny, I just ain't got nothing to give you.'

Trevor sighed loudly. He wasn't in the mood for this. 'Open the door, Charlie . . .'

'Would if I could pay you,' said Charlie. 'You know that, but I ain't got nothing indoors.'

'OPEN THE FUCKING DOOR, CHARLIE!' Trevor heard a window open above him. Some nosey fucking busybody poking their hooter in where it wasn't needed. He heard the latch turn in the Yale and a bolt slide. The door swung open slowly revealing Charlie Marsh, an old lag who'd just got out of the Scrubs after a six-year stretch, his nose red round the nostrils and his eyes watery from a cold. The smell of burnt toast flooded out of the flat.

Trevor spoke quietly – something he'd learned from Ron – drawing Charlie towards him. 'Charlie, what the fuck you talking about?' he asked. 'You ain't got nothing for me? What kind of position does that put me in, eh? What am I supposed to tell Ron?'

'Trev, what can I tell you? I thought it was tomorrow, I fucking swear on me life.'

'You're trying to make a cunt out of me, Charlie.' Trevor shook his head as if genuinely upset.

'I swear Trev, I fucking swear . . .'

'There I am traipsing round in the fucking cold all day while you're sitting snug indoors. Who's being taken for a fucking mug here, Charlie? Who's being taken for a mug?'

'Tomorrow, Trev, I fuckin' swear on me life. I fucking swear it . . .'

'Charlie, I need you to tell me something honestly . . .' As Charlie came a little closer Trevor grabbed the top of the door and slammed it against the old man's head, crushing his temples between door and frame. There was a squeal that intensified when Trevor put his fingers up Charlie's nostrils.

'How you feeling now, cunt?' he asked.

'Oh fucking hell, Trev. Lay off, fuckin' lay off.' Trevor dug his nails into the soft flesh lining the inside of Charlie's nose.

'Oh fuck, oh fuck, oh fuck,' screeched Charlie. 'You win, Trev. You win, Trev, all right? Please, Trev, you win.' Trevor slammed the door on his head once more.

'Now I forgot something as well, Charlie. I forgot how much a sad old blagger like you really gets on my tits when you fuck me about . . .'

'Please, Trev, for fuck's sake, just fucking stop . . .'

'I don't want to hear nothing else from you, you old cunt, understand?'

'Yeah, yeah, 'course . . .'

'This is the second time you've fucked me about, understand?' said Trevor, his voice suddenly calm. 'There won't be a third. Do you hear what I'm saying?' He slammed the door on Charlie again. 'DO. YOU. HEAR. WHAT. I. AM. SAYING. CUNT?'

'I'll have the money for you tomorrow, Trev. I swear it, I fucking swear it . . .'

Trevor could still hear the man's gibbering as he crossed the road back to the Golf. He rubbed his fingers together. They were moist from the inside of Charlie's nose. He hoped he had a box of Kleenex in the motor. If it was still there.

Stoke Newington. He had to go over to fucking Stoke Newington. He hated fucking Stoke Newington, full of Africans and social workers. Bunch of cunts. Wouldn't live there if you fucking paid him.

He'd been to the house before, an old building on the Stamford Hill side of the High Street. He was going to collect from this woman, Belinda Stephens, who lived on the top floor with her three kids.

The mug she'd been living with, some black geezer who was banged up with a couple of mates for indecent assault on a teenage girl, had borrowed money from Ron to pay off a couple of dealers who had become tired of subsidising his coke habit. Unfortunately for Belinda her toerag of a boyfriend had sent word from inside that Belinda would take care of the debt.

Her place was quite nice. Housing Association, which meant that the hallways and corridors got a lick of paint more than once every decade. She buzzed Trevor in and he climbed the flight of stairs to the top of the house where the door to her flat had been left slightly ajar.

Trevor pushed the door open. Three mixed-race kids sat in front of the telly hypnotised by a Sony Playstation. He saw that Belinda had thrown a rug over the settee to conceal its gooey state. Trying to keep up appearances. Trevor closed the front door and walked through to the kitchen. The kids didn't even look up from Original Wipeout. Belinda was at the kitchen counter with her back to Trevor. The kettle was coming to the boil. In front of her were three Pot Noodles – two beef and tomato, one chicken and mushroom. Trevor stood in the kitchen doorway.

'Back so soon?' asked Belinda, pushing a strand of hair out of her eye. She was wearing a white towelling bathrobe that was grey at the cuffs. There was a sticky sound as she lifted the soles of her thin white feet from the linoleum when she moved to turn the kettle off. He could see that her second toes were longer than the big ones.

'Time flies,' said Trevor. She turned to face him.

'S'pose it does,' she said. 'Seems like yesterday Carl was born. He's eight tomorrow.'

'Your eldest, is he?' asked Trevor, feeling in a mood to talk.

'Yeah,' said Belinda. 'Right lot of trouble 'n'all. Takes after his old man. Hope his brothers turn out better.' On cue an argument erupted in the living room.

'Keep it down, you lot!' shouted Belinda. Trevor smelled the food as the water reconstituted the dried noodles. He felt hungry. It was nine o'clock and he hadn't had a chance to stop for a bite yet.

Belinda dropped a spoon and bent over to pick it up. Although she'd had three kids she was still in good shape – her eyes were bright and clear and she had the sexy lived-in skin of a thirty-year-old. Most of all Trevor liked the fact that she was a bottle blonde, not quite platinum, but pretty close. More than that she was the kind of bottle blonde who let you know

66

she wasn't a natural blonde by permanently keeping a track of dark hair running down the middle of her head. Trevor liked that. It was a sure sign of a dirty cow.

'You'll have to wait a minute,' she said, taking the food through to the kids.

'All right, no hurry,' said Trevor.

She came back to the kitchen, got out three glasses and poured three servings of orange Kia-Ora. She filled the glasses from the tap and left the room again.

Trevor looked around and saw the usual kid-controlled provisions that lined the kitchen: catering bags of crisps and biscuits, bottles of Coke as big as HGV fuel tanks. He examined a mug on the side. On it in blue letters was written 'Miami Dolphins'.

'Dennis brought that back from Florida for me last year,' said Belinda. She was standing in the doorway. 'Out there three months and that's what he fucking brought me.' She pulled a small, doleful smile.

'What was he doing out there?' asked Trevor.

'Never said,' she replied. 'Just said he was going, things to take care of. Then three months later called up to say he was coming back. That was it. Didn't send us no money or nothing.'

It was none of Trevor's business so he said nothing, but he couldn't help wishing that Dennis would walk through the door right there so the two of them could sort it out. Right there. Right now. He would have made the cunt fucking apologise to his bird. And to his kids.

'I need the money,' said Trevor. 'Got to make a move.'

'Come through here,' she said. She pushed another door open and followed him into the bedroom. Trevor went over to the window to check the view, make sure the motor was all right. When he turned round Belinda had dropped the robe on the floor and was standing there wearing just a black G-string. He felt himself going hard. Apart from wide hips and a slightly rounded belly she was pretty in a delicate way.

'There's no money, Trevor.' Trevor sat on the bed and beckoned her towards him. There was goose flesh on her thin

67

arms and freckles on her chest and breasts. She knelt before him. He lay back on the bed while she unfastened his trousers.

After he had finished Trevor stood up and went to the other side of the room. Belinda stayed kneeling by the bed, her hands folded over her breasts. Trevor picked up her robe and threw it across the room at her. It landed half on her shoulder, half on the floor. She pulled it over her shoulders.

'Nice job,' said Trevor, leaving the room. 'I'll be back tomorrow.'

Belinda looked confused.

'For the money,' said Trevor.

'You what?' Belinda pulled a pained, uncomprehending face.

'You heard,' said Trevor coldly. There was a thin, icy moment as Belinda's voice curdled into a scream.

'You fucking bastard,' she shrieked at Trevor, throwing a shoe, which bounced off the door frame. 'I told you I don't have no money.'

'Shall I have a word with Dennis, or do you want to?' said Trevor, putting his head round the bedroom door. He sauntered down the hallway idly, whistling under his breath.

'Night, chaps,' he said to the kids, who were still immersed in the video game. 'Look out for your mum, won'tcha?'

'Yeah, later, man,' came the disinterested reply in between mouthfuls of Pot Noodle.

He knew he'd have to knock on John Skinner's door for ages. Old fucker was half deaf. Didn't so much walk as shuffle. He thought he'd keep knocking though, just to annoy the old man, like Woody fucking Woodpecker was at his door. Heh, heh, heh, HEH, HEH. Heh, heh, heh, HEH, HEH.

'Coming, coming,' Skinner protested from behind the door.

'Come on, you old bastard, I'm in a hurry.'

Skin opened the door and took time to register who it was.

'Don't give it that,' said Trevor. 'You know what fucking day it is.'

'Weren't that,' said Skin, irritated. 'Me eyes are bad. Takes time, you know?' Trevor looked bored.

'I've got your money,' said Skin.

'Well, that's good for both of us,' said Trevor.

Skin stepped back to let Trevor in the doorway so that he was sheltered from the eyes of the street. He reached into his back pocket and produced a handful of raggedy notes.

'It's all there,' he said, handing it over.

'Top man,' said Trevor, and changed his tone. 'You ever see Russell Fisher down here?'

'Russell who?' replied Skin.

'Terrible,' said Trevor, like someone had told him a bad joke. 'Try again.'

'Sometimes,' said Skin. Trevor furrowed his brow and pursed his lips in disbelief.

'Areyoushaw? I heard he virtually lived here.'

'A lot of people come through.'

Trevor nodded, suspicious. 'Well we're working together now, so you take care of him,' he said. 'See you later, gotta go.'

Skin watched him climb the stairs. Skin sensed that both he and Trevor would like Russell to be taken care of, but he doubted it was in the same way.

Trouble was coming. Russell had something about Ron's wife – about her past. Skin could sense Russell was up to something he shouldn't be. It was too strong. Nothing good could come of it.

Chapter Ten

It was the smell that woke Zaffir. There was noise – indistinguishable and distant – that circled around him like ginger leaves pitched skywards by autumn gusts, but what sucked him from the drifting currents of insensibility was the harsh antiseptic smell that drenched his body. It was as if he'd been left to soak in a marinade of disinfectant. He felt his eyelids flicker over his pupils, the coolness of the air making them water lightly, and the shallowness of his breathing, his lungs timidly expanding and contracting as if nervous of startling the rest of his rigid frame. His breath hung tangibly in the air like the vibrations of a bell. He didn't want to move. He didn't want to speak. The stillness and the calm were as inviting as a cool pool of water on an August day.

Even with his eyelids closed the whiteness of the light confounded him; he felt girdled by nothing but space and light. He could not imagine what was beyond it, the expanses into which he would float were it not for the weight of his body. It was as if gravity had been removed from everywhere except his own blood which still flowed with the force of life.

Of course much of the liquid which coursed his body was not really Zaffir's, although no one would be asking for it back. Passing through his heart and rippling through his veins was an alien form that was pumped into his arteries from plastic bags the size of human kidneys. Six pints of it. Enough to get you bladdered, if it was strong lager.

Despite the efforts of the council's sanitary department the brown stains left by Zaffir's blood were still visible on the steps of Burlingham Court, like a wash on a canvas, marking the place where Zaffir had been found unconscious by a middle-aged rasta walking his dog. After raising the alarm the dreadlocked man had managed to keep Zaffir breathing long enough to prevent his brain from becoming deoxygenated. The local paper had described him as a hero, but hadn't printed a photo. Zaffir didn't know this. Nor did he know the man had come to visit him, sitting silently for an hour until the nurse told him that visiting time was over.

This was the day before his mother had flown back from Jeddah, fearful for her son's life. And she was still scared as she waited by his bed searching his face for a sign that would offer some hope that he might, one day, open his eyes and smile at her again. She had been praying hard, sure that Allah could not have chosen to take one so young, with so much life ahead of him, instead of a wheezing diabetic like herself. If they could have swapped places she would gladly have undergone a beating to have it that she, rather than he, was punctured with needles and tubes, unknowable through a swathe of bandages.

She waited silently, her feet out of her shoes, the dry skin on the undersides looking like it had been dusted with flour. Her mind circled the muddled message her sister had telephoned to her hotel, how it had taken ages to obtain an international line, the bargaining with the airline staff to get on the first available plane, how her mouth had dried and she'd swallowed her English when the immigration officer held up the queue to ask her questions before reluctantly handing her back her British passport.

And then the sight of Zaffir, his body thin and twisted, his knees propping up the aerated blanket like tent poles, his freshly shaven head wrapped in bandages making him look like a Sikh. Three days now she'd been waiting for a sign of life beyond the sparrow's flutter of his chest. Three days of rank chips and beans at the canteen and sleeping on her sister's spare bed.

She'd seen what the newspapers had written about the attack; the smudged, narrow columns detailing the beating with snatched quotes from 'community leaders' and local politicians; she had received a letter from a man named Goodge who expressed his deepest sympathies and guaranteed that the police regarded such attacks with the 'utmost gravity'.

It made her wonder why they shouldn't. What had happened to her son clearly had greater significance than just another alleyway slapping; obviously it was related to living in an unforgiving foreign land.

The hubbub surrounding the attack, tremors that resounded throughout the press and locality, made it plain that her son's victimisation was a consequence of his race. The irony was heavy on her shoulders. Throughout his life Zaffir had resisted much of what she had thought proper. The death of his father had made things more difficult, both financially and also in the sense that the dominant force within the house had disappeared. She found that her son would not read the Koran, spoke lazy, Anglicised Urdu at home, and slang English to his friends, yet was always loyal and attentive to her. There had been a couple of awkward times when she'd decided that it was time he was married and brokered meetings with eligible distant cousins from Pakistan whom Zaffir had treated with the respect and courtesy he might accord the disabled or mentally ill, despite the encouragement of older female chaperones who clucked approval and grossly over-exaggerated any common ground the youngsters might have.

After the disappointment of her matchmaking Mrs Khan had pretended not to care if she occasionally spied him with white, or even black girls. He never brought girls home to meet her, but sometimes when she was out shopping she might see her son in the street with his arm round some young thing, their faces up close, laughing at some private joke. And though she couldn't approve, Mrs Khan would step into a shop and watch them pass unchallenged, convinced that Zaffir would one day find a nice girl to keep her company in her old age.

It was true that she had thought this far ahead, and had hoped to be useful to her daughter-in-law around the home, looking after the grandchildren and preparing her son's favourite dishes. It would be a simple life but a rewarding one, with quiet surprises and selfless pleasures. This was what she had pictured in her heart and, in ways that she now regretted, expected.

And now she could not think any further than the present.

Her entire body had attuned itself to searching her son for signs of consciousness. It was as if she had been locked in some dark corridor from which she could only escape should her son beckon her from the blackness. A knot the size of a fist had settled in her stomach and was a constant reminder, even during those brief moments when her mind touched upon other subjects – remembering what time her brother-in-law was coming to collect her, the name of the consultant who would smile at her and talk gently after examining her helpless son – that she was alone watching her child die before her.

It was after she had returned from downing a quick, orange-coloured cup of tea in the canteen downstairs that she thought she noticed the slight flicker of Zaffir's eyelids. She leaned forward and tried to remain absolutely still. There were moments like this every day when the pressure on her chest would lighten and she seemed to breathe properly for the first time in years. She concentrated hard on her son's face, trying to ignore the bulging bandages on his head and the tubes that ran from his nostrils and mouth.

She sat still, fearful of over-exciting herself, terrified that this may be another mirage that would leave her, once again, empty and troubled.

But there it was again.

Definitely. A slight but distinct movement of the eyelashes. And there, perched on top of the blanket, his hand. The index finger was quivering as if electricity were passing through it.

Mrs Khan felt as if she had surfaced after being stuck at the bottom of a fathomless ocean. For the first time in years she got to her feet and started to run. There had to be a doctor somewhere.

Chapter Eleven

'I've got a new challenge for you,' Ron had said. 'It ain't exactly the most exciting job, but it's cushy.'

'What is it?' Russell had asked.

'Keep an eye on Sonia, the wife.'

'You what?'

This was unbelievable. Russell shrugged his shoulders. Tried to look disinterested.

Russell and Ron had been cooped up together for a couple of weeks and Russell was beginning to find it difficult to bite his tongue when Ron went off on one. Since the botched robbery a couple of weeks ago Ron had got the jitters, losing his temper for the slightest reason, constantly asking where people were and who they were meeting, gabbing on that things were going to 'kick off big-time', imagining enemies everywhere plotting his own demise and that of his wife.

Just for the record, Russell had protested a little, had made out that he was unhappy to be given such a soft detail, to be so far removed from the seat of power. As far as he could figure it there was no immediate threat to anyone, least of all Ron's wife. Ron had gone on a bit about a need for vigilance and to trust no one and how Russell was to keep an ear open for anyone in the firm speaking out of turn.

Then he'd told him to piss off.

The drive out to Ron's house took longer than Russell had expected, but he got there with time to spare. Throughout his life Russell had hated being late for appointments. Even shit things, like going down the Job Club to be asked why he wasn't working – to 'develop a platform for employability' in the adenoidal DSS whinger's words – he'd made sure he was there on the dot. Only slags turned up late.

Russell crawled up the wide, eerie road where Ron and Sonia Chisholm lived. It was a strange neighbourhood, the kind of place you'd rarely see someone walking, where an Indian dentist lived next door to a kebab-shop king, who lived next door to a Page Three girl, who lived next door to a footballer. A mix of styles like salad dressings: ranch, Spanish, French. Cheesy, hammy interiors; catalogue panache with pick-and-mix appendages plundered from QVC.

Pulling up outside 'Moore House' (named after the England and West Ham captain – nice touch) Russell wasn't quite sure of the etiquette, whether to pull into the gravel horseshoe drive or to park in the road and walk up the drive. He chose the latter. If he had made a mistake it wasn't disrespectful, just naïve, and, when you're with the boss's wife, it's infinitely better to be the latter.

Russell felt uncomfortable with the amount of noise his footsteps made on the gravel. However he placed his feet it sounded clumsy. He felt like an intruder. The cool of the afternoon and the quietness of the neighbourhood made him feel exposed. At any moment a pack of baying Dobermans would scoot round the side of the house with hunger in their eyes.

The letter box had 'Letters' written on it and the doorbell was one of those you pulled, he surmised after pushing a couple of times. Brilliant. Why didn't it have 'Pull' written on it? It played 'I'm Forever Blowing Bubbles' in a heavy, clunking rhythm.

'Who is it?' A woman's voice came through the slatted box on the wall.

'It's Russell. Russell Fisher. Ron sent me.' The sound of the woman's voice startled him. Unconsciously he smoothed his jacket down and patted the crown of his head. Butterflies hovered in his stomach.

Keys turned, locks unfastened and the door opened revealing Sonia Chisholm. She was smaller than Russell had expected, more fragile-looking. She had a pretty, open, face with high cheekbones, sharp green eyes and dark eyebrows that arched high towards the top of her head, which was crowned with thick, salon-assisted honey-coloured hair. Even from this distance Russell could tell she had just washed it; the fragrance of shampoo hung in the air between them.

They just stood and stared at each other.

'My God,' Sonia said eventually. 'Russell. You know, when you said your name . . . you know . . . I thought to myself . . .'

'This I do not believe.' Russell thought he might have blown the line, but he persisted nevertheless. 'It's you, ain't it?' Time had been kind to Jane, he could see that. She looked healthy and she looked strong. Most of all she looked rich.

'Jesus, Jane. I don't believe it . . . but, I, but Ron said his wife was called Sonia. I don't . . .'

She smiled. 'Come in, come in.'

'Thanks.' He walked into the hallway, his hands clasped awkwardly in front of him, his collar sharp against his neck. He felt like he'd come to collect a body. He couldn't believe what he was seeing.

Sonia closed the door behind him and gave him a once-over. 'I'm totally gobsmacked,' she said girlishly. She shook her head in disbelief. 'Look at you. You look well. Hardly changed.'

'Neither have you,' said Russell.

'Get a grip,' said Sonia sarcastically. 'I've put on a few pounds since I last saw you. Still, no grey hairs yet, so I can't complain.'

They stood there, unsure of what to do. He'd prepared for this moment hundreds of times but all his slick lines and smooth words abandoned him. 'This is so strange,' said Russell. 'I mean, what are the odds . . . ? I didn't know where you'd gone, thought you'd moved away.' He looked at her and studied the contours of her face. She was familiar yet unfamiliar. Like turning the locks in a stranger's house.

'Let's go out,' said Sonia finally. 'I think we need to talk. Get reacquainted. I won't be long. I'm just going up to get my things. Why don't you wait in the lounge?' She gestured for Russell to pass through a large doorless entrance to an L-shaped room. 'Jesus, I can't believe it's you.' She smiled. 'I won't be a mo.'

As Sonia disappeared Russell couldn't help a quick glance at her behind. She wore fresh black jeans, a pristine white shirt and faux snakeskin heels with painted toes pointing out. She still had a nice tuche, didn't look like it was melting, like some her age. She moved up the stairs swiftly. Classy.

Knowing that touching anything would inevitably render it into a dozen pieces, Russell wandered cautiously into the lounge. A twenty-foot window provided a vista on to a well-groomed back garden, a triumph of suburbia over nature. Old paintings of horses lined the walls, each one showing a thoroughbred beast in a pose of tense readiness. The paintings seemed incongruous, the rest of the room – carpet, walls, curtains – were a similar creamy off-white, like the dizzyingly airy apartments in *Miami Vice*. If it weren't for the horses this could be the fuck-pad of some Cuban cocaine king. The paintings had been put up by a different person to the one who had designed the interior– they were the work of Ron; Sonia had done the furnishing.

Russell settled into a white leather sofa, but again felt self-conscious about the amount of noise he was making and, scrambling like a tortoise flipped on its back, pulled himself clear of the four-seater. He heard Sonia sashaying down the stairs and pretended to be examining a bronze figurine of a rider and horse coming over Beecher's Brook at Aintree. It was called 'The Brave'.

'That's Ronnie's,' said Sonia. 'All the pictures as well.' She smiled. 'He loves horses.'

'I know,' said Russell, still getting over the idea of someone referring to Ron as Ronnie.

'Of course you do.'

'He's got money in a couple, ain't he? I've seen some of them race,' said Russell, nodding at her encouragingly.

'Have you?' She seemed genuinely interested, not just polite.

'Yeah, over at Haydock last season. They did all right.'

'He's desperate for one of them to win something though,' said Sonia, sounding wistful. 'That's all he talks about. I hear him on the phone in the study – it's next to the bedroom, you see. He's always talking to the stables.'

'Well, he can't talk to the horses, can he?' Russell blurted this out, trying a little too hard. But Sonia seemed far away, staring out at the garden.

'I bet he wishes he was Doctor bleeding Doolittle sometimes', she said dreamily.

'Yeah, he'd make a fortune then. He could have his own animal talk show and everything.'

Sonia gestured towards a cabinet next to a Sony Trinitron the size of a tower block. 'See that? It's full of videos. All of them racing.' She swung the doors open and pointed at each of the plastic boxes. 'Racing, racing, horses, horses, horses, racing, West Ham, horses, racing, racing . . . he's a man obsessed. I don't think he should have married me. He should have married a bleedin' horse.' She closed the doors. 'He says he ended up with a nag, so it makes no difference.'

Russell had to be careful here. He knew what he wanted to say, but the opportunity to chip away at Ron's authority, to print 'wanker' on the back of his jacket *in his own home, in front of his wife*, filled him with a sharp, dry sensation. He knew what would happen next: somewhere between the smell of pink bubble gum and Carpet Magic was a sickness that Russell had once had. It had trailed him throughout his life, ambushing him when he was most exposed, like now. Russell swallowed and reached into his pocket.

'Want some gum?' he asked.

'No, I'm all right.'

'Sugar free . . .'

'Still look after yourself, do you?'

'Something like that. I don't fancy taking my teeth out every time I want to clean them. Reminds me of old people.'

'What's wrong with old people?'

'Nothing wrong with old people. I just don't want to be one yet.'

'Yeah, well stop talking like that. You're starting to sound old before your time.' She fumbled in a Prada bag for her car keys. 'Do you want to drive, or shall I?'

'What are you talking about?'

'Shopping. Brent Cross. Shopping city. I don't fancy Lakeside today. Come on.'

Russell realised that she'd mentioned it earlier, but he'd been too distracted to absorb what she was saying.

'Ron said we ain't supposed to go out unless we let him know where we go,' he said.

' "Ron said, Ron said." ' She put on a voice like a parrot.

'Listen, I ain't being funny but I've been told you're not to leave the house unless it's been sorted with Ron,' said Russell, thinking that he sounded like a copper. 'Anything you need I can bring or have someone collect for you.'

He remembered the look she gave him – somewhere between pity and disdain – from years ago. It made him feel wanting.

'Put some mustard on your burger, Russell. Live a little.'

'But Ron told me . . .'

'So you think everything will be fine if I limit myself to sending out for a couple of pairs of tights and two pounds of Granny Smiths?' cut in Sonia. 'Do you really expect me to sit round watching daytime TV, discovering that stashed away in my attic is a fortune in ageing knick-knacks? Do you want me to grow old eating Quality Street? You think some headcase will think twice about coming after me because I'm tooled up with a TV remote?' Her green eyes met his. 'Russell, I've got to live. I can't pretend that all I want is contained within these four walls. I'm going out to spend some of Ron's money, so are you coming or not?'

Russell remained still. Met her gaze. Lost himself inside her eyes, not quite believing how this had all worked out. She stood with her head tilted slightly to one side, a playful smile across her mouth.

'All I can say is that I've been told certain things, and I'm only doing what I've been told.' Russell jerked his right hand up against his shoulder, as if throwing salt behind him for luck. He wanted it to seem as if he was dismayed to be disobeying Ron's orders. 'Anything else . . . is just talk. Nothing to do with me.'

'Yeah, just talk Russell,' said Sonia sarcastically. 'You're working for me now. So you coming or what?'

At that moment nothing could have stopped him.

As Sonia eased her black BMW on to the silky, silent road she fired up a Silk Cut rescued from somewhere in the door panel.

'You want one?' she asked Russell. 'There's a packet in the glove compartment. I'm sure there is.' Russell fished around amongst the cassettes, yellowing Tiger tokens and empty Ribena cartons.

Of course Russell knew all about Sonia Chisholm. Their paths had separated and Jane had disappeared into the high and low places of the city, masked by mists of members-only circles wherein she had shed her skin and brought into existence a new persona. Russell had kept tabs on her from the shadows: like a sonar operator he tracked her progress from darkness. Although his heart ached he remained respectful, kept a distance. And as stealthy as he was, Russell was no stalker, no Phonecard freak hot-breathing it from a call-box plastered with whore's Day-glo come-ons. Word had come in small doses – a whisper here, a report there. Friends and acquaintances in pubs and clubs and houses passing on sightings, rumours, disclosures, each making his heart thunder with regret.

He'd heard she was looking after a club. He even went down there, see if he could have a verbal, maybe patch things up. They could have at least had a drink or something

But she was gone. 'Oh, you mean Sonia,' the girl behind the bar had said while slicing a lemon. She had dyed black hair turreted on her head and her face was clotted with make-up. 'You've missed her, love. Been gone two weeks. Honeymoon. Only married the boss, didn't she? Tell you, she saw a good thing when she saw it.'

He got drunk. He rarely drank at that time, but that night he hit the Black Prince with Mick and Curtis. The next afternoon he awoke to the sound of a crowd. He rolled out from under a pub bench blighted by Premier League pandemonium. Fucking Tottenham v Man United. He couldn't remember who he hated most.

He walked out of the pub into a sharp autumn afternoon. Two small boys threw piles of leaves at each other, and all he could think of was confetti. That was six years ago, six years of forgetting and dismissal. Six years of suppressing hope. Vaguely he'd been aware of how Jane's life had progressed while he tried hard to shake the spectres of belief and anticipation from his mind.

He had always known that he would come close to her again, that their lives would re-connect. Despite them growing apart, despite her marriage and their separate lives she had never escaped his mind. She had filled his imagination at every dark moment. And as they talked it occurred to Russell that, this time, he was prepared to settle for nothing less than everything.

'You could have driven, if you'd wanted,' Sonia said to Russell, who was sitting deep in his polished black leather seat. Hands clasped in his lap, he watched a bunch of kids shoving each other into the road inbetween mouthfuls of chips. Their untamed laughter and edgy bonhomie made him feel alone, strangely sentimental about his own long-gone schooldays: the smell of the battered, aged textbooks, the thrill of the inquisition, the injustice of punishment. He'd always wanted to go on a school trip, but he'd never made it. Once he'd had to stay in class – with the retards and sad cases – all because his dad wouldn't cough up the £40 he'd been asked to contribute for the week-long trip to the Isle of Wight. All Russell's mates had gone, but his dad said he didn't see the point. Waste of time. Waste of money. Russell skipped school, spent the time playing Defender and Asteroids in the arcade.

'Best days of your life, so they say,' mused Sonia.

'So they say,' replied Russell.

'And you think when they tell you that, well, if these are the best days what are the worst going to be like?' said Sonia. 'You know sometimes when I was a kid I'd just go to my room and pull the blankets over my head and wish that I'd wake up and I'd be an adult. Now I wish I was a kid again. You got kids, Russell?'

'No.'

'There's a difference,' insisted Sonia. 'Loads of blokes help produce kids, but how many of them are *fathers*?'

'Not many.'

'Men are lazy bastards sometimes, aren't they?' said Sonia, as if this were a comment on Russell himself. 'Present company excepted, of course. They get some girl up the duff and like the idea of being a dad. But when the true horror arrives – the screaming and the shitty nappies and the nights in – they don't want to know, do they?'

'Something like that.'

'That's one thing a man's got to have, staying power – and I'm not talking about bed but, you know, long-term stickability. Someone who's going to be there when you need them. That's all most women want.'

Russell watched her perfectly manicured hands. Her cuticles milky white against her purply brown nail varnish. He wanted to ask her if that was why she was with Ron.

'Any fool can make a baby,' said Sonia. 'But only a man can raise a child.' And with that she flipped her finger to some sales rep who'd cut her up in his Rover Vitesse.

Russell didn't have anything to add. He was happy just sitting next to her.

Chapter Twelve

It took longer now to get into Merlin's Cave than before the attack. Ron had got it into his head that danger lurked in every corner. There were now two doors to the club – an outer wrought-iron number and an inner one consisting of three inches of wood with a metal plate set in the middle. Ron had put it about that anyone visiting the club who wasn't welcome would be treated with 'extreme prejudice', some phrase he'd picked up from a Schwarzenegger film he'd seen on video.

The smell hit Russell as soon as he opened the door to Merlin's Cave. It was like someone had eaten a plate of vomit and shitted it out. Twisting his face and fanning his nose as if plagued by invisible flies, Russell headed over towards Frankie who had a red handkerchief tied around his face. He looked like he was just about to rob a stagecoach in some Western.

'What the fuck . . . ?' said Russell. It couldn't be true. Frankie seemed to be sitting at a table covered in newspaper picking his way through a mound of shit.

'Long story, Russell. Tell you, this is worse than watching fucking Millwall.'

'Now you're being silly,' said Russell, speaking through his nose. 'I'm sorry, mate, I've eaten some crap from your kitchen, but I've got to draw the line somewhere.'

'Ain't funny, Russell,' said Frankie. 'Don't think I'm ever going to be able to get this smell out of my nose.' He lifted what looked like a soggy piece of paper from the faeces with the blade of a knife and laid the mess on a napkin to the side, which was already covered with similar scraps.

'You'll never guess what happened,' said Frankie.

'Amaze me,' said Russell, pulling his jacket up so that it covered his nose.

'Well, yesterday Trevor came in with a big pile of cash. He'd just caught up with some slag who owed Ron two Gs. Anyway, he comes in here and I do his dinner. I put the food on the table next to the money while he popped back to his car because he'd forgotten his mobile. The phone went out back so I went to get it. While I was talking I forgot that I'd opened the back door while I was cooking, to let in some air like. Anyway, Trevor came back to find that Barko had come in through the back door and followed his nose to the table. But what was fucking strange was that Barko ignored the food and started eating the money.'

'Fucking clever dog,' said Russell.

'Steady, Russell. Ron went fucking mental, threatened to kill the dog. Reckons Barko ate about six hundred quid. Said that he wanted the money or he'd fucking poison the dog. So my mate tells me that if you can get the serial numbers of the notes the Bank of England will replace them for you. I've had to keep an eye on Barko, waiting for him to take a shit, like. He looked at me real funny when I scooped it all up and went storming back to the kitchen.'

'Wouldn't surprise many of the punters though, would it?' said Russell.

'Behave, Russell.'

Barko was a five-year-old bull mastiff used as an early warning device at the back of the club. He lolled round the back yard drooling to himself and barking at anything passing on the other side of the fence. Kids from the local school made special trips to bait him. Barko was just grateful for the attention.

'How much have you found?'

'Dunno, couple of hundred, tops,' said Frankie, gesturing at the scraps on the napkin. 'I'm going to rinse it off before I go down the bank. Can't wait to see the look on their faces. Gives new meaning to the term money laundering, don't it?'

'And shit money,' said Russell.

'Tell you what, Russ – do us a favour. Let me know if you see Ron feeding little titbits to Barko,' said Frankie with a wink 'I think he's got it in for him now.'

'You should feed him properly, mate.'

'I do feed him properly, he's just fucking mad. He'll eat anything. He's like a goat or something. It was a miracle I managed to scoop up the shit before he ate that. Dog's off its 'ead.'

The stench of the dog shit was getting to Russell. 'Ron in the office?' he asked.

'Yeah,' said Frankie. 'He's phoning round trying to buy some kind of security system for the club. Says we're liable to be attacked at any moment. Reckons there's trouble brewing.'

'What's he talking about? What kind of trouble?' said Russell.

'Shooter kind of trouble.'

'Shooters? Who?'

'Dunno. Ron's been going on that that geezer who got taken care of, one of them that tried to rob the club, the white one, has got some uncle or something who's a bit tasty. Ron's been muttering about sorting out a better security system for the club. Getting cameras and sensors fitted all over the gaff. Don't see the point while we've got Barko.'

'Yeah, well Barko ain't going to be around long if Ron and Trevor got anything to with it,' said Russell. 'Sounds like Barko's gonna get "downsized".'

Frankie shook his head and went back to his unenviable task. Russell knocked on Ron's door. There was no answer. He knocked again before opening the door a tiny bit and peering in. Ron was standing up at his desk with his shirtsleeves rolled up and was gesturing with his panatella at the man on the end of his cordless phone (Taiwanese, knocked out for £30 apiece last summer down Chapel Street). When he saw Russell he furrowed his brow, raised his palms upwards and shrugged his shoulders.

' 'Arry, 'Arry, you've told me about your overheads, you've told me about your expenses,' he said into the phone. 'You've told me about your bottom line, but I'm coming to you as a businessman and friend, someone who wants to put some work your way but feels that we could come to a more mutually acceptable agreement, *youknowoImean*? Listen to me,

'Arry. I've got one question for you. 'Arry, give me your best price. Areyoushaw? *Areyoushaw*?! That sunshine in fucking Florida must have fried your brains. You're beginning to tit me off now. Listen, I'm going to pretend I didn't hear you say that, all right? I'm going to wipe the slate clean. Now you go off and have a think and call me back when you've recovered your senses.'

With that Ron clicked the phone off and stood, arms folded, a smoking panatella in one hand, the receiver in the other.

'All right, guv?' said Russell.

'What the fuck are you doing here?'

'I thought I should check in.'

'You thought, you thought, you thought *what*?'

Russell calmed himself before answering. 'I thought I should drop by and see what was happening.'

'What is probably happening, Russell, is that my wife is probably being raped and murdered by some fucking piece of shit,' said Ron furiously. Russell tried not to laugh at Ron's absurd paranoia.

It struck Russell that there was now a new overpowering odour. Since the botched robbery Ron's office had been completely redecorated – lick of paint, new carpets, new furniture, the works. The place stank of solvents, emulsion, fresh plastic and glue.

'She told me that she was going to her health club this morning so I should come down here,' explained Russell.

Ron gestured to the heavens, shaking his head. 'Who fucking runs things round here? Her, or me? Eh? Who fucking runs things? *I do.* I fucking run things round here, so don't start acting the smart cunt, all right? You're on the firm now, Russell. Everything you've done up to now has given me cause to trust you. But this, this is fucking out of order. "She's going down the health club." Areyoushaw? *Areyoushaw? Yeravinalaugharncha?* As far as targets go my wife and home are as soft as a virgin's tits. That is why I sent you over there – to keep an eye on things.'

While Ron was ranting at him Russell switched off. He

didn't hear the abuse. He thought of something else. He thought about Ron's wife. He thought about Jane or Sonia or whatever she was calling herself. He wondered if Ron spoke to her this way. If they argued and fought, or if, when he got home and heaved on his slippers and activated his movement-sensitive alarm system, he became a pussycat before his wife. He thought not.

But he knew that anyone used to having their way, used to running things, anyone who could lose it as quickly and easily as Ron, couldn't just switch off. He felt protective towards Sonia; not the paranoid grand-gesture protectiveness of Ron, who would, no doubt, use his wife simply as a way of getting into a ruck, but with a warmth that circulated inside him and made him feel good. Russell attempted to tune back into Ron's bollocking, trying to ignore what was going through his head. He'd been burying that kind of thing the best part of his adult life, and for good reason: he knew what kind of trouble it could get you into.

Chapter Thirteen

Zaffir was told that he'd been unconscious for eight days, but it was not something that he could verify, except by looking at a calendar. Everything that had happened since he last focused his eyes and felt sensation could have occurred over a period of seconds, years, or a lifetime. It was all so indefinite, he couldn't put a finger on it. He just felt like he hadn't been *there*. Not that he knew quite where he'd been, or what he'd been doing. There are no explanations for such things, only darkness accompanied by the green hiccup of a monitoring machine.

The churning of his mind – the only sensation he could recall – had been disrupted by urgent, demanding voices. There was something going on, and even if it meant throwing off his tiredness and evacuating his state of deep, fuzzy tranquillisation, he felt a need to clamber from the well of numbness, if only to see what all the shouting was about.

Most of the time he slept – as if he hadn't slept enough over the preceding few weeks – his mother eyeing him fearfully, concerned that his falling lids might be the overture to further horror. But this hospital business was tiring him out: first he was woken at dawn by the breakfast trolley, after that sadistic cleaners clanged huge drum-like machines around his bed before groggy nurses busied themselves with his ablutions. Before he knew it there was a crowd at the end of his bed – usually a doctor or consultant who didn't address him directly, trailed by a bunch of earnest-looking students who wouldn't meet his gaze.

Then there was the police. A couple of detectives had turned up – a short, portly old boozer and a formal young geezer with a ginger crop, old before his years, speaking in unnecessarily elaborate sentences. They told him they were still investigating the case, but were making slow progress, and anything he could remember would help them a great deal. The doctor had told them that Zaffir was still not strong enough to be submitted to a formal interview and that the detectives should wait a week for him to recover some more.

Zaffir just stayed shtoom. Best not to say anything until he'd had a chance to clear his head. One thing was for fucking sure: there was no way he was going to tell them who'd put him in hospital. He wasn't stupid. They'd eyed him warily, suspicion traced in their eyes, but they'd been on too many be-nice-to-the-Pakis training schemes to push it any further. They'd nodded sombrely at him underneath the strip lighting, the ginger one taking notes. They'd left a card on his bedside table, uttered some encouraging words and told him to give them a call 'if anything comes to mind'. Zaffir had let it sit there next to the bottle of Ribena, hadn't even looked at it. No point, really.

Since he'd slipped from the coma Trevor Chisholm had become Zaffir's companion whenever he closed his eyes. He came primarily at night, stalking him at home, harassing him at the pizza parlour, bullying him at college. There seemed to be no facet of his life to which Trevor did not have access, no lock that he could not unpick. But this was his inner life, the expanses within which he travelled alone.

His mother brought him large parcels of food from home, big greasy containers filled with vegetables and rice and breads wrapped in silver foil and greaseproof paper. They hadn't talked about the events on the steps, Zaffir pretending he didn't want to upset her by reviving bad memories, his frail body on the hospital bed serving as sufficient reminder. And how to say it? The woman had been beyond the bounds of reasonable suffering. He would leave her to bury the pain without disturbing her further.

It was after another week, when the boredom uniquely occasioned by institutional life had really kicked in, that his mother arrived for her evening visit with a middle-aged man. His thinning hair was stuck to his pate by the sweat from his walk up four flights of steps (only the service lifts were working, cash had dried up) and he patted his head with the heel of his hand absently as he walked along the glossy NHS floor alongside the beaming Mrs Khan.

'Zaffir,' she said. 'This is Mr Rasheed.' Zaffir nodded at the man who was standing by his bedside clutching a leather briefcase, his breathing audible.

'I'd like to extend my sincere sympathies to you,' he said. 'What has happened is a shocking crime and an indictment of our violent times.'

Zaffir looked at his mother. Anxiety passed across her face. She looked from her son to Mr Rasheed at her side. 'Mr Rasheed is here to help us,' she said grasping her son's lukewarm hand. Zaffir lay there dumbly. A large group of Cypriots were laughing and joking noisily in Greek opposite him, here to comfort a fat man in his mid thirties who'd been hit by a joyrider while crossing the road. Both of his tree-trunk legs had been hauled up in traction. On his night table he had pictures of his three daughters which he kissed before going to sleep at night. Zaffir liked the way he would give the thumbs-up to other patients who went by, his rump steak forearms plastered with thick black hair.

His own corner of the ward was considerably more sober. His mother and Rasheed had seated themselves on the moulded seats at his bedside and had the look of counsellors about them, like a couple of soft-touch supply teachers.

'I hope that you do not find this an intrusion, Zaffir, but I am here with your mother's blessing,' opened Rasheed, his index finger tapping his briefcase. Zaffir did his best to look as if he was kindling attention from deep within his exhaustion. 'I realise that you are still tired from your ordeal but I contacted your mother after hearing about your situation, should there be anything I could do to lend assistance.'

His mother reached over to the jug of water at his side and poured her son a helping, gesturing with the glass for him to sit up and drink something.

'She tells me that you have yet to speak of the night you were injured.' Rasheed left a charged silence, a theatrical delicacy, letting it linger over the scrubbed linoleum. Zaffir, I appreciate that there are occasions when, for very good reasons, one feels one must be reticent, when time is needed before it may be possible to speak openly and honestly about events, that pain only subsides over weeks and months and that recounting events can be as agonising as the happenings themselves.'

Mrs Khan reached over again and held her son's clammy paw. Rasheed continued, acknowledging the woman next to him with a soft nod. 'However, for those who love you there are still many questions in their minds about what happened to you that night. Questions which only you can answer. It would come as a great comfort to them to know what happened. And let's not forget that there are countless others in the community who have heard about these events and are pondering their significance.'

Watching the portly man hunched over his battered brown attaché case Zaffir realised what he was being asked. He'd known about Rasheed for a while now, knew he had influence, got in the papers, did a lot of shouting, could stir things up a bit. But he, Zaffir, involved in all this politicking? It was not something he had ever thought about, nor did he like the sound of it.

'It seems unlikely that the motive for the attack was financial,' continued Rasheed. 'There was no money removed from your body as you lay on the floor, was there? If your . . .'

'I can't remember anything . . .' said Zaffir faintly, his eyes trailing along the ward. 'It's all a blur.'

'Yes, it seems so,' said Rasheed, persisting. 'It must still be difficult for you, my boy, I understand this. But is there not any detail which you can identify which may help you to recall matters of significance?'

Rasheed surveyed him cannily, knowing what he knew and keeping it to himself.

It was probably the wrong thing to do but Zaffir couldn't help but look at his mother, to meet her bay eyes that were slightly yellowed by age. As he watched her, round-shouldered yet attentive, her right hand gripping a comforting tissue; he knew he would have to say something, to offer an explanation for what had brought them all here, to strengthen the contours of their grim supposition. This knowledge wearied him virtually beyond tolerance but, like the late-night driver opening the windows and turning up the car stereo to drown out sleep, he knew that it was the only way home.

'Ham and pineapple,' said Zaffir as if he were naming the real killer of John F. Kennedy. Rasheed and Mrs Khan looked at each other and then back at the young man in the bed, his brown, mottled skin resting on the sheets that someone else would be lying on soon.

'That was what I was delivering. Ham and pineapple.'

Chapter Fourteen

In a devastating attack on Council Leader
Malcolm Goodge yesterday Councillor Abdul
Rasheed confirmed that many Asian voters
are questioning the council's commitment
to stamping out racism in Illingford.

'When there is a crime of this seriousness, nothing is done,' Rasheed said from
his home. 'The police and council officers
are utterly uninterested when it comes to
finding the thugs who assaulted a young
Asian man who was delivering pizza in
order to buy medicine for his sick
mother. How does that make us feel?'

Asked who he blamed for the attack on
Zaffir Khan, 17, Rasheed replied, 'It is
clear that Asians in Illingford are considered to be second-class citizens. This
kind of thinking is what causes these
kinds of attacks. However Malcolm Goodge
can no longer fob us off with excuses. We
are sick and tired of being treated in
this way and this time we will not accept
excuses. We want a tangible commitment
from the police and council and we want
to see justice for Zaffir Khan.'

Rasheed revealed that his own pressure
group, the Community Action Group, is now
thinking of breaking away from the ruling
Labour group and fielding its own candi-
dates at the forthcoming local elections.

> Research demonstrates that eighty per
> cent of Asians voted for Goodge at the
> last election.
>
> Saul Briffa of the political analysts
> Fulcrum estimates that should Goodge's
> support drop below forty per cent of
> Asians this would be enough to force a
> coalition with the Conservatives. 'If the
> CAG get organised and appeal to Asian
> voters, then they could hold the key to
> the election,' said Briffa.
>
> And Rasheed has an even bleaker message
> for Malcolm Goodge. 'Despite our best
> efforts the young do not seem terribly
> interested in the CAG. For them it does
> not seem very exciting. They'd much
> rather try and remedy the situation on
> the streets.'

Malcolm Goodge slammed the paper down next to his poached egg. A wave of Earl Grey rode over the lip of his cup and sank into his stripped-pine breakfast table. Things were beginning to look grim. This whole CAG thing was getting out of hand and the more it gathered pace the more his situation became precarious. He needed to deal with Rasheed soon, put him in his place, and he knew just the man to do it.

Chapter Fifteen

When Russell strolled into Ron's office that morning the big man put down his paper and took a swig of tea before resting his heavy chin in his hand. When Russell asked him if he was all right, Ron could only sigh and wonder, out loud, whether his words of the previous day had actually penetrated his skull. Or did Russell just think that he was running his mouth? What narked Ron the most was that Russell seemed to have no fucking idea how much shit they were in, the sheer irregularity of such an occurrence, of two slags breezing in to his club trying to mug him off. Most worryingly, Russell didn't seem to grasp the gravity of the situation, as if it was something that didn't involve him.

For Ron it was simple: two geezers had tried to take him out on his own manor, *in his own club*. It was out of order, it had transgressed the unwritten rules, it was a fucking liberty. Still, the scum had got their just deserts. According to Trevor – who had taken a great interest in the body disposal process – teeth had been removed and crushed so that even dental identification would be impossible.

Ron picked up his letter opener – a German bayonet his old man had picked up during the War – and started scraping the dirt from beneath his fingernails. At least the incident had given Russell the chance to show that he could take care of himself. Ron felt good about that; he'd been looking for someone reliable for a few months now, tried a few faces but things hadn't worked out: they'd been too mouthy, too stupid, too indiscreet. Most commonly they'd been too willing to get involved in fisticuffs. As much as Ron needed people who could be a bit handy, who could put it about a bit, what he didn't need were knuckle-scarred bruisers who might attract unwanted attention. There was no need for that kind of thing. The people who needed to be taken care of would be taken care of, and the kind of people who needed to know that Ron and his people could take care of themselves would make it their business to know the score. Word gets around. Russell had done the business when it mattered.

'What the fuck are you doing here?' he asked Russell. The younger man looked over his shoulder.

'Yes, you, you mug.'

'What are you talking about, Ron?' Russell offered Ron his palms. 'I don't get it . . .'

'Well, you ain't the one who's gonna get fuckin' got, are you?' said Ron angrily.

Russell sat silently.

'Russell,' said Ron, 'this ain't fucking *Mastermind*. What have I asked you to do for me, Russell? What have I trusted you with, eh?'

'I'm looking after Sonia.'

'Good.' Ron put down the knife on the desk and flashed a sarcastic smile. Russell nodded at him expectantly.

'So what the fuck are you doing sitting in my office at nine-thirty in the morning, then?' His voice was as quick and harsh as an upper-cut.

'Came by after I'd been to the gym, didn't I?' said Russell. 'It was on my way. Sonia told me to meet her at the health club.'

'I told you different, Russell,' said Ron testily. 'Told you to look after her. That's the job I wanted done, Russell, and you're not fucking doing it.'

'But she said . . .'

'And I said different, Russell, and as far as you're concerned that's the only thing that matters.' The volume of Ron's voice was increasing. ''Cos, remember, you're responsible for her welfare when I'm not around. I've put trust in you, Russell. See to it that you don't let me down. You don't want to let me down, Russell. Never. Now get the fuck over there before I lose my temper.'

Russell skimmed his upper teeth with his tongue as if thinking for a moment.

'And next time you're up the gym you can tell that fucking

degenerate Skinner that if he so much as thinks about missing a payment then my little brother will not be his usual understanding self,' added Ron, turning the knife.

'He ain't a degenerate, Ron,' said Russell without looking Ron in the eye.

'What did you say?' asked Ron. The room seemed suddenly to turn cold.

'I said he ain't a degenerate.'

Ron pursed his lips as if he were about to whistle. 'You know, Russell, I think you might have a point. John Skinner ain't a degenerate, he's a sad fucking old loser with a problem with the gee gees.'

Russell looked at the man sitting behind the desk with anger brewing in his veins. He left the room without saying a word, a fact that vaguely saddened Ron who felt that he hadn't had the opportunity to let himself go properly.

The phone rang. Ron put the receiver against his ear and carried on cleaning his nails.

'Yeah,' he said.

'Ron?' The voice was firm and well-rounded. Someone who was used to being listened to. Ron recognised the voice. Waited a couple of seconds.

'Ron?'

'Who's calling?'

'It's, er, Malcolm, Malcolm Goodge.'

Ron smiled to himself, feeling in control.

'That would be Councillor Goodge, would it?'

'Absolutely.' The smile in his voice had returned. 'How are you?'

'Getting by. What can I do you for?'

'Well, I wanted to know if you could meet me for a drink.'

Ron had been waiting for this call for a few months now. He hadn't thought it would come like this, though. He'd expected some flunky, some nerd in Doctor Marten shoes with herbal tea on his breath popping in with a nervous invitation. But then Goodge probably wanted to limit the number of people who knew about this call to a small and intimate circle of people; namely himself.

Their history was brief, going back only a couple of years. While he'd been in the process of applying for late licences for Merlin's Cave and three other nightclubs, Ron had read in the local rag about Goodge's acrimonious divorce, how his estranged wife had hired some shyster lawyer who had taken Goodge for all he was worth – put him in a position where he had to apply for a council house in his own borough. Ron had got Trevor to have a quiet word in Goodge's ear to see if he might help steer through the late licences in return for a cash donation of £10,000 that would help him get back on his feet. An unsolicited gift from a local businessman who shared Goodge's vision for the borough. He remembered meeting Goodge to donate the money. The councillor virtually shook his hand off when their palms met. Couldn't be helpful enough. Ron had made it clear that he hoped Goodge would not hesitate to call if there was any other way he could be of assistance.

Now he knew that if Goodge had decided to call him, if he was the only person Goodge could turn to, then something was up. Ron had got a result. This was good. Obviously something that Goodge couldn't handle himself. Something he probably shouldn't be up to. And the more things Goodge did that he shouldn't be up to that Ron knew about, then the more firmly he had him by the gonads.

'When?' asked Ron.

'Tomorrow night.'

'Can't do it.' Lies, of course, but he wanted to make Goodge work.

'What about the day after, Thursday?' suggested Goodge.

'That'll do.'

'How does seven o'clock sound?'

'Yeah. Meet me here.'

'At the club?'

'Yeah.'

'OK, er, I'll see you then.'

'I'll get the beers in, Malcolm.'

Chapter Sixteen

The traffic was a bitch. Scabby kids and pikeys appeared at every junction offering to smudge Russell's windscreen with their clotted rags. He usually shook his head when they approached with their scrapers and sponges, but when one of the kids went ahead and did it anyway the sight of his tatty threads and third-hand trainers forced Russell to wind down his window with some cash in hand. Invariably the kid would nod thanks as he casually dodged the traffic and disappeared among the exhaust fumes.

Nudging his black GT Turbo north along the suburban A-roads Russell thought about the change that had come over Ron since the attack. His sense of assurance, the regal bearing, had disappeared, replaced by an introverted tetchiness. Where his gestures had once been grand and inclusive he was now preoccupied and insular, snarling at people rather than convincing them. His transformation from popular dictator to despot had only one constant – pride. With his bullish shoulders and cropped hair Ron had always appeared robust enough to knock down a bad building. But recently his upper body movements had become troubled and groggy, like a wasp recently woken from winter slumber.

Although thoughts about Ron's mood gnawed at the back of his mind, Russell found it simple to distance himself from the looming crisis. From Ron's perspective he was just doing his job. The way he saw it, he was spending time with Sonia, biding his time. It kept him away from Ron's wavering moods and distanced him from Trevor, who always regarded him with sinister thoughts in his eyes. There was an insolence, an oppressive menace about Trevor that worried Russell, yet still he found he could not look away when challenged by that flat stare. Trevor came into the club irregularly and when he did beetle in he was always on the way somewhere and needed just a few seconds of his brother's time for a taut, whispered communion. Somehow Russell knew that it was Trevor's footsteps, not Ron's, that he should listen for at night.

The Oakheart Health Club and Spa was situated in an odd wedge of suburban north London that masquerades as countryside, but whose denizens would shudder at the thought of dismounting their four-wheel drives for a nature ramble. This was a London in which suburban semis gave way to the odd stretch of rapeseed squeezed between DIY superstores and renovated theme pubs with car parks the size of football pitches and menus with wipeable surfaces. Here families gave their daughters pony lessons for their birthdays and turned a blind eye when their teenage sons got laid by their continental au pairs.

As he strolled through the health club car park Russell noticed that nearly all the cars that surrounded him were either saloons or four-wheel drives. They were what was known as 'birds' cars' – perfectly acceptable motors but for the odd detail (wrong colour, wrong upholstery, kids' safety harness, wet wipes stashed on the dashboard).

Russell stepped through two sliding smoked-glass doors and was greeted at the reception desk by a girl in her early twenties who looked like she was dressed for a Miami beach in June rather than London in February. Her hair was dyed the colour of egg yolk, her arms were trim and tanned and her breasts, which were supported only by a Lycra halterneck top, sniffed the air like a couple of gun dogs.

'Hi!' she said as Russell leaned on the desk. 'How can I help?' Her bouncy, life-embracing attitude had been lifted directly from a celebrity-endorsed aerobics video. Russell felt dowdy and grey in her presence. He tried to give his voice a lift.

'Hi.' It just didn't sound right. 'All right. I'm here to meet Mrs Chisholm.'

The girl looked down at a list in front of her. 'Sonia

Chisholm. OK. Let me see. Now I know that she usually does Buns of Steel on Tuesdays. Yes, I'm afraid that she's still in a class. She won't be long, it only lasts another five minutes. I'll page her when they finish. If you go through you can wait in the Revival bar, you can get yourself a juice or something.'

Russell mumbled appreciation.

'And who shall I say is waiting for her?'

'Russell.'

'OK, Russell, if you can sign the visitors' book I'll let her know,' said the girl with a peppy little smile. 'Enjoy.'

The girl seemed so happy to be alive, so thrilled to have had the opportunity to help Russell out that he couldn't help but wonder what would have happened if she'd actually cared about him. God only knew what she did when she saw her boyfriend. It was enough to take Russell's mind off the pastel-clad female forms working out on the machines as he headed for the café. He felt oddly conspicuous wearing his outdoor clothes, as if he had something to hide, as if, beneath his black MAl jacket, lurked a shameful secret.

The air-conditioned, carpeted plushness of the place was a far cry from Skin's gym. The sounds of grunting and leather against leather were replaced with vapid handbag house music and hard-bodied instructors who barked, 'Move it up!', 'Get busy!' and 'Go for it!'

He wasn't thirsty, but Russell still thought he ought to buy a drink if he was going to wait in the café. A camp bloke in his forties, who had spent so much time under sunlamps that his face had the quality of an old-fashioned lace-up football, asked him what he wanted. He asked for tea.

'What kind?'

'Just tea.'

'OK,' said the man pointing to a blackboard on which a menu had been printed in different coloured chalks. 'We have camomile, peppermint, raspberry and lemon zing . . .'

'Just normal tea.'

'Earl Grey, Darjeeling, Kenyan, Assam or English Breakfast?'

'English tea.'

'Is skimmed milk all right?'

'As it comes, mate. Two sugars.'

'The sugar is on the tables,' said the man dismissively.

Russell sat in one of the director's chairs beside a rubber plant that had been polished so much he could make out his face in it. The music continued to pump round the building like some factory generator that never went off, even when shifts came in and out. A group of women walked down the passageway talking amongst themselves. All of them glowed a little, but none were actually sweating. Most had towels placed round their necks, as if this was what one did after working out. Most were in their thirties and forties and the majority were in good nick, spent a lot of time here torching calories, getting tanned, massaged, hair coloured and manicured. Their gear was pristine, only the odd dark sliver of sweat giving away their practical rather than leisure function.

Sipping at his tea for something to do rather than stare, Russell noticed that one had broken from the group. She was headed in his direction.

'What the hell are you doing here?' It was Sonia.

'Ron sent me.' Russell placed the cup back in its saucer a little too loudly. Sonia had her hair pulled back in a ponytail. She was slightly flushed but not out of breath. She had her hands on her hips and shook her head slowly, her bottom lip drawn up slightly. Some of the other women were looking over.

'Oh, come on. This is getting stupid, Russell,' said Sonia impatiently.

Russell puffed his cheeks out.

'I know it's not you,' said Sonia, exasperated. 'But what's he thinking? Jesus Christ, this is a health club, not West Ham. What does he think is going to happen – I'm going to get slapped about by my aromatherapist?'

Russell didn't know what to say. It was hard to know what was going through Ron's mind. Anyway, if anyone should know Sonia should.

'He just wants me around.'

'But what about me? Do I get a choice or are you going to be shadowing me for the rest of my life?'

'I'm sure it won't be for long,' said Russell.

'Too right it won't,' snapped Sonia, and raced off up the corridor. Russell waited for a few moments to see if she'd return. He felt the eyes of some of the other women on him. They were pretending to chat, but each had tuned in her antennae to his and Sonia's frequency. Her resistance to his presence wasn't too encouraging. He was going to have to work a bit harder at being congenial – the last thing he wanted was his marching orders back to Merlin's Cave.

Sonia came back clutching her slim mobile. 'He's turned his mobile off,' she said. 'Look, I'm going to get changed. We'll talk about this after. I'll see you in the car park, all right?' She walked off towards the changing rooms. Her body, Russell noted, was as hard and firm as a dolphin's.

She arranged to meet him at a Chinese place in Totteridge. Although she shot ahead through the ugly traffic Russell didn't think that she might pull a runner. Sure enough, when he walked into Wing's Palace there was a plate of sesame prawn toast and a Coke on the table with his name on it.

'What kept you?' she asked. Russell smiled. 'Look, I'm sorry about shouting at the club like that. It isn't you, Russell, it's just that sometimes I want to run my own life.' Russell bit into his prawn toast, thinking it wise to redirect the conversation.

'You hear one of Ron's horses is running at Leicester tomorrow?'

'No,' said Sonia, uninterested.

'You going?' continued Russell.

'You've got to be joking,' laughed Sonia. 'I can't think of anything more boring than watching a lot of horses running round a track. Ron's taken me a couple of times, but it was like torture. I know he's disappointed that I don't want to go again, but he's just going to have to lump it.'

Ron lumping anything was a novel idea to Russell. He didn't seem like the kind of geezer who just lumped things. Maybe he only lumped things where Sonia was concerned. The waiter brought sweet and sour prawns, ginger chicken, beef in black bean sauce and some special fried rice.

'You're hungry,' said Russell.

'Not really. I ordered it for you.' She still seemed pissed off. 'Go ahead, I'll pick when I feel like it.'

Russell glanced at the table. He had the option of knife and fork or chopsticks.

'Use the knife and fork,' said Sonia, 'or you'll starve.' Hungrily Russell scraped a large portion of each dish on to his plate and got stuck in.

'How is it?' asked Sonia.

'The business.'

'So you and me, Russell, looks like fate has brought us together again.' Russell nodded, not wanting to speak while his mouth was full. 'How long do you think this is going to go on?'

'Don't know. Few weeks. Until Ron thinks things have cooled down.'

'Jesus, it's no way to live really, is it? All this?' said Sonia. 'Most of my friends have normal lives – take care of the house, go to the health club, go shopping, pick up the kids from school, go out for a meal with hubby. Most of them think that's what I do. If only they knew.' She sighed, picking at one of the prawn toasts. 'How long do you think we're going to be together, really?'

'Told you. No idea.' Russell kept shovelling food so that he didn't have to talk. There was so much he wanted to say to her, but he needed more time, didn't want to push things too hard.

'Bet Ron tells you about as much as he tells me – nothing.' Sonia looked him in the eye. Russell turned his face to his plate, scooped up some rice.

'It ain't my business really. I just do what I'm told.'

'How long have you been working for him, then?'

'Few weeks.' Russell sensed they were moving from business to personal. They had some catching up to do. He wanted to unburden himself, but he didn't have the heart to tell her everything.

'And what were you doing before Ron entered your life?'

'I was a sparky.' Russell started laughing.

'You were doing that when I knew you. I can't believe you didn't blow yourself up.' Sonia joined in the laughter and undid the band that had been holding her hair back. She shook her hair and Russell watched it fall and settle on her shoulders. He felt a little more relaxed with her now.

'Well, you know,' he said. 'I sort of enjoyed it. There was regular work and it was OK money.'

'Electrifying,' said Sonia.

'I was plugged into things,' said Russell.

'That's enough now,' she said.

'You ain't gonna tell Ron, are you, about us?' he asked.

'What do you think, Russell?' said Sonia, lighting a cigarette.

'Well, I think you should keep quiet,' said Russell. Sonia snorted as if it was the most stupid thing she'd ever heard.

'How long have you been married then?' He knew the answer, but he though he'd better ask.

'Let me see now,' said Sonia. 'It'll be six years in July. I was a blushing bride of twenty-three when I was hauled off to the altar. My parents were not happy bunnies. Ron was fifteen years older than I was and he'd been married before. My mum was devastated when she saw all his mob turn up to the church with their broken noses and gold jewellery, thought I was throwing away me life. My dad didn't say much, just kept going "It's your life, girl. You make your own decisions." And then at the reception some of Ron's mob had a bit too much to drink and got out of hand. There was a lot of food thrown about and one of the silver service waiters got a kicking. They kept on coming over and saying things to me like "If anyone bothers you, you let me know and we'll sort them out." Just a bunch of leery pissheads, but not the kind of people you want to bring home to mum.'

Russell thought for a while before he spoke again. 'So why did you marry him?' he asked.

'This might sound stupid, but it was because he asked me,' she said dreamily. 'He was exciting, charismatic – they all said that. Charming, you know. Always buying me stuff and having people seat us in the best places. I used to work at this club he owned.' Russell looked down at his plate, embarrassed. 'Cocktail waitress, and the day after we first went out he sent me a bouquet of flowers as big as a house with a note. It said I didn't have to work as a waitress no more. That I was running the place now. I kind of knew then. Knew this was different. That things might be different, that I could have a better life than the one I had.'

'I know how you feel,' said Russell obliquely. 'What about the name then? I liked Jane.'

'Oh, all the girls had different names at the club. Put punters off the scent. Mine sort of stuck and Ron liked it, so . . .' She wiped her ash in the glass ashtray. 'What did you mean just now, about knowing what I mean?'

'Oh, right, you know, all this business it ain't really me,' said Russell, turning his index fingers in to point at himself. 'Just because they think I'm a bit tasty on the pavement doesn't mean to say I'm like Ron and Trevor.'

'What? You in touch with your feminine side, then?'

'Well at least I'm part of the same species as women.'

Sonia drained her Diet coke and swilled an ice cube round in her mouth. 'So what do you want, Russell? Do you know?'

He couldn't give her a truthful answer to that right now, so he busked a little. 'Never thought about it. You know? Never really thought about it. I suppose I'm as boring as the next mug – wife, kids, nice house, 'nuff money. Reckon that's why I'm doing all this, so that when the right girl comes along I'll have something to offer.'

'But Russell, when the right one comes along she'll be interested in you, not your money,' said Sonia. He couldn't tell whether she was joking or not. He looked at her, trying to read her eyes.

'Well some of them are, some of them ain't,' he said noncommittally. 'Takes all sorts, don't it?'

'So the right one hasn't come along yet?' asked Sonia.

'She's out there somewhere,' said Russell. 'I've just got to find her.'

In the background Lionel Richie was singing 'Easy'. Russell worked away at his meal, taking care to listen to Sonia as she voiced her opinions on the Eurotunnel and weight machines as opposed to free weights. After the dishes had been cleared away her mobile trilled. She had a short, clipped conversation. From her tone Russell could tell she was speaking to her husband.

'Ron,' she said folding away the phone. 'Said he's on his way home. You know, I do think that he could be affectionate – if he was provoked.' She offered an empty smile. 'Anyway, Russell, you're relieved of your duty. He wants you to go back to Merlin's and make sure everything's sorted tonight.'

Russell stretched. 'You know, I could get used to this,' he said.

'What's going on tonight then?'

'Drum 'n' Bass,' said Russell, raising his eyebrows. 'There was a little bit of bother last week. Two different sets of dealers. Mugs, really. And I suppose Ron wants to get an early start tomorrow, what with the race and all.'

'Yeah, I suppose he does,' said Sonia. 'Looks like I'll be watching racing videos all night.'

'Beats *EastEnders*.'

A waiter brought the bill. Russell reached for his hip but Sonia waved him away. 'I'll take care of it. My treat.'

'Thanks.'

'Oh, don't thank me, thank Ron.' She fumbled around in her bag and pulled out a roll of twenty-pound notes. 'Jesus, I'm fed up with walking round like a bloody cash machine. Ron just won't be doing with banks.'

'They say cash is cleaner,' said Russell.

'I'll tell you something, Russell, it's downright embarrassing. Last year I had to pay my annual subscription to Oakwood in cash. The bloke looked at me like I'd just robbed a bank.' She laughed to herself. 'Ron probably had. Can you imagine the shame, Russell?'

They wandered out to the car park. The sky was low overhead, an odd mauve colour that only ever seemed to occur in late afternoon in winter. Russell walked Sonia to her car. 'Thanks for the meal,' he said.

'A pleasure,' said Sonia. 'Don't worry about me, I can make the Dukes of Hazzard look like a couple of learner drivers.' She pecked him on the cheek. 'I'll drive straight home and take evasive action if there's any snipers on top of Marks & Spencer's.'

She got in the car and started the ignition. The electric window slid down. Russell stood there for a moment feeling the wetness of her mouth on his cheek.

'See you tomorrow,' she said and was gone.

Russell pursed his lips and smiled to himself. Maybe he was getting somewhere. Maybe he was getting in too deep.

Chapter Seventeen

Valet parking. Russell could live with that. As he skipped out of the car he handed a fiver to a fresh-faced youth wearing a red waistcoat. An older, military type wearing a dodgy green top hat held the glass door open for him and nodded in a grudging kind of way. Yanks and Japs love that shit. Makes them feel like royalty.

Enjoying the click of his shoes on the marble floor Russell surveyed the airy lobby. On the atrium above glasses flashed and waiters flitted in the contented babble of the restaurant. Friday night and the expense account crowd were lavishing corporate entertainment on their nearest, dearest and sometimes their husbands and wives.

'I'm here to see Ron Chisholm,' he told the receptionist, a young Chinese who nodded abruptly and tapped something in to the computer below the desk.

'Certainly, sir,' he replied. 'Mr Chisholm is in our Mayfair suite, which is situated on the top floor of the building. If you turn left when you leave the lift it'll be right in front of you. Go straight up. Mr Chisholm mentioned that he was expecting guests.'

The call from Ron had come late in the day. Russell had been hoping for a quiet evening. He was cream crackered after fucking last night and all he wanted was to watch some telly, maybe go down the Black Prince if he could summon the energy. But Ron had been insistent. The phone connection was poor but Ron had been shouting excitedly. Russell told Sonia he had to go. She just shrugged and broke open another can of Diet Coke, hopped the channel over to MTV. They had just come back from Blockbuster with *Forrest Gump* and a bar of Dairy Milk.

There was a buzzer outside the suite, like it was a flat. The cool, halogen-lit corridor stretched into the distance. The mute hum of the hotel reminded him of the bowels of a cross-Channel ferry. Russell heard laughter and music from behind the door. He stared into the plastic stud that housed the security viewer. A chain slid through its casing and the door was opened by a chuckling, red-eyed Frankie; whether this was from alcohol or laughter Russell couldn't tell. Frankie said nothing, beckoning Russell inside, laughing to himself. Russell found himself standing inside another, much smaller hallway. Immediately to his right was a large gilt mirror in which he saw Frankie was shielding a spliff behind his back.

'Frank. What's going on, mate?'

Frank burst out laughing and clapped his hand on Russell's stiff shoulder.

'What isn't going on, mate?' he sniggered. '*What isn't*? You've come to the right place. Come on through.' He gestured Russell to follow him past a table bearing an enormous vase of lilies. As Russell entered the living area the smell of marijuana hit the back of his throat, causing him to cough slightly. It was a vast room housing three plush sofas and two armchairs arranged in a kind of horseshoe round a television set. The decor was ersatz Georgian – striped pastel-coloured wallpaper, watercolours of English pastoral scenes on the wall, reproduction furniture stained a burnt orangey-brown, lavish overstuffed cushions piled on every conceivable surface. A drinks cabinet in the corner looked as if it had haemorrhaged bottles of booze, glasses, straws and slices of lemon all over its counter. On the glass table little neat lines of cocaine had been chopped up with a SIM card from a mobile.

Ron was sitting in the centre of the sofa holding a can of lager. His shirt was undone down to his navel but he still had his jacket on. A gold chain as thick as a salami nestled among the clouds of grey hair on his chest. Beside him a half-caste girl dozed quietly. The buttery colour of her skin contrasted with the snow white of her underwear. At Ron's feet a young white girl no more than eighteen rested her head on his knees. Her dyed blonde hair was betrayed by the swirl of mousy pubic hair that was visible over the top of her crooked leg.

Next to her was a man in his late thirties with tight curly hair and a broad flat face whom Russell had been introduced to a couple of times. He was something to do with Ron's horses, a fact betrayed by the battered Barbour jacket that hung behind him on the sofa. To his right was an older white woman. The slight traces of crow's feet round her eyes made Russell think she looked about thirty-five She wore black knickers and stockings and cheap black patent leather heels. She wore no bra and had small, pink nipples A shoreline of white round her breasts betrayed the phantom traces of a tan over the rest of her body.

On the sofa sat Terry and Mark, their Nautilus-enhanced bodies making them look stiff and ungainly on the feminine sofa. The dry scarlet slashes and yellowing bruises on Terry's face served as a reminder of the attempted robbery. They sat silently drinking beer and watched a porn movie in which a woman with improbably large breasts was being taken from behind while fellating a plumber.

'She must feel like a fucking kebab,' laughed Frankie, skipping back to his seat next to the half-caste girl. At the back of the room a pale, thin girl with thick black hair sat in a chair on her own smoking a spliff. She wore a bra and a short black skirt. She seemed oblivious to what was going on around her.

'Russell, my son!' said Ron, standing up suddenly. 'We won! We fucking won! Rustler's Rump came in! Thirty to one! A right old result! You should have had a few sobs on her, son. What did I tell you? *What did I fucking tell you?*' Ron grabbed him in a bear hug and lifted Russell from the ground. Russell heard Ron's rough face rubbing against the shoulder of his jacket. He broke away.

'Come over here. Come on. I want to show you something.' Ron went to the back of the room and picked up a green canvas bag. On the way back to Russell he ruffled the hair of the girl sitting on her own. She didn't even blink.

'Take a look in there, son,' said Ron, unzipping the bag. 'How much do you reckon is in there? Go on. How much?

How fucking much?' His eyes were crazed, like some evangelist searching for a convert.

'Ron can buy Alan fucking Shearer with that lot,' cracked Frankie from across the room.

Russell shrugged and looked at the mound of neatly bound twenty and fifty pound notes. Given that the last time he'd seen Ron he'd been on the wrong end of a bollocking it was all very strange. 'I dunno, twenty grand?'

'Twenty grand? Twenty fucking grand? Areyoushaw? *Areyoufuckingshaw?*'

'Fifty?'

'Kids' stuff, Russell.'

'Hundred?'

Ron shook his head and smiled so fiercely his face almost seemed to double in size. 'You ain't even close, son. Do the maths. Go on. Odds of thirty to one. I pre-paid me tax and put on five grand.'

'One hundred and fifty thousand pounds. Fuck me, Ron.'

'I hit the fucking jackpot, so we're having a little celebration. Just me and the boys and a few friends.' He leered at Russell. '*KnowotImean?* One of them is even a brewer,' he whispered.

Russell frowned. 'What the fuck is that?'

'She'll do it without a condom.' Ron winked at him. 'You want some, Russ? She's in there at the moment with Trevor.' Ron gestured to a doorway on the left of the living area which led through to a bedroom.

'I'm all right, Ron. I could use a drink though.'

'Help yourself, mate. Fucking hell, look at that.' Ron gestured towards the television screen. Terry and Mark were hooting with laughter as the porn queen got shafted in three orifices at the same time. 'Who's a clever girl then?' laughed Ron.

Locating a tall, clean glass, Russell filled it with ice and tonic water and took a quick wander round the suite. Classy. There was a Jacuzzi in the master bedroom's ensuite bathroom. Russell ran his hand over the soft white towels piled up by the bath. They were as big as bales of hay. Anyone wanting to go home with one would have a job closing the suitcase. He wandered through the living area. Everyone seemed to be falling asleep except for Terry and Mark who were crouched over the glass table snorting coke through the plastic casing of a Biro.

Forgetting what was going on in the other bedroom, Russell peered round the door. He flinched and stepped backwards. Trevor was sitting on the bed, trousers round his ankles, red-faced with his eyes closed, while a naked black girl bobbed up and down on her knees before him. Russell suddenly had a feeling of entrapment. He wanted to leave but thought it might anger Ron if he gave it the off immediately. He'd stick it out for half an hour and then make some excuse about having to pop over to Bowler's, Ron's club in Poplar.

'We're going for a jacuzzi,' said Ron, gesturing to the half-caste girl and the young one. 'You want to come?' A shallow laugh escaped him as he realised what he'd said. He gathered up some glasses, a couple of joints and a bottle of champagne. The young girl stood naked on a woven rug and smiled thinly at Russell. Her skin was flushed between her breasts.

'I want to get another drink, Ron,' said Russell, gesturing towards the drinks cabinet. 'I might come through in a bit.'

'*For* a bit, more like it,' said Ron as he disappeared into the bathroom with the girls. Filling his glass with tonic Russell looked out of the window across London. It just seemed to keep rolling, the lights a jumble of contours shaped by a drunken cartographer. Despite living his whole life in the city Russell was still amazed how indistinguishable most of the buildings were, how it was grey areas rather than specific landmarks which best defined the place. A train crept across the night, like some fugitive making a run for the Home Counties. Russell suddenly felt a pang of loneliness. The deepest ocean was hardly more solitary than this dark place. The air in the room had curdled and Russell looked in vain for a window to open in the sealed building.

The girl with the black hair was still sitting alone, legs crossed, staring at the ends of a strand of hair that was stretched between her fingers. Russell went over to her. She smiled, but not in a way he liked. Her face was workaday welcoming, like a girl on a perfume counter. Standing next to her Russell didn't know what to say. He thrust his left hand into his trouser pocket and held his drink in his right as if enjoying a Sunday afternoon on the nineteenth hole. Looking down on her from above he noticed that her hair was very thin. It was parted down the middle and the white strip that crossed her scalp looked like cream cheese between two slices of black bread. The girl's left foot bounced a couple of times and she shook her high heel loose until it was balanced on her toes.

'Aren't you going to have a Jacuzzi, then?' she asked. Russell suddenly felt uncomfortable standing, as if he was purposefully trying to dominate her. He crouched down and looked from below. This close he could see two parallel strips of blood just below her knee, the legacy of a rushed shaving job.

'Nah,' said Russell. 'Don't fancy it.'

'Not in the mood?'

'Something like that.'

'A lot of them are like that.'

'Like what?'

'Don't fancy it.' The girl shrugged. 'Just want to talk. Boring stuff usually, how their wives don't understand – blah, blah, blah . . . Some of them are different, though. They've got really good jobs, in the City and that.'

'Well it's not like that with me.'

'I bet you don't work in the City.'

'I didn't mean that,' said Russell. 'It's just that I don't want to.'

'What, fuck me? Is that what you mean?'

'S'pose,' said Russell, laughing at her bluntness.

She sighed. 'Well that's a fucking relief. I'm not in the mood myself. No offence.'

Russell shifted legs. His left thigh was beginning to go numb.

'No offence,' said Russell, taking a sip of his drink.

The girl stopped playing with her hair. 'It's like anything, isn't it? It's a job. I used to work at Top Shop and some days I got up with the joys of life in me. Other times I just wanted to stay in bed.'

'Except now you get to stay in bed all the time.'

She laughed. 'It ain't exactly like having a kip.'

'What's your name?' asked Russell.

'Well, when I'm working they call me Sophia, 'cos it sounds Spanish and they like me to take care of the punters who like the Mediterranean type of girl. But my real name is Tara.'

'I'm Russell.'

'You work with horses then?'

'Horses?' Russell was confused. 'Oh, right. No, no, I work for Ron . . .'

'Fat one in the Jacuzzi?'

Russell smiled. 'Yeah, the fat one in the Jacuzzi.'

'Always wanted a horse when I was a kid. Well, not a horse, a pony. Had pictures of ponies all over my room. Bit of a waste of time, really. Don't know where you'd put a pony in Finsbury Park.'

'You left it in the park it would probably get eaten by pit bulls.'

'Never got a dog neither,' she rubbed an itch on her nose. 'Not even a little one. Mum said we didn't have the room.'

'Do you want a drink or something?' asked Russell.

Tara giggled. 'You know what? I've smoked two spliffs in the last half hour and now I've got the munchies. Anything to eat over there?' She pointed at the bar.

'I'll have a look,' said Russell. 'Tell you what, if you fancy it we could get some room service up here. Get you a sandwich or something. Get some meat on those bones.'

Tara looked away, embarrassed. 'You sound just like my mum. She was always trying to feed me up. Blah, blah, blah. I've always been like this. It's the way I am. See if there's some crisps or something in the bar, will you? Oh, and I'll have a Diet Coke if you're there. Please.'

Searching through the cupboard Russell discovered three packets of dry roasted peanuts. He struck gold in the fridge, where a Toblerone cooled its heels among the cans of Heineken. He presented Tara with her Coke and nuts before putting his hands behind his back.

'Guess which hand and win a prize.'

'What's the prize?'

'Find out.'

Tara bit her lip as if suddenly worried.

'I ain't going to bite you,' added Russell. Tara tapped his right arm. Russell transferred the Toblerone from his left hand to his right.

'You win tonight's star prize of a bumper bar of Toblerone,' he said, pulling it from behind his back. 'What you reckon – the new Bruce Forsyth or what? S'pose I'm not ugly enough. I'd have to turn orange first.'

'Oh, it's all cold,' laughed Tara as he handed it to her.

'It was in the fridge.'

'I love Toblerone, but I never buy it,' said Tara. She seemed to have perked up a little. 'You know how you get into buying something and you can't buy nothing else? I'm like that with Marathons. Yes, I know they're called Snickers now – I'm not stupid – but I still can't get used to it. They'll always be Marathons to me.'

Trevor appeared from the bedroom wearing jeans and a white Lacoste polo shirt. He pulled at his crotch, organising his package. The girl followed him, loping uneasily, a combination of cocaine and red high heels. Trevor looked over at Russell, raised his left hand to his face and sniffed his forefinger and index finger. Russell met his gaze until he could bear Trevor's smugness no longer. For the first time he felt hate, rather than just distaste, for Trevor.

'Used to think that if there was only one thing that I was allowed to eat for the rest of my life it would be chocolate,' continued Tara, oblivious to what had just gone on. 'But now I'm not sure. I think it might be those prawn mayonnaise sandwiches you get at Marks. I've got a thing for them and cheese and onion crisps. Walkers, of course.'

'Yeah, it's got to be Walkers, ain't it?' agreed Russell. 'Funny you know, when I was kid all we ate was Golden Wonder, and now all we want is Walkers. I'm a cheese and onion man myself.'

'Do wonders for your breath, don't they?' said Tara, grinning. 'I love kissing a bloke after he's had a couple of packets of cheese and onion. You can even feel the bits of potato that have lodged in his teeth.'

Russell noticed that they'd been conducting their conversation over the noise of another porn film in which the male lead seemed determined to embroider his performance with vocals that made him sound like a baboon calling its mate.

'Look, I ain't being funny, but there's no one in the other bedroom now if you fancy going in there, just to talk like,' said Russell.

Tara thought for a moment before standing up, folding her arms over her breasts and crossing the room to the bedroom which was drenched with the funky smell of sex. Russell followed her, carrying her Coke. He braced himself for comments from the group who were still crashed out in front of the video. He only breathed out when he got into the bedroom. Tara was lying on the bed propped against the headrest. Russell stood in the doorway and took a sip from his drink.

'Where do you want this?' he asked, brandishing her drink.

'Listen,' she sighed. 'If you want to have sex, you can. That's what I'm here for, but I don't do anything kinky and you'll have to wear two condoms. Extra strength.'

Russell's stomach felt hollow. He felt like he'd played a cruel trick that he now regretted.

'That's not what I had in mind, honest,' he said. 'I was just getting fed up with standing. And all that bonking was getting on me nerves.'

'Yeah, bonking gets on my nerves as well sometimes,' said Tara flatly. 'Come and sit next to me.'

Russell got on the other side of the bed, leaving a foot between them. Tara moved a little closer to him. 'Nice in here, ain't it? Bet you'd get a really good night's sleep here.' Russell looked at the framed watercolours and felt the plumpness of the pillows against his back. The light was soft and restful. He wondered how many German industrialists and Japanese financiers had been lulled to sleep by the cool colours of the room. He wondered how many of them had been lulled to sleep by someone like Tara.Russell closed his eyes and felt the harshness of the day recede.

When the door opened it seemed to shatter all the peace that Russell had ever accumulated. He looked at his watch. He had only been asleep for about ten minutes, and now he felt even more tired. Trevor stood in the doorway, his head cocked back, his eyelids hovering slightly over his grey eyes.

'Oh, how sweet,' he slurred. 'Ain't interrupting anything, am I? No, 'course I'm not. The tart and the tosser. What a lovely couple.'

'Give it a rest, Trevor. Piss off and watch your film,' said Russell.

'You're the one who's been taking a rest,' said Trevor. 'What, you knackered after a hard day's fetching tea for Sonia? Or have you been busier than that?'

'Door's behind you, Trevor.'

'I'll be off in a moment, don't you worry.' He turned and looked at Tara. 'Come on, slag. Get off your bony arse. Time to go to work.'

Tara slid her legs off the bed wearily. Trevor smiled to himself. 'There's a good girl,' he said.

Russell reached over and held Tara's arm. 'She ain't in the mood, Trevor,' he said. 'Go back in the other room and find someone else. She's staying here.'

'You fucking what?' Trevor smirked as if he'd never heard anything so ridiculous.

'She's staying here with me.'

'Don't be silly, Russell. This girl loves getting shafted. Why's she going to stay in here with you? If she wanted a baby carrot she'd go down Tesco's.'

Tara looked at Russell, torn between duty and choice. Russell could see that she was uncomfortable, would rather go with Trevor than sit through the confrontation. Feeling Trevor grabbing at her shoulder she shouted, 'All right, all right, I'm coming, I'm coming.'

Russell stood up on the other side of the bed. Trevor let go of her shoulder. 'Look at that,' he said. 'She's so lovely I'd eat me chips out of her knickers.' He put his arm round the shrinking girl who was trying to put her feet in her shoes. Russell could see that she had made her mind up. She was silent and stoical, ready to suffer dispassionately any of the injustices that had become her lot in life. Russell tried to claw through the film of indifference that had settled upon her.

'Listen, Tara. You don't have to go if you don't want to,' he said. 'It's your choice.'

Tara shook her head and walked from the room. She stopped in the doorway, turned and said to him, 'Don't be a fool, Russell.' There was no bitterness in her voice, only fact. Trevor raised his arms in the air and waved both hands at Russell.

'Love to stay, Russell,' he said, 'but I've got to go and shag your bird. See you later.'

'You're a fucking animal, Trevor,' said Russell.

'And I love it,' said Trevor, then shrugged and left the room. Russell thought about punching the wall, but he couldn't even summon the energy to slam the door behind Trevor. In the silent room exhaustion swept through him like an illness. He stumbled to the bed and fell on the warm spot where Tara had lain. The pillow still smelled vaguely of her hair. He turned the light off and removed his clothes in the dark. He was asleep almost before he stretched out between the thick cotton sheets. Sometime during the night Russell felt Tara warm beside him. In the morning she was wrapped around him, her hands clutching his shoulders while still in the soft, silent embrace of sleep.

Chapter Eighteen

'You hungry, Ron?' asked Frankie.

'Listen to me, I'm going to tell you something now,' said Ron, sitting at the bar in Merlin's Cave. He pointed at Barko who looked back hopefully. 'That dog needs to go on a diet. It couldn't catch a fucking one-legged cat, let alone guard the gaff.'

Slumped over the table, Frankie looked up from his paper like he hadn't really heard what his boss had said. Ron still had it in for Barko, but he really couldn't be dealing with it now, what with no sleep last night.

'You peckish, Ron?'

'Had a pizza when I got up,' said Ron. 'Someone got it off room service last night. It was all cold so I shoved it in the trouser press to warm it up. The business. Mr Fujifuckinwara is going to have a bit of a fucking shock when he shoves his Aquascutum strides in there overnight.' Ron patted his stomach. 'Can't believe I don't feel worse,' he said. 'By the time we got to the hotel I was well bladdered. After a couple of joints I was ready for a kip, but after I slid up that coloured girl's guts I woke up. Couldn't get enough.'

'Nor me,' said Trevor. 'Fucking dream come true. Cunt on tap. Tell you what, though. That one with blonde hair: she was a good fuck, but she was so lardy you could use her sweat to fry chips.'

Ron laughed. He was partial to his brother's vulgarity.

Trevor lit a Marlboro. There was another still smouldering in the ashtray. 'What was wrong with Russell last night?' he asked Ron.

'What do you mean?'

'He'd got the hump,' said Trevor. He took a sip of tea. 'Didn't get himself a portion. He ain't a ginger, is he?'

Ron shook his head, suddenly grave, as if the question was too alarming to contemplate. 'No, he ain't a ginger.'

'Didn't seem interested in the birds,' said Trevor.

'I thought he shtupped the one with black hair,' said Ron. 'The Itie tart.'

'Nah, she said nothing went on. They just talked.'

'Birds like that,' said Ron. 'Listen to me, Trevor. I'm going to tell you something now.' He sat up straighter for emphasis. 'Don't know what it is between you and Russell, but I don't like it. For all I care you can hate the bloke, detest the sight of him. But as long as you're both on the firm you're going to get on, because I tell you you're going to get on. I ain't asking you to go out on the piss together, suck each other's knobs, just get along while you're working. That's all. It ain't no big fucking deal. *KnowotImean?*'

Trevor blew a big cloud of smoke into the room, watched it disperse across the dance floor.

'I tell you, Trev, when things ain't working right around here I take it personally.' Ron was beginning to get annoyed with his brother's bored expression. 'Show some fucking courtesy. Have you got a fucking problem, or something?'

Trevor was silent, flicked some ash on to the table.

'That's what I'm fucking talking about, Trevor. Would you do that indoors? Wudja?'

'Maybe,' said Trevor.

'Areyoushaw? *Areyoushaw?*'

'Probably not,' said Trevor with a distinct lack of conviction, his voice thick with resentment.

'You would too, wouldn't you? You dirty cunt. Listen to me, Trevor. You're doing good business at the moment. Things are handsome. I wouldn't want no one else taking care of collection at the moment. You're me brother and all, and you'll always be me brother, but I've got a business here. Don't put me in a fucking position. I mean the geezer's hardly ever here, so there ain't no reason why you can't work together, is there?'

Trevor sucked on his Marlboro and shook his head slowly, smoke streaming from his nostrils.

'*Is there?*' shouted Ron.

Trevor remained silent. Ron stood and leaned over the table so that only a cigarette paper could have passed between his and Trevor's noses. 'Trevor, if you don't fucking answer me,' he whispered, 'I am going to tear you another arsehole. You've got me well vexed. So tell me, is there any reason why you can't work with Russell?'

'No, Ron,' said Trevor. 'Everything's pukka.'

'Stop playing the wanker, all right?' Ron thrust a thick index finger towards Trevor. 'You're driving me fucking mad. Believe me. No wonder Mum went to an early grave. It's just fucking courtesy, Trevor. Fucking courtesy.'

Trevor lifted his chin by way of acknowledgement.

'All right?' insisted Ron. In the kitchen the sound of a plate being scraped clean bounced around the tile and aluminium. Frankie lurched into a wandering couple of lines of 'In the Air Tonight'.

'Shut the fuck up, Frankie,' bellowed Ron. 'You're giving me a headache. You're giving me a fucking brain tumour!' He ran his fingers over the top of his shiny head and examined his hand as if to see if any more hair had abandoned his dome.

He turned back to Trevor. 'You got any outstanding this week?' He sounded calm again. It seemed that this was the sole reason he employed Frankie, as a whipping boy. Someone he could kick about without fear of retaliation. But even during his blackest moments Ron never sustained an attack on Frankie for more than a few moments. For some, Ron would eclipse the sun, make the sky fill with darkness, but Frankie only ever suffered occasional, passing thunder clouds.

'Couple. But we're well up,' answered Trevor. 'That fifteen Gs I gave you for the safe is just Thursday through Tuesday, and that ain't even counting Station Harbour.'

Ron smiled to himself. There was a lot more than fifteen grand in the safe, but Trevor didn't need to know that. 'A lot of good payers this week, or are you just being your most persuasive?' he asked.

'Giro week, innit,' said Trevor matter-of-factly. 'Anyone with any sense pays before I make a call.'

'What about the paperwork?'

Trevor tapped his jacket pocket which contained the black book into which he scrupulously recorded every transaction in a code he and Ron had painstakingly constructed. Ron insisted that all the paperwork was transcribed into a ledger he kept in a safe in the office. He pored over the tabulations and calculations, his stubby fingers quizzing every entry. Any deviation between the money lent and the amount of interest that was being charged that week, any inconsistency in Trevor's mathematics, concluded in an antagonistic interrogation.

'It'll be done by Friday.' Trevor realised that he'd better get scribbling when he got home as he was going over to Manor House that night. Promised a bird. He felt restless, the thumping beats of the sound system prematurely echoing through his guts. He started to move his head from side to side very slightly as if the house music was already within him. Better sort some pills out.

'What's fucking wrong with you now?' asked Ron.

'I've got to give it the off, Ron. Get grafting.'

'I want that paperwork first thing Friday, you hear me?'

Trevor nodded. 'Later, Ron.'

As Trevor's footsteps thudded up the stairs Ron reached for his cigarettes. Sparking his gold lighter he fired up a B&H and manoeuvred his bulk out of the booth. He went up to the bar and shouted through to the kitchen.

'Oi, Frankie! Stop shagging that fucking dog and make me a cuppa rosie.' He walked back to the booth but stopped half way and returned to the bar. 'And make sure you wash your hands first.'

The buzzer by the bar sounded. As the picture on the screen became sharper Ron made out a fish-eye image of Malcolm Goodge. The man had stepped as close to the camera as possible. Not an unusual habit for a politician. Ron crossed the club to the DJ booth. The buzzer went again. Ron was in no hurry. He energised the amp, which hummed to life, and located a David Morales compilation tape one of the DJs had mixed. He hoisted the volume so high it was loud enough to ensure that two people having a conversation would have to be practically kissing.

It was an old technique of Ron's that he hoped would foil any attempts to record the conversation, plus it had the added benefit of disorientating and intimidating the enemy. That is, unless the enemy were house music lovers. Ron had Goodge down as a Bob Dylan or Rolling Stones kind of bloke. A bad dancer, kind of person who only got on the floor when he was drunk 'for a bit of a bop' and stumbled through an awkward repertoire of stamping and gyrating whatever the music. Ron's line of work meant that he was one of the few people of his age who liked house music. Couldn't stand that techno shit, though.

'Make sure the door is closed firmly behind you,' he said into the speakaphone before pressing the release button. 'And watch yourself on the stairs. The lights ain't on.' Frankie had got to fix that fucking fuse.

'Hold the tea, Frank,' he shouted into the kitchen. He went to the bar and fixed two drinks: one vodka and tonic with a substantial measure of spirit, one neat tonic. As he plopped in the ice and lemon Goodge appeared at the bottom of the stairs. He squinted across the club at Ron before recognising him and waving diffidently. Ron gestured him over to the bar and watched Goodge walk self-consciously across the dance floor in his dark double-breasted suit and belted mac.

'Evening, Malcolm,' Ron said softly. Goodge leaned in close, embarrassed.

'Sorry?'

'I said evening.'

'Evening, yes. The music's very loud, isn't it?' he said almost apologetically, like some suburbanite apologising to his neighbour about the racket from his daughter's sixteenth birthday party.

'Sound check.' Ron shrugged, still holding the two glasses. 'They've had a problem with the amp, so they're testing it out.'

'Oh,' said Goodge.

'I hope you'll join me for a vodka and tonic,' said Ron, handing Goodge a glass. 'Cheers.' He raised his glass and savoured the bitter sweetness of the neat tonic. He watched Goodge looking around club as if he was a prospective buyer, trying to appear calm. Ron said nothing but walked over to a booth and waited for Goodge to follow him. He was settled back in his seat smoking another cigarette by the time Goodge had removed and folded his raincoat and settled himself. He leaned forward, his arms resting on the table, hands firmly cupped around his glass.

'So how's business?' he asked Ron.

'Swings and roundabouts, Malcolm,' said Ron with a sigh. 'Swings and roundabouts. Sometimes we're up, sometimes we're down. One thing's for sure, it's tough being an independent businessman in this day and age. *KnowotImean?*'

'I thought the nightclub scene was booming.'

'There are a lot of punters coming through the door, that's for sure. But you've got to look at the overheads.' Ron looked down and brushed a piece of lint from his lapel. 'We've got to take care of security and maintenance of the property, pay the bar staff. Most of the punters just drink water all night because they've dropped an E – before they come on the premises, of course. And then there's the prohibitive taxes we pay to your good self and central government – both directly and indirectly. It ain't easy, Malcolm, it ain't easy.'

'I understand, Ron,' said Goodge, happy now that he could lapse into one of his prepared speeches. 'That's why the council has implemented several key policies to try to encourage small businesses. For instance, we've had talks with all the local banks to try and ensure that before any business is liquidated both parties come and talk to us to see if there's any way we can reach a mutually agreeable settlement.'

'You're taking the piss, aren'tcha?' said Ron. Goodge wasn't sure whether Ron was genuinely upset or just messing with him. 'You fucking strangle us to death and then try and revive us and then make out we owe you a favour. *Areyoushaw?*'

'We do our best, Ron, for all the people of this borough.'

'So why do all the council homes go to Pakis?'

Goodge tried to slip from the tightening noose. 'I don't think that's fair, Ron. Neither to refer to an ethnic group as "Pakis" nor to make a sweeping statement of that nature. If you look at the statistics . . .'

'Bollocks. Statistics are bollocks,' snapped Ron. 'You can make up what you fucking want.' He stared hard at Goodge, impatient now.

'Even so, Ron, that hardly warrants the kind of racist remark . . .'

'It ain't racist if I'm telling the truth,' said Ron. 'You can't get a council flat in this borough if you're white. Even the old people who've been paying taxes all their lives, went through a world war for this country, what have they got? Fuck all, that's what, because the likes of you are too busy implementing positive fucking discrimination so that the likes of us get squeezed off our own streets. I ain't being racist, I'm being realistic.'

Goodge let the words settle a little. Waited for Ron to nurse his drink for a while before he said, 'I thought you told me you'd moved out to Hertfordshire?'

'That ain't the point, is it?' barked Ron. 'That ain't the point. I'm talking about the old people who are stuck here. Not everyone is as lucky as I am, not everyone is good at business.'

'Nor is everyone as well connected as you, Ron.'

'Yeah, well, on that front I'm unbeatable.' Goodge's flattery had melted Ron's increasing iciness. 'Better connected than the Underground. *KnowotImean?*'

The music throbbed in Goodge's head. The man across the table was too dangerous to mess about, too unpredictable to trust, too greedy to be loyal. Even so . . .

'Ron, I've a favour to ask you.'

Ron did not react He looked at Goodge with a steady, proud stare. 'Although we're in different camps we both understand each other's business,' Goodge continued. There was no reaction from across the table, no acknowledgement or encouraging words. 'We both recognise that maintaining a positive image in a competitive world is of the utmost importance and that it's very tough in this day and age to go about one's legitimate business without making enemies.'

At last Ron nodded. 'Sharks lurk in even the shallowest waters, Malcolm.'

Relieved, Goodge went on. 'Quite, er, absolutely. As you know I have tried my utmost to work for the people of this borough to make both social and economic conditions good for all, but have recently come under attack from a section of the community, following a shocking, er, racist attack on a young Asian man. Yesterday the *Record* published what was pretty much a verbatim interview with Abdul Rasheed, a malicious busybody who is whipping up unrest while fallaciously pretending to represent the interests of a section of the community. Of course, he represents only himself. Rasheed is a vindictive man and should he and his group, the CAG, succeed then it will be bad for all of us.'

Goodge paused for a moment and pressed the fingers of both hands together. 'It's a very difficult time for the council. We are trying to balance a budget that has been slashed by central government while maintaining our commitment to providing first-rate services. We are under attack from our political enemies as well as certain sections of the media.'

Ron nodded, yet Goodge was unsure whether this meant he understood, or whether he was just trying to get him to come to the point.

'So this Rasheed geezer, or whatever he's called, is trying to put the frighteners on you?' said Ron.

'Yes,' said Malcolm, already regretting the use of the word 'attack'. Ron's concept of the word was slightly different. 'In a manner of speaking.' For Goodge, dealing with Ron was like digging in sand – no matter how hard he tried he didn't know quite know where he stood; words always came between them.

'And?' asked Ron. Goodge realised that Ron was making him work hard for what he wanted, making him spell out his request in words of one syllable.

'If I, er, we lose the election then, I hate to say it, there are going to be a lot of changes. The opposition are promising to crack down on crime, they're making a play for the scared voters who are worried about what's going on on street level. Your kind of business is seen as a threat because of the amount of drug dealing that goes on in some establishments and the inevitable kinds of problems that arise from having gangs of young people out on the streets late at night. Your business, Ron, is an easy target for people like that, you see, as even legitimate, law-abiding businesses will be tarred with the same brush.'

Ron sat as still and cold as a stone Buddha.

'I'm sure you're aware that should we be re-elected then small businessmen like yourself can rest easy. I'm so keen to support your kind of venture that when your late licence is up for renewal I can assure you it will receive my full consideration.'

Ron regarded his cigarette for a moment. 'So you want me to sort out this geezer?'

Goodge raised his hands. 'I wouldn't put it like that. Just try to persuade him that he should reconsider his position.'

Ron raised his glass and emptied it. 'I suppose it ain't beyond the realms of possibility, Malcolm. Name again?'

'Abdul Rasheed.'

'Sounds like a nonce,' said Ron.

'No mess though, Ron, eh?' said Malcolm nervously.

'We're professionals, Malcolm,' said Ron. 'Don't you worry about a thing. We're good as gold.' And with that he reached over and put his hand round Goodge's upper arm and gave it a firm squeeze. Through the vodka gauze Goodge began to feel slightly nauseous. Ron, on the other hand, was beginning to wish he hadn't turned down Frankie's offer of a fry-up.

Chapter Nineteen

They were not there. Rasheed scanned the school gates again but he could still find no trace of his two daughters. Clustered around the wrought-iron gates – cheerfully striped in garish colours – was the usual collection of mothers and the occasional father standing on his lonesome, away from the mums discussing the soaps and the continuing closure of the leaky school hall. Rasheed was a bit of an anomaly when he came to collect his daughters. There were not many Asian fathers who would show up at school. This, after all, was women's work.

He pulled his Toyota up just beyond the white zig-zags that protected the school kids like a giant pair of dragon's fangs and waited for a second to see if the girls had observed his arrival from a place of secrecy. That was it. They were probably hiding.

Still nothing. He picked up his security lock and fastened it through the steering wheel, cursing to himself. He was beginning to grow anxious. He felt the first flowering of nervous heat in his stomach. As he clambered from the car his jacket caught on the security lock. He gritted his teeth and moved back into the car to free himself. Standing in the road he scanned up and down the perimeter of the school to see if any of the high-pitched squeals and shouts were from his daughters.

He had broken a sweat and his heart had upped its tempo. Trotting along the pavement he asked the first group of mothers and their ragged collection of kids if they had seen his daughters. His anxiety elicited concerned looks, but heads were shaken all round. The women stopped talking and watched him run over to another group who cooed and shrugged at his questions. He ran through the school gates, but stopped when he realised that he had no idea where to go for help. Usually there was a member of staff around, keeping an eye open for molesters and perverts.

Maybe they had gone home on their own? Maybe their mother had walked down to pick them up? It was implausible, it broke a routine that had continued uninterrupted for three years now. His daughters were sensible, and Asian kids – especially his – were usually not as prone to the schizophrenic hot dogging of their cola-fuelled, burger-bred white classmates.

He was at a loss at what to do. Maybe they had been delayed for some reason. Were they in some sort of trouble with a teacher? He should calm down, there was probably a good reason for this. He decided to wait in the car for ten minutes and if they didn't show up he'd phone home.

He walked back up the road. A silver Golf GTi sounded its horn. He started and looked round. A young white man with a ponytail sat with the window open, nonchalantly smoking a cigarette. He raised his eyes to Rasheed's. It took Rasheed a few seconds to realise that the movements in the back seat, the two children waving and laughing, were in fact his own daughters.

'You're late,' said Trevor.

Rasheed was divided between the young man and his daughters. He reached for the handle of the back door and began to tug at it.

'Open this damn door,' he said, his mouth dry with anger. 'What the hell do you think you're doing?'

'Now you just keep your hair on and calm down,' said Trevor. 'They're all right. For now.'

'Open this damn door!' insisted Rasheed.

'Stop moaning,' said the young man, flicking his fag butt into the gutter. 'Now listen to me.' Rasheed continued tugging at the door. 'You're upsetting some friends of mine. They're sick of you fucking whinging on and causing trouble. They want you to stop, all right? Shut it. Shut the fuck up. Understand?'

The expression on his daughters' faces had changed. They

could see that their father was upset, that this wasn't fun any more.

'I swear that if you don't open this door I will knock you into next week,' shouted Rasheed.

The white man smiled slightly and shook his head. 'No you won't. I just wanted to let you know that you should keep an eye on your kids. There are all sorts of nutters around.'

Trevor pressed a button by his thigh. The door lock clunked open and the two girls clambered out into their father's arms. Leaning from the car Trevor slammed the back door and screeched up the road. He was gone before Rasheed could raise his head from embracing his daughters.

Chapter Twenty

There he was gunning through the contraflow just north of Scratchwood, Mary J. Blige simpering away on the stereo, with some fucking sales rep in an SRi (jacket hanging from a peg in the back) virtually hammering on the boot to get him out of the way, when the mobile chirruped.

'Yeah?' said Russell, trying to stuff the device under his chin.

'It's Ron.'

'I'm on me way. I'll be there in fifteen.'

'Hold up, hold up, that ain't what I'm calling about.'

Russell followed the curl of the cones, like an orange funnel channelling the bumper-to-bumper vehicles away from the inactivity on the other side. He had not seen a single workman, one perspiring Paddy, in six months, just big green trucks, with 'Murphy' painted on the side, standing idle.

'What's occurring then?'

'Remember that time when you first came down Merlin's, there was that bloke . . .'

'Pikey?' asked Russell.

'Right. Well, there's a situation. Micky Ison brings word that he's been running his mouth. That he's been going round giving it the verbal.' The line disappeared somewhere for a moment, choked on the London fug.

'Russ? Russ? Fuckin' hell . . .'

'Still here, Ron. Line ain't good though.'

'Listen, then,' Ron said impatiently. 'I've banned him.'

'Banned him?'

'Banned him.'

Russell couldn't imagine that Pikey would be considering visiting Merlin's Cave in the near future.

'From what, Ron?'

'From the manor.' Russell's neck was beginning to ache. He swapped the phone over to his other ear. 'Say that again, Ron.'

'He's banned from the manor,' said Ron. 'If he shows his boat he's got me to answer to. I ain't having it, Russ. I ain't having it. I ain't going to be mugged off.'

'Yeah, yeah,' said Russell, swerving into the outside lane to get past some flat-capped codger in a Rover who, without a doubt, would not be shifting out of the middle lane until he needed to empty his bladder at the next Welcome Break.

'So if you clock him I want him dealt with,' emphasised Ron. 'No excuses. *KnowotImean?* I don't care if he's with his bird, his kids, whatever. The man needs to be sorted. Teach him a thing or two. Spill some claret.'

'All right, Ron,' said Russell. 'Might see you later on.' Russell laid the phone back on the passenger seat and shook his head.

'Man's gone fucking loopy,' he said and turned the volume on the stereo back up. At that moment the sales rep in the SRi crept abreast of him and pipped his horn. Inside the smoky interior a spotty kid in his early twenties was making wanker gestures with his right hand. Russell stared, unbelieving, for a moment before the kid shot off doing over a ton, his white Next shirt stuck to his back with perspiration. Russell took a deep breath. 'Whole world's gone fucking loopy,' he sighed.

'What do you reckon then?'

Russell was still wiping his sparkling Nikes on the doormat when Sonia spun round before him, her hands placed on her hips, like Cindy gyrating on the catwalk.

'Very nice,' said Russell, slightly confused.

'Dolce & Gabbana,' she said. Russell was still trying to work out whether he should be admiring her chocolate brown fitted shirt or the jeans-cut black satin trousers. Could even have been her shoes (black stilettos with three patent leather bands crossing the middle). What the boys down the Black Prince called 'fuck-me' shoes.

'You don't think they make my arse look big, do you?'

Sonia asked, her head twisted to examine her behind in a mirror.

'No. No.' He meant it, but what else was he going to say? Sonia's mind seemed to stray. It was all Russell could do to try and stop himself from jumping her there and then.

'Oh, I'm sorry,' she said. 'Listen to me, "Is my arse too big, Russell?" Talk about lack of breeding.'

'No, no, it's OK,' said Russell. 'I think they really suit you. The whole outfit is the business.'

Sonia smiled. 'I'm glad you like it. You know I've had my beadies on these strides for, oh, God knows, probably a month now. Saw them in a magazine – *Vogue*, I think it was, maybe *Harper's & Queen* – you can see how posh I've got, can't you?' She smiled self-deprecatingly. 'Anyway, when I saw them,' she started guiding Russell through to the kitchen, 'it was like a voice was issuing me with an order. "You shall have those trousers!" it said to me. Ron was indoors yesterday so I dragged him out shopping. He was so bored I knew that if I promised him we could go home he'd buy me these.' She winked at him. 'Who's a clever girl then?'

'I can't imagine Ron being a lot of fun schlepping down Sloane Street,' said Russell, entering into the spirit of the moment.

Sonia looked embarrassed, as if she'd suddenly remembered something. 'You eaten, Russell?'

'Well, not really. I had a pint of semi-skimmed in the motor, and a banana.'

'Beefing up, are you?' Sonia juggled her eyebrows. It made Russell feel self-conscious. He didn't want her to think he was a meathead, some goon who crushed his bollocks every time his thighs brushed together.

'No, I just try to stay in shape,' he answered, more self-consciously than he wanted to.

'So you won't be wanting a fry-up then?' asked Sonia, mock-examining her nails.

'Does the Pope shit in the woods?'

They sat at the breakfast bar in the snow-white kitchen,

Russell resting his elbows on the cool marble worktop, savouring the fry-up that Valerie, Sonia's maid, had knocked up in the microwave. Sonia sat sipping a cup of black coffee, a Marlboro Light in one hand. A heavy gold chain dangled from her wrist, rattling like a jailer's key ring.

'You know, the best sausages I ever had were in Germany, about five years ago,' she said as Russell polished off his second Wall's Lincolnshire. 'Ron and some of his mates decided to go to Germany, to Munich, for the – *watchamacallit*? The beer festival, the, er, Oktoberfest, that's right. So all the wives went 'n'all, and the boys would go out drinking and we'd go shopping or go to a café or something. Anyway, one night we all go out to this traditional restaurant, and we had these German sausages, from the region we were in, Bavaria, and they were fantastic, just melted in the mouth. Can't get anything like them here though.'

Russell finished off a mouthful of mushrooms. 'You know what?' he said. 'I only know one phrase in German: *"Mochten Sie einen Regenschirm kaufen?"* '

'Mokten zee imen raygunshirm cowfen,' Sonia tried repeating. She had cupped her hands round her face, resting her chin on the heels of her hands.

'Nah, nah, it's *"Mochten Sie einen Regenschirm kaufen?"*,' explained Russell, turning on the Sunday afternoon war film Hunhead accent.

' *"Mochten Sie einen Regenschirm kaufen?"*,' repeated Sonia.

'Something like that,' laughed Russell.

'And what does it mean? Something dirty I assume.'

'It means, "Would you like to buy an umbrella?",' said Russell, wiping his mouth with a paper napkin. 'You see, a few years ago now, I was selling swag to tourists on Oxford Street – moody perfume, sunglasses, snide Polo, cheap fucking tat, excuse my French – and it had been banging it down with rain for a couple of days. Pissing down, and this geezer I know knocked me out some umbrellas, just off the boat from Taiwan. So I made a point of learning the French, Italian and German for 'umbrella' – 'cos if you get a punter talking you're bound to get a sale, they feel terrible otherwise. Anyway, this one Kraut teaches me this phrase

"*Mochten Sie einen Regenshirm kaufen?*" and it's just stuck, you know, the way some things just stay with you?'

'The square of the hypotenuse is equal to the sum of the angles on the other two sides,' said Sonia. 'Python's theory or something. I didn't even get maths CSE or whatever they're called now, but I can still remember that. 'Course I've no idea what it actually means, but it's still lodged up in the porridge.'

Russell took a sip of his tea. 'It's strange all the things you remember. Like TV theme tunes. I can remember TV theme tunes like they were yesterday. All the cartoons I watched when I was a kid.'

'But what about the stuff you forget?'

'There's too much of that,' said Russell. 'I can sit and listen to, say, the weather. Me eyes are open, me brain's working, but if someone asked me what it was going to be like I couldn't tell them. I might as well have been watching *Power Rangers* or something.'

'I try not to watch too much TV,' said Sonia. 'Don't want to end up like one of those housewives who takes the kids to school and then settles down with *Richard and Judy*, a Cup-a-soup and two Valium for the day. Just to get through it, like. I think what did it for me was lying on the sofa watching David Hamilton tell Nerys Hughes his recipe for tandoori chicken. I thought, life's too short.

'Ron watches the sport – seems like there's football on every night now – but we tend to go out and eat. I like going to the pictures, but Ron can't get into it, moans about people sitting in front of him, fidgets all the time. Means I can't enjoy the film myself, so we watch a lot of videos. Mind you, Ron knows people so we get all the latest stuff. Moody, of course. Quality's terrible though sometimes, 'cos they've been filmed at a cinema in America, you know, with a video camera. You can hear people talking, people getting up and walking around. Can't stand it, breaks your concentration.'

'I sold those for a while,' said Russell. 'Couldn't stand watching 'em. They flicker so much I thought I'd have a fit or something, end up in the loony bin. Geezer I was working for, he's inside now. False accounting. I can't believe he kept any accounts, let alone cheated on them.'

Surveying the empty plate resting beneath his elbows Russell leaned backwards slightly to signify he'd finished. 'That was blinding,' he said.

'Now do you want anything else?' asked Sonia, stubbing her cigarette. 'I've got enough food to feed an army in here. Keep Sainsbury's in business, we do.' She carried his plate towards the sink.

'Nah,' said Russell, gesturing her to sit down, 'you're all right, you're all right, sitdahn. *Sitdahn.*'

'Don't be silly,' said Sonia. 'What do you think the dishwasher's for? I tell you, I could never go back to doing everything by hand.'

She took the plate and rinsed it under the tap.

'Mind your new strides,' said Russell. Sonia turned and smiled but Russell saw only a kind of sadness in her mouth, her eyes effortful and straining. In the garden a couple of sparrows bickered, their tiny claws gripping the bars of the griddle that was stickied by blackened barbecue detritus. In the kitchen both Sonia and Russell were silent for a moment, as if pausing for breath during the white heat of an August afternoon. Russell realised then that she was feeling as strange as he was. Knew things could never be the same.

'Another cuppa, Russ?'

'Sweet as,' said Russell, glad for the prop of the mug. Sonia filled the kettle.

'So you had a good time the other night then, Russell?' said Sonia in an offhand way. Russell narrowed his eyes in her direction.

'Thursday night, after the race,' she reminded him.

'Oh, right,' said Russell, aware now that he was being tested. 'Yeah, it was a laugh.' He tried to shift the conversation. 'Good news about Rustler's Rump, eh? Never thought she had it in her. Think even Ron was surprised.'

'So was I,' said Sonia. 'He didn't come home that night.' She puckered her lips slightly, her face hardening.

'Well, you know, we had a few drinks, that turned into a few more and before we knew it the sun was coming up.' Even

Russell was unconvinced by the tone of his explanation.

'There's no need to make excuses, Russell,' said Sonia, not sounding annoyed, just tired. 'You're not responsible for Ron.'

The kettle clicked off and Sonia filled two mugs and pulled the teabags out, plopping them into a pedal bin. Russell thought about excusing himself for a slash, maybe even sitting in the toilet for a while to let Sonia's mood pass. He didn't know how to handle this, didn't want her to be disappointed in him.

'I'm not such a mug that I don't realise what's going on,' she said. 'The kind of business he's in it's par for the course really, isn't it?' She carried the teas over to the counter and sat down. Russell mouthed thanks.

'There's bound to be booze and nights out and the rest, and if you ask me there's not a man alive who'd keep his strides on if he was given an opportunity to get them off.' Russell kept quiet, stirring a couple of sugars into his tea slowly. 'We've never been a particularly affectionate couple. I mean he'll put his arm around me if we go out to a restaurant or a party or up West or something, but only because he's staring down any mug foolish enough to flash a look at my tits. No, we're more of a unit really, more like two people who do things for each other – I take care of him and he takes care of me. I suppose it's pretty fair in its own way, but he likes me to stay out of his business.'

Russell really didn't want to hear this. He nodded indifferently, and blew steam from his tea. He had no idea what to say. He'd never really thought about the practicalities of getting back with Sonia, had only really imagined their life to be in the future, away from Illingford and Ron. Now the very thought of what he was getting himself into made his neck stiffen with tension. He didn't want to push too hard – didn't want to wreck everything – but he knew he'd never be able to live with himself if he didn't reach Sonia somehow.

'Now I know you work for Ron, so I don't expect you to say anything,' she said. 'And I know him well enough to know that if you suggested to him that I ever said what I'm going to say then the next person to see your body would be the captain of a dredger somewhere downriver of Canary Wharf. I'm not being funny now, but have you noticed a change in him? Over the last few weeks he's gone a bit weird, you know, into himself, distant. And, no offence, Russell, but what the bloody hell is this all about? I thought he'd get fed up with the idea after a few days. It's been what, three weeks now?'

'Something like that,' said Russell.

'Well it's not really on, is it? I mean, has he gone completely off his rocker? Is he going to get down on all fours and start barking?' She was joking now, the corners of her mouth rising slightly, but Russell could still feel the undertow of seriousness. 'I mean what does he think he is, the bloody Godfather?

'Over the weekend he hardly said a word. Even when we were out shopping and then went to get something to eat, it was like he'd been struck mute. When we were indoors he just sat there on the recliner sipping V&Ts and watching telly. And guess who had to keep getting up to make them for him? I mean, I know he likes his sport, but it was ridiculous. I felt like I'd gone invisible or something.'

Russell knew what she was talking about. Ron had become guarded and broody, cloaking himself with a sinister irritability that masqueraded as pride or indomitability. Yesterday Frankie had annoyed him by making some shite joke about Ron's shoes (something along the lines of 'Don't those usually come with callipers running up the side?') and Ron had totally lost it. Went Radio fucking Rentals. He stood up, clambered out of the booth and gestured Frankie towards him with his frankfurter fingers, shouting, 'Come on then, you cunt! You want some, cunt? Let's 'ave ya! Let's fucking 'ave ya!' Bemused, Frankie had sloped off to the kitchen and bleached the surfaces. After Frankie had disappeared Ron had stood for a few moments eyeing the others, waiting for a challenge, for someone to utter disapproval. None had come. Everyone had examined their nails or got lost in their beers. Trevor sat there smirking, probably thinking of the money Barko had eaten.

'I wouldn't worry about it. He's had a lot of agg recently,' said Russell, not wanting to be too specific. 'Maybe he's feeling the pressure a bit, he's got a lot on his mind.'

'Enough to justify him fucking teenage prostitutes?'

Russell iced over. Tried to contain his shock. Watched the digital clock on the microwave turning over.

'I have a pretty good idea what went on on Thursday night,' said Sonia. 'He's done it before. He likes 'em young, does Ron.' For a horrible moment Russell thought she was going to turn on the waterworks. 'He'll do it again. Just look at me. I'm almost young enough to be his daughter.' She laughed. 'Christ, what a fucking mess. I'm thirty-two years old and look at me. Look at me. Jesus, I've got more money than I know what to do with and a lifestyle like me nan – the only difference is that she shops for cat food while I buy Gucci.'

Russell thought it was all right to laugh at the last comment. This wasn't some red-eyed plea for help from the bottom of a bottle of gin. He couldn't get involved. But this was all good. Sonia's words had taken them into new territory, put them on a different footing. She was telling him things, taking him into her confidence, and that was hopeful. It would be difficult for her to retreat from this level of intimacy. But he had to be careful, had to keep his guard up. Publicly he had to pretend that this was nothing to do with him. Sonia lit another Marlboro Light. Russell envied the short, hungry drags of thick smoke she sucked into her. He really fancied a snout.

'Listen to me going on,' she said. 'You must be bored witless.'

Russell waved her away. 'Don't be silly,' he said. 'You know I'm a good listener.' He smiled at her as kindly as he could. He was more than happy to sit and absorb as many injustices and humiliations as she cared to list. It was too early to reveal his intentions but he was content to be in this germ-free testament to kitchen cleanser nodding at her every word. In the garden the sparrows continued to bicker.

Chapter Twenty-One

Since Russell had been taking care of Sonia, Ron, out of choice, had been doing his own driving. It would have been easy enough to find a replacement for Russell; plenty of young geezers on the manor desperate to get behind the wheel of a flash motor, put the pedal to the metal given half a chance. But Ron wasn't in the mood for company. Hadn't been for a couple of weeks. There was a tension in his neck, a heaviness that had settled upon him, made him irritable, intolerant. He didn't want to sit in the motor listening to some mouthy slag giving it loads. Besides, you couldn't trust no one these days. Even Frankie, the mug. If he opened his gob again Ron would fucking shut it for him.

Which made it all the worse when he stepped from his car outside Merlin's and that shifty cunt Malcolm Goodge stepped out of his Saab and waved a paper in his face. Ron didn't talk on the pavement; he'd worked on it for long enough. He was a businessman now. He looked skywards for a moment. It wasn't raining, but there was water in the air like the other day, like someone was spraying him with the mist attachment from a garden hose. Too fine to form droplets, just hanging in the air. London air. Air you can see.

'Have you seen this?' Goodge demanded. 'Have you fucking seen this?' The cunt's bottle had gone, no doubt about it.

'Come inside.' Ron pulled the keys from his pocket and headed for the club. Goodge pulled at his arm. Ron looked at him. He couldn't believe it. Bang out of order. First he looked at Goodge's hand, pink and ugly on his camel coat, secondly he bored deep into the cunt's piglet eyes. Goodge's face altered until he looked like he'd trodden on a rattlesnake. He slowly pulled his hand back, regaining his senses.

Ron said nothing more. There was no need. He turned and walked to the club, unlocked the door and held it open for Goodge who walked in sulkily, the newspaper clutched beneath his elbow. Ron locked up after him – he took no chances these days, drove around the block before he got out of his car – headed down the stairs and disappeared. Goodge, not knowing what to do, kicked his heels in the middle of the dance floor.

He waited for a couple of minutes, sure that he was being watched. He heard a clattering of cutlery and realised that Ron was in the kitchen. Self-conscious in the middle of a dance floor Goodge went and leaned on the wall, studying the framed poster of Marilyn Monroe, her skirt billowing upwards in a still from *The Seven Year Itch*.

Blowing on a mug of hot tea Ron strolled out from behind the bar and gestured for Goodge to sit at one of the tables. He hadn't even wasted a glance on the damp councillor. Somehow Ron had dried off, as if he'd done a sneaky change of outfit. There was no tea for the visitor.

'Ron, I . . .' Ron held up his hand. He had yet to look at Goodge.

'You should be fucking ashamed of yourself,' said Ron. 'Have you taken leave of your senses? Eh?' He looked at Goodge in the way he might regard the contents of his handkerchief. 'You should be fucking begging me for forgiveness.'

'I really . . .'

'No, no, no,' said Ron, slicing his hand horizontally through the air. 'You are well out of order. Turn up here unannounced . . . You took a fucking liberty accosting me in the street.'

'I hardly . . .'

'It's a miracle you're even in here talking to me. You should be lying on the fucking pavement with your nose spread from there to there.' Ron pointed from Goodge's right ear to his left.

'Well, I, er . . .'

Ron stirred his tea slowly. 'Yeah. Reckon you might have a headache explaining that one away in the council fucking chamber. See, you might think to yourself, "I'm unhappy about this, I'll go and have words with Chisholm", but what you've got to understand is that when you come to me you are stepping from your domain into mine. Where you come from you might be top boy, but over here you're fuck all. Over here there's only one top boy and do you know who that is?'

Goodge hung his head. He hadn't come here for this.

'Do you know who the top boy is round here?' Ron's voice was quiet, but insistent.

'Aaagghh!' Goodge screamed and clutched his hand, examining a red welt. Ron pointed the scalding teaspoon at him.

'It's just a question of respect, you see,' said Ron, somehow calmer. 'If you try and mug me off I'll slap you, no questions. *YouknowotImean?*'

'Sure, Ron, there's no question of that, there was no disrespect intended. We're both honourable men and I came here in good faith, with no intention of causing you grievance whatsoever.' Goodge was settling a little now that he could hear his voice bouncing around the dark club. 'It's just, I suppose, that I came here in a state of concern, I was very keen to talk with you, to gauge your reaction to something.' He listened to himself talking to some smartarse second-rate thug like he would the borough finance committee.

'Well, what the fuck are you waiting for? Talk to me. Don't waste my time.'

'Sorry, yes. It's the newspaper this morning,' said Goodge, flattening the soggy object on the table. Ron picked it up and brought it closer to his face; his eyesight wasn't as good as it used to be. A headline ran: 'Rasheed: Race Hate Thugs Nearly Killed My Kids'. Beneath it, in the introduction, it read, 'Abdul Rasheed blames council inaction'.

'So?' said Ron.

'Well, the thing is, Ron, last time we met I discussed my concerns about Rasheed.'

'And . . .'

'I came to you for help.'

'And . . .'

'And . . . well, it doesn't look like we've achieved much, does it?'

'Areyoushaw? *Areyoushaw?*' boomed Ron. 'Rasheed's been spoken to.' He paused for a moment. 'You ain't waving that paper in my face, are you? Are you?'

'No, Ron . . .'

'Took care of my end. Now if you can't take care of business at your end, if you can't take care of the local fucking press on your own manor, then I hardly think that I'm to blame. Or am I wrong?'

'Well, I was just a little disappointed that Rasheed seems to be at the centre of this,' said Goodge slowly. 'I thought that someone was going to speak to him.'

'Someone had a verbal with him. But he seems not to have taken any notice.' Ron shrugged. 'Ain't my problem. I've done my bit. Reckon you've got the fucking problem. You've got to decide whether you want to have this taken care of properly or whether you want this cheeky cunt to run around making you look like a mug for any longer.'

'Well, it was never my intention . . .'

'Don't come the pious wanker with me,' said Ron, his voice hushed and firm. 'You're in this now. Deep. You may not know it, but the water's above your bollocks and rising. Believe me.' He looked at the tip of his fast-fading cigarette. 'Kidnapping kids is a criminal offence, even for the leader of the council. Think about it. You can't lose your bottle now. You want to get mugged off twice? Get fucked by Rasheed *and* end up nicked for conspiracy? Is that what you want? Is that what you want? So what's it going to be, Malcolm? Have you got the bottle, or are you just another shitter?'

'I can't possibly contemplate further action of an illegal nature,' said Goodge.

'*Areyoushaw?*' asked Ron. 'If you were a comedian you'd fucking starve. You've already made that decision. You've crossed the line. You're fucking well beyond "illegal nature".'

'But I don't need to cross it again.'

'Depends, don't it. Now I get the feeling that this Rasheed geezer is giving you serious grief. It's up to you, innit? You either let him drive you out of the town hall or you sort him out. It's a simple question. All it needs is an answer.'

Goodge pushed himself back in his chair. The boyishness, the halo of confidence that had elevated him beyond the leaflets and tombolas of local politics, had melted away. Ron noticed a slittishness to his eyes which were puffy with tiredness.

'You know, Ron, I've always tried to do what I thought was best for the people of this borough,' said Goodge. 'Thought there might be something I could do to improve things. But, you know, I'm not so sure any longer. Sometimes I wonder if democracy even works.'

'Very touching. That's hardly news to the average mug in the street,' said Ron impatiently. 'You cunts at the town hall couldn't even agree on the colour of shit. And while you're scoring points over each other the rest of us get on with our lives. It ain't no big deal. We ain't heroes. It's only because we have to. So why don't you do just that? Make a decision. 'Cos I'm getting sick of listening to your bleeding heart.'

Chapter Twenty-Two

He was gutted. There was nothing Russell hated more than sweating it out for a couple of hours first thing to find that the showers at the gym were on the blink. Wiping off the hot slick with a towel wasn't good enough. Skin had come up with some lame excuse that a plague of rats had forced the water authority to take drastic measures and the water was off for most of the day. Russell thought it more likely that it was just good old-fashioned British utilities incompetence. That, or Skin's dodgy plumbing.

He had an Italian shower – smothering himself with thick gusts of aftershave – but the absence of hot, steaming water from his morning routine threw him into a prickly temper. An itchiness spread under his skin making him feel rank as a puddle of puke in Dalston.

After necking a cup of Red Label with Skin Russell headed back to the car, his black gym bag slung over his right shoulder. Busting a right by a hardware shop he came to an abrupt halt. There was a fraction of doubt in his mind but he could have sworn that the man he clocked loping towards him was familiar. Maybe he was a face from the old days, some Intercity bully boy he'd run with during his years of hooky labels, soul weekenders and white knuckle away-days. He tried to fit the face to some shadowy memory, some tangible instant from a murky past.

He drew a blank. The man slowed down himself, eventually coming to a halt about eight feet away, outside a Chinese chippy. Alone in the cold, clear early morning, the two men eyed each other, like two unfamiliar dogs. Russell could feel a stickiness beginning to spread down his torso from his armpits. Those showers had better be working tomorrow.

Then it came to him.

'Pikey, ain't it?' said Russell.

There was no response. The man's eyebrows beetled a little and he scratched the back of his ear.

'Merlin's Cave. You came to see Ron.' Russell realised that the second part of the sentence was redundant. Pikey was hardly likely to have forgotten his last visit to the club. Russell took a couple of steps towards Pikey but halted instantly when the other held open the left side of his leather reefer jacket to reveal the handle of a five-inch screwdriver, the defensive weapon of choice these days when being caught carrying a blade could mean a stretch.

'Just fucking walk away,' ordered Pikey. 'Just fucking go unless you want some.'

Russell opened his arms, trying to look less threatening. He shook his head. 'Listen I ain't interested in all that,' he said. 'I just want a word.'

'How about two words? Fuck off. Don't want to talk to you. Just walk away before you get hurt. On your toes, son.'

'Nobody's getting hurt,' said Russell.

'Ain't telling you again,' said Pikey, quickly looking round, aware that they were standing in a public place. Russell didn't move. Just waited. 'What do you want?' asked Pikey.

'Wanted to warn you,' said Russell.

'Warn me. Warn *me?!*' crowed Pikey. 'On yer bike son.' Russell could see that the swallow tattooed on the skin between the thumb and forefinger of his right hand was fluttering slightly.

'Ron says you're banned from the manor. He said if we see you then we've got to sort you.'

'Ron says, Ron says . . . bollocks. Tell me something new.' Pikey laughed.

'Ain't threatening you, just telling you,' said Russell as calmly as he could. 'Giving you a bit of advice. Don't be a fucking fool. Lie low for a bit, it'll all blow over.'

'Chisholm thinks he can act like God he's got another think coming,' said Pikey. 'He's living in a fucking dream world. He's just a sad old man who's lost his bottle. It's all over for him.'

'You should take more care,' said Russell.

'Just visiting me brother. He's got a pub round the corner.' There was silence between them now. The atmosphere had passed, it was as if they had both been waiting for something to happen that never did.

'I'm going to turn round now and walk away,' said Russell. 'Far as I'm concerned this never happened.' He pulled the sports bag on to his shoulder and started back the way he had come. The other man said something behind him as he walked away. He wasn't sure, but it sounded like 'I'll be seeing you.'

Russell thought he'd grab a Big Breakfast once he'd had his meeting with Ron. These days their talks always went the same way, Ron's mood unravelling ever more as he gabbled on about every infringement, every insult heaped upon his crumbling empire.

'I ain't standing for it no more, Russ,' he would grumble. Russell considered telling him that if he was so worried about the business then it was a lesson in futility him bodyguarding Sonia when there was quite clearly absolutely no threat to one of the tousled, teased, bleached hairs on her sun-bedded, gym-toughened body.

But Ron wouldn't have had any of it, might even have read treachery into his words, so Russell continued to do as he was told, collect his folding, keep Ron sweet, maintain a low profile. This way he could enjoy an easy life up in the Hertfordshire/London borders without fear of any of his boss's enemies or the boss himself. And, more importantly, he got to spend time with Sonia.

As he parked outside Merlin's Russell clocked the pink and black poster tacked inside a plexiglass frame.

EVERY FRIDAY. MIND EXPANSIONS. DJS ON THE NITE: LINDSAY D, THE ERADICATOR, VINYLRIDER WITH SPECIAL GUEST MICHAEL UNSUNCIO FROM NEW YORK. LADIES FREE ALL NITE. MEN: £5 AFTER 10.

The Ecstasy thing was still knocking a big hole in their bar takings, the trim, loose bodies, high on amphetamines and hallucinagens, just drank water all night. The bogs were constantly flooded from people dunking their heads in basins full of cold water, like there was some apple-bobbing competition going on. Bar takings had plummeted along with the agg, they were all touchy-feely instead of being desperate to kick seven colours of shite out of each other like young people are supposed to. But even though there was little money being taken behind the bar Ron hadn't stopped smiling since he'd got a good, cheap connection and a couple of lads working the floor. The word went around among the kids that there were good pills inside the door.

For a while charlie had made a come-back. So the dealers were given a different product, security was lightened on the bogs (Ron, charitably, described it as a 'special needs' situation, one of his business manual sayings) and bar takings got back on the road again as ice lager and shorts made a reappearance from behind the Thirstade, psychoactive tonics and premium mineral waters.

It was a sign of the times that sometimes you'd get rich kids coming down for a bit of rough. Notting Hill trustafarians slumming it. Blonde birds with their mums' faces toking on dodgy spliff peddled by Trevor's mate Tiny Tony (who was, of course, as big as an articulated lorry) and getting hit on by shaven-headed black lads who could scent a score as soon as it swished through the door.

Boxes of some new tonic chock full of caffeine were stacked in the entrance. Over-priced drinks were the last thing on Russell's mind as he locked the door behind him; soaked to the skin by a mixture of his own sweat and the pygmy rain, all he wanted to do was blow the steam off a nice cup of rosie. Judging by the dark stains that marked the soiled synthetic carpet tiles two sets of shoes had passed this way not long before.

He took the stairs. There they were, tucked into one of the booths in shoulder-to-shoulder urinal-style intimacy, muttering plots and promises. Their double-breasted familiarity was such that Russell thought the men long-term associates – Jesus, maybe Ron's even got a spar. But no, the other is up and leaving, his handshake formal and rigid, the tilt of his chin too sober for that. Russell copped a good butcher's at his boat and

– Jesus, twice in the same morning – knew the mug from somewhere: a boyish forty years old, a face trustworthy and ready to smile, eyes a little too watery, slightly red around the edges. It could just have been another of Ron's tooled loafered associates, but Russell sensed something different.

The man disappeared in a rustle of water-proofed cotton mix as he wrapped his raincoat around himself and offered Ron a final nod, before they both remembered that, in fact, Ron would have to accompany him up the stairs and unlock the door once again. Russell watched the man in the raincoat disappear up the stairs. Ron stopped the man while they were still in sight, put his hand on the man's shoulder and said – quite clearly for Russell's benefit – 'Good doing business with you again, Malcolm.' The other pulled himself away and carried on up the stairs, his footsteps suddenly heavier.

Ron came down the stairs a couple of minutes later and joined Russell. He was rubbing his hands together absent-mindedly.

'Russell,' he said. 'I've got a job for you.' His mood was sour. He was searching Russell's eyes for dissent, hoped there might be a chance of a row.

'See, Trevor had an unfortunate encounter with a young man over on the Merrivale Estate a few weeks ago.'

'The kid in the paper, Ron?' asked Russell as inoffensively as he could muster.

'Don't see the papers, Russell,' said Ron offhandedly. 'Anyway, he still owes us. Think it's better if Trevor lets this one slide, knowotImean? So I'd like you to take care of it.'

'Do what?'

'Encourage him to clear his debt, Russell.' The words, as ever, were little more than a whisper – like a snake tasting the air. Russell knew that he was not flush with options, and nodded conspiratorially to get Ron off his case.

'Make sure you take care of it, Russell,' he added.

Russell nodded again, feeling Ron's eyes boring into him.

'Where's Frankie?' asked Ron. Russell could sense he was looking for someone to bully.

'Dunno, Ron.'

'Bet he's taken that fucking dog for a walk.' Ron glowered at Russell. 'I don't pay you to sit on your arse. Go and find that Paki kid.'

'What about Sonia?'

'She's visiting friends until this afternoon. Meet her at the health club at three. Tell her I'll be home late. Working.'

Russell slid from the booth and made to leave. He couldn't wait to see Sonia at three. First off though he needed a drink, relax his mind.

'And Russell,' said Ron. 'Don't ever let me down, understand?'

Chapter Twenty-Three

An assault on a man in Illingford, East London, has raised fears that extreme right neo-Nazi groups may be mounting a campaign against the local Asian community.

Mr Abdul Rasheed, a community and political organiser, was attacked outside his home yesterday evening as he returned from prayer at the London mosque in Mile End. His right leg was broken when struck by a man wielding a baseball bat. His head and upper body were severely bruised. It is not known how many assailants were involved in the attack.

Speaking from his hospital bed Mr Rasheed, 43, said that he saw nothing. 'I got out of my car and before I'd even had a chance to lock it everything went black,' he said. 'The next thing I knew I was in hospital.'

Police have condemned the attack as 'vicious and cowardly'. As yet they have no leads and are appealing to local residents to come forward with information.

This is the second suspected racially motivated attack in a month. On February 4th Zaffir Khan, 17, was attacked on the Merrivale Estate while delivering pizza and suffered serious head injuries.

As news spread of the attack Asian

youths gathered in gangs and stoned police. Running battles between police and youths flared intermittently throughout the night. No arrests were made.

Community leaders are now appealing for calm and renewing their calls for the local council to liaise with the police to offer better protection from racist attacks.

Speaking from Paris, where he is on a fact-finding mission regarding the borough's planned transport improvements, council leader Malcolm Goodge commented, 'This [attack] is an insult to all decent members of the community. People capable of committing such an act as this have no place in a civilised society.

'I am a great admirer of Mr Rasheed and will do my utmost to ensure that his attackers are caught so that all people in the borough may go about their business in peace.'

Mr Rasheed is an outspoken critic of the ruling Labour group and leader of the Community Action Group, an Asian pressure organisation which has threatened to withdraw its support from the ruling coalition. 'People are scared to walk the streets,' Rasheed stated at a council meeting only a few weeks ago, 'and Malcolm Goodge does nothing to help us.'

His sentiments were echoed yesterday by a neighbour of Rasheed's, who wished to remain anonymous. 'None of us feels safe any longer, even in our homes,' she said. 'It is unbelievable that the council and the police are allowing this to happen and not taking any action.'

Chapter Twenty-Four

Lunchtime drinkers at the Crown & Anchor were a funny lot. Once the two pints of Fosters and a lamb balti crowd had snuck back to the office before their bosses got the hump the boozer boasted the usual assortment of early afternoon detritus: men leading PAYE-free, roll-up lives, grumbling through the *Sporting Life*, scratching notes and marks to themselves with stubby plastic Biros half-inched from Ladbrokes.

Old geezers taking toothless slurps from lukewarm McEwans, punctuation marks to break up the hours, seeing off the long afternoon. Gee-gee schemers and lottery dreamers clambering above the water level with increasing difficulty. Even at three o'clock a place like the Crown & Anchor, largely sheltered from the fast-forward laminated liteness of the new service sector, offered purchase in an increasingly worrisome world.

Which was why Russell came here. There were no American-style Bar-B-Q burgers in baps, a marked absence of Punjab Pot Pourri bar snax, and punters didn't have to watch abseiling from Latvia on a sports channel while sitting on a wood-effect stool that had been screwed to the floor. It was an old-fashioned pub (meaning seventies, which is as old-fashioned as pubs get without interior stylists having breezed in yard-of-ale glasses or dried floral combinations); a place that had yet to join the revenue-per-square-foot handwringing of the new leisure nation.

No cranberry juice, no jugs of sangria, no clean toilets, no Australian bar staff, no fucking karaoke or pub quizzes. Just booze, pork scratchings, darts and a ruck at the weekends.

'Old man's pub,' was how Russell usually thought of it, but it was a good place to sit and think as long as you kept your distance from the coffin dodgers who tried to tax you for fags and bitter in return for some luck-free life story divested at a snail's pace.

He couldn't believe what Ron had just asked him to do. There was no sense to it: Trevor had hospitalised some kid, had given him a beating he could never forget – that would stalk him whenever he left home – and now Ron wanted him to do another number on the kid, turn the screw. Russell knew that there was more to this than money. Ron could afford to let it go, but it was gnawing at him like a bad tooth because it was another symbol of decline, of lack of respect. An insult.

There was no way Russell was going to take care of the kid. He'd known that the moment Ron asked him. It wasn't right. He remembered Ron's words – 'Don't ever let me down.' That was what this was about. It was personal. Had nothing to do with the kid. It was about him and Ron. It was a test, a test that Russell had no interest in passing.

Russell was hunched over 'Sunsport', well into his second whisky and Coke when he picked up one of the old boozers in his peripheral vision. The man had come and sat right next to him, locked on target.

'What's the news, then?' the old bloke asked. He had a nose the colour and texture of a ripe raspberry.

'Not much,' replied Russell, his eyes fixed on the page.

'Those Manc cunts still running away with it?'

'Looks that way, dunnit.'

The old man took a drag on his thin, smokeless roll-up. 'You wouldn't happen to have a few spare pence to buy an old man a drink, would you?'

Surprise, surprise.

'Sorry, mate.'

'Or a cigarette?'

'Don't smoke, mate.'

The old man seemed satisfied by this. No hard feelings. Life was shaded like this. The sting over, he settled in to tell Russell a thing or two about life.

'Been drinking here for over forty years now.'

'Really,' said Russell. 'And you still ain't pissed? Slags must be watering the beer down.' The man entirely missed the joke, ploughing his own furrow.

'Yeah, 'course it's different now to what it was. This one,' he indicated the portly man dunking glasses in a sink behind the bar, 'has only been landlord for the last ten. We get on, we do. You see he's the money man and I'm the ideas man. Take that fridge.' He indicated a stainless steel vault with a glass front door. A Castlemaine XXXX sticker was peeling off at the side.

'Fucking good fridge, that. I told him to buy that,' said the old man proudly. 'I told him to buy that fucking fridge, and it'll keep anything fucking cold, that will.'

Russell wondered how long this was going to carry on. He signalled to the barmaid for another round.

'And what about the fucking lottery, eh? Fucking swizz, that is. You know anyone who's won? I don't. Reckon it's all a fucking fix and all those cunts in the paper are a bunch of swindlers.' The old man took another draw on his cigarette. 'Tell you what, though. I won a million quid, I wouldn't spend a fucking penny. Not a fucking penny. Know why? Because if I did I wouldn't be a millionaire no more.'

And with that the old man stood up, opened and closed his mouth a couple of times, as if unsticking his tongue from his palate, drained the soapy dregs of his drink and wandered out on to the pavement.

Russell gave the barmaid a knowing wink. She giggled back at him before going back to her *Puzzlemaster*.

Halfway through a sensational exclusive about calamity and broken beer glasses at an Essex country club disco involving a rising star at Arsenal, Russell felt a slap on the back.

'All right, Russ.' He turned to see Mark Thorpe, an old school friend who he still had a drink with occasionally.

'All right, mate,' said Russell. 'What you drinking?'

'Pint of Carling, mate.'

'Pint of Carling, please love, and another whisky and Coke.'

'Thought you never drank during the day,' said Mark.

'Just fancied one.' Russell shrugged. He thought a couple of drinks before seeing Sonia might help his cause, relax him.

'You still seeing that bird I saw you with last time?' asked Mark.

'Who was that then?' asked Russell.

'Listen to him.' Mark raised his eyebrows. 'Red-headed bird. Tall.'

'Oh, Mandi. Nah, we split up a while ago.' Russell had quite liked Mandi but had got fed up with the little-girl-lost act that she played the whole time. She'd needed the kind of man who was going to spoil her rotten. Russell had heard she'd started going up Stringfellows on the prowl for someone older with a bit of wedge.

'You still married?' asked Russell. Mark had married Melanie Squires, Russell's class's favourite wank fantasy.

'Yeah, still married. Mel's got another one on the way.'

'Up the spout again?' said Russell. 'You randy old bastard. How many's that now?'

'It'll be the fourth. Got two girls and a boy.'

'Any good at football?'

'Give him a fucking chance, Russ, he's only eighteen months.'

'You've got to get 'em young though, Mark. He could be in the Premiership in fifteen years.'

'Yeah, but West Ham fucking won't be.'

Enough said. Both men shook their heads as if remembering a long-lost friend.

'What you up to these days then?' asked Russell.

'Still shopfitting. It's all right, pays the rent,' said Mark, casting his eyes around the bar. 'You're doing all right though, aren't you? You're well Ralphed up.' Mark indicated Russell's outfit: Polo shirt, Hilfiger jeans, Polo jacket and Air Max trainers.

'Well, I'm earning all right, I suppose. Working for this nightclub geezer, Ron Chisholm. He's got some arcades and a couple of pool clubs as well. Wine bars. Does all right for himself.'

'Yeah, I heard. Bit heavy, though.'

'S'pose.'

'You work with a geezer named Trevor.'

'Trevor Chisholm, yeah.'

'Right fucking headcase? Ron's brother?'

'That's the one.'

'He used to be mates with my cousin Wayne,' said Mark. 'You know, maybe I'm out of order here but ... Wayne bumped into Trevor down the boozer a couple of days ago and he said that Trevor was banging on that he just sorted out some geezer with a baseball bat, broke his legs. He was going, "That Paki got what he deserved". Made me think of that geezer in the papers.'

Russell was jerked from his mildly drunk state as if an alarm bell had rung. 'You sure, Mark?'

'God's honest. That's what Wayne said. Said Trevor was going on about fucking up anyone who messed with him.'

'He's probably just all mouth,' said Russell, knowing otherwise. 'Giving it the large.'

'Yeah, that's what I thought. He was well pissed up, probably just mouthing off, playing the hard man. Steven fucking Seagal. Another one, Russ?'

'I've got to give it the off, mate. I'll speak to you later on. Send my best to Mel, eh?'

'Good luck, mate.'

Good luck, thought Russell. Good luck. Strange how everyone round here wished each other good luck.

Outside he looked up at the sky. Strange. It was cloudy but bright. Schizo London weather. He got in his car, settled into the leather upholstery and sat silently for a moment. Ron. Trevor. Zaffir. Rasheed. He knew who that other man was now, Malcolm, the one Ron had been having the verbal with. He leaned back against the headrest and took several deep breaths, felt his lungs filling and emptying. The whole thing was going pear-shaped. His mind felt scorched. He thought about Sonia. It was payback time. Time to rewrite history.

Chapter Twenty-Five

'Can you tell me where Mrs Chisholm is, please?' asked Russell, jangling his car keys impatiently.

The tanned girl with the pastel pink lipstick and snow-white sweatshirt with 'Oakheart Country Club – Pleasure and Leisure' stencilled on it eyed a chart on her left.

'She's just gone into Ab Attack in the studio area. You can wait for her in the Revival bar if you'd like to sign in.'

'Yeah, thanks.'

'It's through two sets of doors and on your left, er,' she turned the signing-in book upside down, 'Russell.'

Heading straight for the studio Russell passed the trophy wives and retired DIY millionaires straining on pec decks and lat pulldowns, their groans making the rooms sound like bedlam, presided over by toned-out, zoned-out, chipper trainers with firm words and meaty thighs.

Hearing the soul lite of Diana Ross's 'Chain Reaction' Russell knew he was on the right track. Peering through a glass window in a baby blue door he clocked Sonia in a co-ordinated group of stepping and stretching women. The instructor had her back to the door, but Russell could see in the mirror at the rear of the room that she was oriental, her heavy black hair swaying with the music before falling perfectly into place.

Not wanting to wave, in case some of the other women spotted him and thought he was some gusset sniffer who hung around women's workouts, Russell stuck his boat flush in the middle of the window, hoping Sonia would see him.

From the set of her face he could tell that she was concentrating hard. Her hair was tied back and she wore a black two-piece outfit with white socks and Nike trainers. Russell waited. She had good balance, transferring her weight from foot to foot with a dancer's lightness. She shook herself abruptly when she noticed Russell and lost her rhythm earning a 'Work that body, Sonia,' from the instructress.

Russell gestured to her madly. At first she shook her head but, after a failed attempt to regain her rhythm, sneaked round the back of the class, fanning herself with her hand, and left the room.

'Your timing really is spot on, Russell. You know that?' She was slightly out of breath, her chest rising and falling in a pronounced manner.

'Look, I'm sorry to drag you out of there, but there's been a bit of bother at the club.'

'What kind of bother?' Sonia wiped the moisture on her brow with the back of her hand.

'Nothing too serious . . .'

'Has Ron been hurt?' Her tone was double-edged. Concerned and expectant.

'It ain't like that,' said Russell, not quite sure why he'd said all this. 'Go and take a shower. We'll talk when you've freshened up.'

'Russell, I've only just got here,' said Sonia, irritated by his obscurity. 'Is it really that urgent? Can't you just wait until I've finished?' Russell could see that she was perplexed, annoyed even. He didn't want to push it. He had no idea why he'd interrupted her. No idea what it was that he wanted to say to her. What he knew was that Ron had lost it, was floating around in cloud cuckoo land meeting the council leader and imagining enemies and conspirators round every corner. He knew that Trevor was a psycho and he knew that he wasn't going to beat up the kid. It was all too much for Russell. He wanted out, but he wanted the money. Most of all he was scared beyond anything he'd ever felt before. He was scared because he knew he had to lay his cards on the table. Like some lucked-out Las Vegas chancer down to his last few chips, he knew it was all or nothing.

'No. It can't wait,' he said, and leaned forward and kissed her. She was hot and sticky and Russell couldn't tell whether the thumping of her heart was due to his advances or the workout. He put his hand through her hair on to the back of her neck and the cold of his hands made her flinch slightly, but she didn't draw away.

They parted and stood for a moment regarding each other, aware that, even though they had remained unseen, somehow they were both implicated in some terrible deed. Russell suddenly thought of those films he'd seen about nuclear war and how it always took two people turning keys simultaneously to lock the procedure into some irreversible countdown. He could almost hear the numbers declining in his head . . . 10, 9, 8 . . . before Ron burst through the doors with Trevor and a couple of vengeful sadists bent on teaching him a lesson he'd never recover from.

But Ron didn't come and the two of them just stood there, Russell composing an excuse in his head. Sonia tilted her head to the left a little, narrowed her eyes and said, 'I think I'd better go and get changed.'

He followed her in the car all the way back to Moore House without once cranking up the Blaupunkt. Hearing only the hum of the engine and whistle of the radials he trailed Sonia, watching her golden pony tail as if its busy little swing could point the direction they should both follow or could make what was coming any easier.

Russell had never known her to drive as slowly as she did, barely over thirty, stopping at the faintest trace of an amber light, waving old grannies and welfare mothers across pedestrian crossings. It was unnerving, reminded him of the slowness of a funeral cortège.

Yet it was also sexy. Like unwrapping a present slowly, wanting to take in every detail, every moment of newness, of hope and novelty, savouring every fleeting minute of what would soon become a gilded memory.

It was a strange sensation, the danger. He had never had a thing with a married woman before, had never found himself tied up in the half-truths and shady living of affairs. He didn't want to acknowledge the little bubble of hope that had surfaced in his heart that there was more to their relationship than the rekindling of the cold ashes of love. He didn't want an affair. He wanted a beginning, something tangible, a shelter of hope in a harsh world. As he lay there in bed, in Ron's bed, Sonia's skin warm against his, the smell of sex upon them, Russell felt a peace he had not known since those summer days at the reservoir.

Sonia lay beside him stroking his arm. No words had passed between them since the health club. Like two somnambulists they had parked their cars and drifted up to the bedroom. Russell had not asked her if he could unbutton her white shirt and remove her hipsters. And even though he'd expected it when he saw what he'd always known: little fading knots of blue flesh, one on the ribs, one on the shoulder – sharp reminders of Ron's rage upon her – it still sickened him to the stomach.

She sensed him staring at the marks and drew closer to him to stop him looking. Their lovemaking was controlled and smooth. There were no little hitches, an absence of the minor misunderstandings and embarrassments that can disrupt the rhythm of an initial coupling. He tried to remember how it had been before, but his memory was adrift on the chemical clouds of pleasure drifting through his body.

And now, deep in the full flush of their togetherness, there was still nothing that needed to be said. She rolled over and sat astride him, the white cotton sheet wrapped around her midriff, her hair falling helter-skelter about her shoulders. Her tongue reached out and pulled a strand into her mouth. She stared into Russell's eyes while he reached up, stroking her small brown breasts.

All that passed between them was their togetherness, in the large bedroom with its cut-glass chandelier and fitted wardrobes with mirrored doors. Her mood throughout had been difficult to gauge, passive yet passionate, troubled but relieved, perhaps contemplating much the same as Russell, that life could some-how never be the same after the happenings in this room with its nude watercolours on the walls. The room had smelled odd to Russell at first; there was a smell that he associated with being somewhere else. Now he knew what it was – Ron.

As he stretched upwards to kiss Sonia that was what Russell was thinking: now Ron's bedroom smelled of him.

Chapter Twenty-Six

Malcolm Goodge looked at his watch and wondered how much longer this was going to go on. Throughout the evening's council meeting he'd been tapping the end of his pencil on the table like some rhythmless drummer. He was aware that he was doing it, registered the irritated glances of his colleagues, yet couldn't stop himself from bouncing the eraser off the desk in front of him, playing out some secret beat.

It was strange, all this knowledge, knowing that he was inches away from ruining his life. There, pressed against his chest, folded neatly into thirds, right here, *right now*, two simple documents with black helvetica 12 minutely raised on their surfaces that permitted Ron Chisholm all-night licences at two of his clubs and bars. The pages were seemingly innocuous, but each sheet was as deadly to his career as a tabloid call-girl exposé or an internal putsch among the rank and file.

The Rasheed news stories had begun to tail off, although he still had to run the gauntlet of a few weedy looking *Socialist Worker* whingers with their 'Black and White Unite and Fight' placards. But he wasn't rattled, they could do nothing to touch him.

Goodge had kept his head down after the attack on Rasheed. There was plenty of incoming, but also plenty of time spent on camera and in print, an opportunity to get his profile as high as possible. And that, he realised, was when he sparkled, when the electricity of life fizzed and crackled in his veins. Christ, how he hated the tiresome meetings of pedants and local busybodies, the interminable hours of agendas, motions and amendments, the power games of teachers and plumbers exercising their democratic rights with all the impact

163

of a gnat on an elephant. They were just a distraction, a mild impediment in his running of the borough and the far more important business of getting him selected for a safe seat at the next general election. After all, he didn't want to be stuck in this shit hole for ever. He'd served his time in the trenches.

In the beginning he hadn't seen a problem – rubber-stamping a late licence for a couple of Chisholm's places was really no skin off his nose. The chances of him being brought to book were slim. No one on his side of the fence had any idea who Chisholm was, and even if they did there was no way they could forge a link between Chisholm and Rasheed. Any connection would be purely circumstantial, nothing he couldn't survive by lying low for a few weeks and playing it dumb, disappear somewhere on a fact-finding mission. There was the possibility of danger – a little loose talk from one of Chisholm's boot boys, an extra snoopy journalist – but the chances of anything rearing up and sinking its fangs into him were slim; he wasn't losing sleep over it. Only natural disaster could capsize his assault on Westminster.

He thought back to his meeting with Chisholm, that mad old lag with delusions of grandeur, how his partly digested management speak made him like some cut-price Don Corleone meets Anthony Robbins. It occurred to Goodge that Chisholm had made a huge effort to make him uncomfortable when he visited the club, how he kept him waiting, pumped up the volume of the music, mixed extra-strong drinks, made huge, lumbering efforts to maintain control of the conversation. Did he really think he could have done that without his own complicity? Did he not realise that the business of politics was as dirty as any other? How you acted a part in certain situations to get what you wanted – even if it involved playing dumb, rolling over, taking a dive, swallowing?

He smiled at the thought of Ron's self-importance, this absurd middle-aged goon on the brink of hysterical anger, a terrifying lump of a man with his bull's head and champagne chins. Goodge explained it to himself this way: all he was doing was encouraging local business by aiding Ron in his quest for revenue-earning opportunities – even the top carnivores sometimes needed some luck with their kill.

And that was why he was sitting listening to some tedious amendment about increased security in schools after some tyke had got stabbed by a schizo who should have been locked up anyway. Some in the chamber might have mistaken his pencil tapping as the impatient gesture of a political player who was convinced of the righteousness of his path and just wanted to get on with the business of legislation.

But it was his own security that weighed upon his mind and, as cock-sure as he was about controlling his end of the deal, the thought of others holding sway over his destiny made him more jumpy than a cage full of lab monkeys. More than once a terrible scenario had flashed across his mind: during the long nights he was scared of getting caught, scared of getting strapped on to the inevitable tabloid ducking stool ('LOONY GOODGE ON MURDER RAP', 'COMRADE MALCOLM'S MAFIA HIT'), scared of his career going to shit before the ultimate opportunity of getting his nose to the trough was realised. Most of all, ferreted deep within his mind, he was spooked by Ron Chisholm. Sure enough, he was convinced that he was Chisholm's intellectual superior, that Chisholm wasn't smart enough to consider him a threat. He even hoped that Chisholm might consider him enough of a player to accord him a certain level of respect, maybe even protection.

But there was still that hitch in his breath, a clamminess to his palms that came with a certain knowledge that Ron's mind appeared to be scrambling information fed to it. As much as Ron masked it, played the smart-as-a-button-geezer-business-man, Goodge could sense an instability to his manner, an edginess in his voice; trace a paranoia that belied his confident guv'nor exterior. And it was this that made him sweat into the Dunlopillo at night: the understanding that Ron Chisholm could not be relied upon to make rational decisions any longer, could not be trusted even to protect his business life by seeking the route of least conflict. Ron was on the edge, his eyes ablaze, his breath fevered – and it scared the shit out of Goodge. Scared him worse than a room full of tabloid byline bounty hunters.

Chapter Twenty-Seven

Little in life had prepared Russell for the situation in which he now found himself. When he was a youngster he had disengaged himself from his parents' parched and loveless marriage by lying low, ducking the whole ugly mess. As an adolescent, his spell of lawlessness had been essentially a means of kindling the spirit inside, something that made him feel so vital that it temporarily masked the tense slipper-and-sofa shackles of his home life. Yesterday's events at Moore House, however, had given him the feeling that life had caught up with him. There was nowhere to run. All of a sudden it felt as if things were happening to *him* rather than just to other people, like it was his turn to be the rabbit hanging in the butcher's shop window.

Just as today's cycle courier is tomorrow's organ doner, Ron was losing it, recently developing a nasty habit of pulling his top lip over his teeth when annoyed that gave him a cadaverous menace, his eyes speckled with an unsettling wildness.

They betrayed his state of mind as surely as Russell and Sonia were now knotted together. The sex hadn't been just some blow and grope romp, some hot-breathed attempt to escape workaday tedium. Sonia hadn't articulated her feelings about what had happened between them but, headed for the Black Prince on a cold Friday night with the smell of her still on him, Russell felt an inevitability about their coupling, a sense of togetherness that signified a beginning and not an end. His years in the cold may have come to an end, but now he'd found himself right in the middle of a raging fire.

It was clear that their relationship could continue on the basis of afternoon fuck sessions deep in the pebbledash prairie

166

of suburbia. If it was just about the sex they could continue to extinguish long afternoons between the sheets without fearing the dark shadow of Ron cast over their entwined bodies. But Russell knew that the questions rolling around his head were about more than that; like the hook of a catchy pop song playing at the back of his mind, he kept turning the mess over, playing out the scenarios, sure that there was the possibility of another dimension to their relationship. It nestled there between them, somewhere between longing and compulsion.

Although he still could not be sure, he sensed that there was more going on in Sonia's mind, that her hopes and sense of self had altered in some way, that her gossamer-thin expectation had grown beyond the confines of its plush interior-decorated prison. Something hopeful was going on in Sonia's life and he fancied that the hope might be him.

As terrifying as the whole situation was, what caused him most alarm was that he had engineered the whole thing or, at least, not discouraged it – like the boy burning down the pigsty and discovering roast pork. There lay the real cause for fear. Banging the boss's wife – even if your boss happens to be a minor hoodlum – is a situation from which you might be able to extricate yourself. In Russell's case it probably meant leaving the manor, maybe moving somewhere gentile out of London. But opening your life to someone, making a commitment to them beyond banging them a couple of times a week, that was what was making his mind race.

It was odd, but he was beginning to like the idea, and thought that maybe she did too. After all, she had as little to lose as he did. Only money. Her marriage was in darkness – a cheap, market-stall version of a snappy designer outfit. She needed escape as much as he did. Maybe she was sitting at home pretending to sign her name 'Sonia Fisher' just to see what it looked like. Maybe she thought about him as Ron slid between her legs (although – despite never having given it much thought – Russell couldn't imagine Ron anywhere but underneath). Russell hoped they didn't even do it.

Even if she wasn't thinking of him every waking moment, there was still something significant happening. A woman like

Sonia didn't lightly rupture her life beyond all repair. Should Ron discover his wife's betrayal it was clear that he would exact retribution – this was not a man with a highly developed sense of forgiveness. Ron's sense of self was founded on his ability to make those around him, such as his trophy wife and recently recruited employee of the month, do exactly as he decreed. And his method of enforcing this could not be relied upon to deliver impartial justice.

The easiest solution was to have Ron removed from the equation with as little fuss and bother as possible. Maybe he should call the papers – a Sunday morning exposé nestling amongst the Frosties and marmalade, featuring a council leader, a local thug and a racist attack, a juicy slice of sleaze would be as lethal to Ron as lacing his PG Tips with arsenic.

With his form it was unlikely that the courts would look on Ron with a great deal of leniency. And while he was doing porridge Sonia and Russell could make their own plans, disappear some place where Ron and Trevor would not think to cast their harsh and edgy eyes. Ron would serve his time with the stoicism of the born-to-be-incarcerated, keeping his head down and running things through whispered phone conversations in hallways ringing with institutional stench. And when he came out the ache of betrayal would be deadened by the attentions of some good-time girl only too happy to swap stripping in pubs for a bit of wedge and the occasional drunken beating.

Russell wondered what would happen to Malcolm Goodge. Once the newshounds got bored with the story he'd be transferred to some open prison, a former air force base where Old Etonians shared bunks with Essex fraudsters; where investment tips are shared among tomato vines and cloched marrows and white-collar daredevils slip away to West End nightclubs and friends in the night.

Goodge would pay dearly for his swim with the sharks in terms of his political career, but Russell knew he would haul himself up from the bottom of the well before his lungs filled with water. From what Russell had read of Goodge his sense of persecution would serve him well as he stared at the bulging pale green walls of his cell: he seemed like the kind of man who would plead his innocence no matter how overwhelming the evidence brought against him, like the kind of man who goes to a boxing match and complains when a fight breaks out.

And what of him, Russell Fisher? Russell knew that going to outsiders was out of the question, unless he wanted never to be able to close his eyes again. They would come for him. Somewhere, somehow, they took care of grasses. Even shtupping the boss's wife was considered a minor misdemeanour in comparison. Sonia Chisholm was what he had longed for over the protracted years and perhaps more than he had expected from life. Despite stumbling across her within the eye of a hurricane Russell felt that Sonia's existence was proof to him that he might feel whole, might step beyond the limited concerns of his current fortune; that there might be a future for him away from the hurly-burly.

Chapter Twenty-Eight

Russell couldn't shake the thought out of his mind – Ron was a wife-beater. Hurt those who loved him most. He knew the breed – self-justifying wankers who always felt the world was against them, that somehow they'd got a raw deal. Sanctimonious cowards, too up their own arses to feel pity for their victims.

Over the next two weeks Russell slept only fitfully. Every time he ebbed towards sleep he had the same vision: Ron's eyes. Cruel, unblinking eyes, burning with the intensity of a welder's torch. The eyes *knew*, they reached into Russell, felt his pain, his weakness, knew his fear. And Russell's fear was that he didn't know where all this was going, couldn't put the story together in his head. But he knew that if he looked closely into Ron's eyes he might witness his own fate.

Russell entered the club quietly, closing the metal door gently, like putting a baby to bed. He turned the keys in the mortice before stepping, hands in pockets, down the stairs like a ballerina, toe first, then heel. He'd driven round the block a couple of times, couldn't see Ron's car (this week the Cheese had sorted him a black Lexus: 'ABS, dual air bags, the dog's'). He'd looked in all the usual places, but drew a blank. Ron couldn't know anything, he was sure of this. But somehow it seemed worth tiptoeing down the stairs anyway. He was still suspicious that Russell claimed not to be able to find Zaffir, that the kid had done a bunk. Russell could do without another interrogation.

He reached the unlit basement and searched the darkness for the eyes. All he could feel were the stares of Jimmy, Marilyn and Bogey, the long dead of Hollywood's monochrome past, frozen in character for all time. He thought he heard a chair scrape, but it was just water moving along a pipe. The place was littered with the ticks, creaks and grumbles of an old building.

A match flared.

Frankie's face glowed orange. The end of his cigarette fizzed for a moment and the flame went out leaving the glowing tip bobbing in the darkness like a firefly.

'Frank?' said Russell. There was nothing for a few seconds, only the sounds of the old building and Frankie's intake of breath. 'What you doing?'

'Barko's brown bread,' said Frankie, his voice flat, kippered by tobacco. 'Ron killed him.'

Russell walked over to the booth and slid in, feeling a slight stickiness beneath him where the cleaners had failed to mop up a Coke spillage from the night before.

'He didn't say nothing afterwards,' said Frankie. 'Just dropped that bayonet of his and walked out, blood all over his strides.' He pulled on his cigarette. 'You want a fag, Russ?'

'Nah.'

'Had that dog seven years,' said Frankie slowly. 'Good dog as well. Good fucking guard dog. 'Course it wouldn't harm a bloody fly, just yapped a lot.'

'And ate money,' added Russell.

'Yeah, stupid git. I reckon that's when Ron took against him, when he ate all that folding. Trevor grassed Barko up. Ron went fucking spare. Said he was going to kill him then.'

The two men fell silent, the darkness guarding their secrets. Russell put his face in his hands, kneading his temples.

'He didn't need to do it like that, though,' said Frankie.

'He said he was going to poison him, that wouldn't have been so bad. But he didn't need to do that. There was no need for it.'

Russell waited to see if there was any more, but Frankie just sat and smoked.

'What happened, Frank?'

He exhaled through his teeth. It was laughter of a kind.

'I didn't see proper,' he said. 'I was in the kitchen, defrosting the freezer. I just heard him come in, heard his shoes coming across the floor here. I shouted out 'Oi, oi,' but he didn't say nothing, just went in the office. So I thought he'd got the nark about something, didn't want to talk. So I carried on with what I was doing, reckoned nothing of it. Dog was asleep round the back, lying in the doorway. Just been fed.

'Then Ron comes past me, real quick like he was chasing after something. And I hear this yelp. Strange sound, more like a yawn than anything else. By the time I looked up, over the counter like, all I could see was Ron's upper half. He was bending his legs and hitting the dog in the head with this thing. I couldn't tell what it was.

'I scooted round the back, but before I could get there he'd pushed past me. I tried to catch his face, but his head was bowed, looking at the claret on his strides.' Frankie paused for a moment. Let out a deep, smoke-saturated breath.

'Barko was twisted in this horrible shape with his legs all over the place and he didn't have no head no longer. I mean there was stuff there, but it didn't look like a head. I could see the snout and his ears. But when I picked him up to see if there was anything I could do the thing just sort of fell apart. There was all this fur matted with blood, and bits of skull and pink fuck-knows-what. It was horrible, Russ, really fucking horrible.

'And I turned and knocked a bottle of milk over and the milk mixed with the blood and it looked like that stuff, *whatdyacallit?* Calamine lotion. And I just watched this stuff moving across the kitchen floor, just watched this pink stuff covering the floor.'

Frankie drummed his hands on the table. Russell could see the orange tip of his cigarette had grown closer to his fingers. 'He didn't say nothing. He just walked out of the place. Nothing.' The back of Frankie's hair brushed against his collar over and over. He was shaking his head. 'It defies belief, Russ. That dog never done nothing to him. I mean he ate the money, but he's only a dog. He don't know no better.'

'The money ain't important, Frank.'

'That's right, Russ, it ain't important. Not compared to a dog's life.'

'I didn't mean it like that, Frank,' said Russell, still working the tension out of his forehead. His back was beginning to ache again. 'I meant that I think Ron would have killed Barko anyway.'

'What? He don't like dogs?' offered Frankie, stubbing out his B&H.

'No, I mean that he had his own reasons for doing it. He just did it because he wanted to. Simple as that.'

'I don't know how he could do it, I really don't,' said Frankie. He sounded suddenly distanced. Like he was watching a film and commenting on something that had happened to someone else.

'Been on me own for a few years now,' said Frankie, his voice suddenly spiritless. 'Wife ran off with this salesman. Flash bastard, travelled a lot. Thought a dog would be a good idea, bit of company. Don't think I could have another one now though. Not after this.'

His eyes had grown used to the dark now and Russell realised that there was a dog-sized bundle wrapped in a yellow travelling rug on the scalloped-backed seat. One end was slick with blood, as dark and shiny as freshly laid tarmacadam. All Russell could think of was where Frankie had got the blanket from.

'What are you doing here anyway?' asked Frankie. 'Ain't you supposed to be with Sonia?'

'Meeting her later on. She's gone to the shops on her Jack Jones – but don't tell Ron.'

'Not likely to, am I?'

'Trevor told me to meet him down here,' said Russell. 'Told me that Ron wants me to take something over to some geezer on Essex Road. Slot machine company or something.'

'Well I ain't seen no trace of Trevor.'

'That ain't the end of the world.'

'You two don't get along, do you?'

'I don't think he gets on with anyone.'

'Yeah, well, watch yourself,' said Frankie. 'He ain't a good enemy to have. I've heard stories.'

'And so have I,' said Russell firmly. 'Most of them from

fucking Trevor. I've seen worse, Frankie. I've seen a lot worse.'

'That's the trouble these days though, innit? Any mug who can pick up a Stanley gets leery, thinks they're a fucking hero. Just remember, Russell, I've been with Ron on and off for twenty years now. I ain't being funny but I've seen others like you. Good at fisticuffs, bright as a button. They all got worn down in the end.'

Russell leaned forward on the table. 'Why don't you leave, Frank? Piss off and do something else. Just fuck off.'

'Simple, son – I ain't really got nowhere to go. This is sort of like family now. Where I belong. I ain't ever seen Ron quite like this before, but I ain't got no choice but to see it through. When you get to my age, son, your options begin to run out a bit, just like old Barko here.'

Russell realised that this was the first time that Frank had made reference to the dog's corpse. The stillness of the room was broken by the trill of Russell's mobile. Through the static he heard Sonia's voice.

'Russ, Russ, can you hear me?'

'Yes, Mrs Chisholm.'

'Don't give me all tha . . .' Her voice trailed off for a moment into telespace. 'Oh, oh, I see. Russell, I need a walk, need to clear my head. Meet me at Regent's Park at eleven, at the entrance to the zoo. And bring some peanuts. For the elephants.' The line went dead.

'Mrs Chisholm,' said Russell unnecessarily.

'I heard,' said Frankie. 'Imagine the shit she has to put up with. Fucking hell, I hope he makes it worth her while.'

Russell folded the mobile away and put it back in his jacket pocket. He felt claustrophobic. Like Ron was coming back. He had to leave.

'You all right with that dog, Frank? Need an 'and burying it?'

'No, it's all right, mate, I'm going to take it over the Marshes, bury him over there, bury it deep so the rats can't get him. I'd prefer to do it on me own.'

'You're the boss,' said Russell, and reached over and patted

Frankie on the back. The man flinched. Perhaps it came as a shock, perhaps he had a sore shoulder. As Russell disappeared up the stairs he heard another match flare in the darkness.

Chapter Twenty-Nine

'Here,' said Russell, giving Sonia a blue vacuum-sealed foil packet of peanuts. Sonia took the bag, laughed and slipped her arm through his.

'Joking, aren't you?'

'What are you talking about?' asked Russell, perplexed.

'These are ready salted. You can't give an elephant ready salted. They don't agree with them.'

Russell looked at her, not quite sure if she was messing with him. 'What are you talking about? Elephants eat all kinds of shit.'

'Oh, listen to David Attenborough here, reporting from central London, teeming with wildlife.'

'Teeming with rain and filthy pigeons, more like,' said Russell. It was a crisp March day, not quite cold enough for them to be able to see their breath, but chilly enough out of the sun to make them want to keep moving.

'I'm going to tell you something now, Sonia,' said Russell. 'Did you know that rats carry seven diseases communicable to man, whereas your average pigeon flying around London can pass on thirty-seven diseases communicable to man?'

'And don't tell me,' said Sonia, 'you're never more than ten yards from a rat in London.'

'Reckon that's an under-estimation,' said Russell. 'Dunno if that includes the human kind as well. I know loads of geezers with whiskers and long pink tails.'

They reached the entrance to the zoo and Sonia stopped and tugged on Russell's arm. 'I don't want to go in there now, Russ. It's too spooky. All those bored animals in cages give me the creeps. Let's just go through the park. Feed the ducks or something.'

'What, with peanuts?' Russell asked.

Children rushed round the pond cheering excitedly as their balsa wood boats lurched through the stagnant green water. Sonia and Russell watched one small boy burst into tears as others pelted his miniature yacht with stones until it keeled over and dipped its white sail in the water and floated there amid curious mallards and drakes.

A park-keeper was eventually alerted to the boy's predicament and rowed out to fish the sad craft from the water. The blubbering boy was reunited with his boat and, to the delight of his peers, rushed back to his au pair who was sitting listening to Oasis on her Walkman, blissfully unaware of the whole incident.

'Kids are cruel bastards, ain't they?' said Russell.

'They're just in training to be adults,' said Sonia. Russell threw a shower of crumbs at a noisy collection of ducks.

'Some are worse than others,' said Russell. 'Sonia, you know, it's been on my mind. What I saw the other day. We can't let it happen again.' He was talking about Ron beating her. He crossed his fingers in his pocket – like a twelve-year-old telling a fib – hoping he wouldn't drive Sonia into herself.

'You must think I'm a proper victim, Russell,' said Sonia, pulling her black wool coat around herself more tightly, sinking her chin into the collar.

'I don't understand,' said Russell. 'You ain't the type. I can't imagine you putting up with it.'

'Neither could I,' said Sonia. 'I never thought I would put up with it.'

'So why do you?' Two geese came over the trees and landed on the pond, their wings outstretched, reddy-orange feet sliding along the surface of the water like water skiers. The other birds clucked disapprovingly, seemingly upset by the disturbance.

'I remember the first time he did it,' said Sonia, putting her arm through Russell's. 'We'd only been married a week and he got upset because I'd used all the hot water and he'd come home wanting a bath. He pushed me into the bathroom and threw me in the bath and ran the cold tap. And he was slapping me in the face and shouting, "This is what it's like having a cold bath, bitch. This is what it's like."

'And then he just left and didn't come back all night. And I didn't know what to do. I felt hurt and humiliated and angry and all that stuff, but I also felt guilty, like I'd done something wrong. Driven him away. And then he came home and brought flowers and chocolates and apologised, said he'd had a bad day at work and was looking forward to having a nice hot bath. And that he'd just got angry and that he was sorry, and could I make sure that there was always plenty of hot water when he came in.'

The wind picked up a little, blowing some dust in their eyes. Sonia blinked a couple of times. 'That's playing havoc with my contacts,' she said, wiping the corner of her right eye. Russell thought that he didn't know she wore lenses. She didn't used to. Wondered how much other stuff there was to discover. 'Anyway, I thought to myself "Well, he regrets what he's done and there's a reason, so I can understand why he did what he did".'

'You forgave him?'

'I suppose I did. I mean it wasn't like I hadn't seen it at home when I was a kid.' Russell thought back to his own childhood, his father taking off his rubber-soled slipper to give his mother a whipping for forgetting to iron his work shirt.

'And over the years I suppose I almost forgot about it, took it for granted,' said Sonia. 'I'd know when I was in for it from the way he walked in the door, from the way his face was set. I almost came to expect it, so I didn't think of it as that unusual. And he'd always apologise afterwards and tell me what drove him to it and that he hadn't wanted to do it. So I just took it as normal, thought that this was the way things were.'

A grey bank of cloud swept across the sky, moving so quickly it seemed to be hurrying away from something. Momentarily its shadow fell across Russell and Sonia.

'Come on, Russ,' said Sonia, 'let's move around a little, get the blood flowing.' Russell sat for a couple of moments too long – like a child being contrary – before he laboriously raised himself from the bench.

'You're getting old before your time,' said Sonia, wrapping her arm around him. 'You want to start taking care of yourself.' They continued round the pond, dodging the large green gobs of goose shit deposited, seemingly purposefully, on the path.

'Sonia,' said Russell. 'What are we going to do? All this, at the moment, it ain't good for anyone.'

Sonia produced a tube of lip salve from her pocket, applied it and pursed her lips.

'What's brought this on?' she asked.

'Don't be like that,' said Russell. 'Come on . . . It's obvious. I'm running into a lot of trouble . . . *we're* running into trouble. Things could all go wrong. Big time. I don't know what's going to happen if I get more involved with you.'

'You already are, Russell,' said Sonia, putting the lip salve back in her coat pocket. They walked in silence for a while. 'So what are you going to do then? she asked.

'I dunno,' said Russell. 'I don't really have a lot of options, do I? Maybe go away. Get out.'

'So that's it, is it?' asked Sonia. 'You get yourself in a spot, you just piss off. Screw those left behind. More fool them.'

'It ain't like that . . .'

'That's *exactly* what it's like, Russell, that's exactly what it's like.' Sonia stopped for a moment. 'And how do you think that sounds to me: "Oh, sorry, Sonia. Thanks for the shag, but no hard feelings, eh?" Exit stage left.'

'You know it ain't like that,' protested Russell. 'What else am I supposed to do? I can't expect nothing from you. I can't expect you to just up and change your life. Move in with me in a ratty bedsit. But I know we can be good together. I've known it from the start – way back, the first time. Believe me. But I know you've got a life that it ain't easy to give up. What am I supposed to think?'

'Depends what you want, Russell, depends what you want,' said Sonia. There was a harder edge to her voice. They stopped walking. Facing him she put her hand on his and left it there.

'What would you say if I told you I was sick of all this as well, wanted out, just as much as you, *more* than you because you've not had to put up with the shit I've suffered for as long as I have – and don't tell me you have.'

'I dunno . . .'

''Cos I do, Russell. I'm sick of my life here. I'm sick of my marriage, I want to change things . . .'

'You can't just . . .'

'I've been thinking about it for a while now . . .'

'Just walk out . . .'

'And what's happened between us has really made me think about what I want, made me realise that there's too much in my life that I've just tried to ignore . . .'

'It's a huge step, just to up sticks . . .'

'Put up with.' Sonia stopped for a moment and bit her lip. She smiled, but her eyes shone with tears. 'I can't hide any longer, Russell. I'm just so . . . tired, so fucking tired. I've got to go. Got to get away, just got to go from here.'

Russell watched as a small tear escaped from the corner of her eye and traced a trail through her blusher. He leaned forward and kissed her. They parted.

'Come on,' he said.

Chapter Thirty

'What's the matter with you then?' Skin asked Russell. 'You've been sitting there with a face like a slapped arse for the last quarter hour.' The two men sat on Skin's settee, illuminated only by the blue light of the television.

'I'm all right,' said Russell defensively.

'No, you ain't,' said Skin. 'You're even quieter than normal. Look like you're gonna get executed tomorrow morning.'

'That ain't so far from the truth,' said Russell into his mug of steaming Red Label. He shifted on the lumpy sofa, trying to get comfortable. They sat in silence for a few minutes watching the evening news. Skin scratched at some dried food stuck to the front of his lumpen grey cardigan.

'You ain't been down here much recently,' he said.

'Been busy,' answered Russell, not meeting Skin's gaze. There was another silence before Skin coughed loudly, like something was lodged in his throat.

'So Ron's got you running round then?' he asked.

'S'pose,' said Russell.

'Thought you said you were with his wife most of the time.'

'Most of the time,' said Russell. 'Some evenings I'm in Merlin's keeping an eye on things.'

Russell reached over for the paper to check the TV listings. Wanted to see which games were on *Sportsnight* later.

'Tell you, that must be so fucking weird,' said Skin dreamily, watching a car plunge down a ravine and burst into flames.

'What?' asked Russell without looking up from the paper.

'You going out with Ron's wife,' said Skin. 'You being there first and Ron don't know.'

Russell sat up and closed the paper. He looked directly at Skin for the first time in twenty minutes. 'Who told you that?'

he asked. He sounded concerned.

'You did, you mug,' said Skin firmly. He sounded annoyed, like he'd just been accused of something he hadn't done.

'I never.'

'You did, Russell, you fucking did. You just can't remember.'

'What you talking about?'

'You can't remember, can you?'

'Do behave.'

'One evening you came down here all excited,' said Skin patiently. 'You'd just met Ron's bird and you were banging on about the fact that she used to be your bird but that you ain't seen her for years and that she'd changed her name.'

'Fucking hell. This ain't happening,' said Russell. He pursed his lips, annoyed at himself.

'There you go,' said Skin, satisfied. 'You remember now, don't you?'

Skin was beginning to get on Russell's nerves.

'Look, there are things that need to be kept quiet, all right?' said Russell. 'Some things ain't for public consumption.'

'All right, son, all right,' laughed Skin, enjoying Russell's discomfort.

'I ain't being funny, Skin, but you're bang out of order.'

'Calm down, calm down,' said Skin. 'No need to get in a fucking lather.'

'I mean it Skin,' impressed Russell. 'This ain't a fucking laughing matter.'

'Little bit tetchy, ain't you?'

'Leave it, Skin.' Russell tried to ignore him, turned back to the television.

'What you doing then, slipping her a length?'

Russell turned to face Skin. His eyes were wide and his mouth twisted with anger.

'I said shut the fuck up, Skin,' he said. 'I fucking mean it. You are well out of fucking order.'

'Come on, Russ. Only a joke.' Skin was laughing to himself but he knew the joke was over, that he'd pushed Russell too far. 'Only a joke, Russ.'

'Just belt up, Skin. Leave it.'

The news ended and a trailer for a programme about children growing up in Beverly Hills blotted out the silence between them.

'Look, Russ,' said Skin. 'I'm sorry, all right? Maybe I was out of order. I don't know, but let's forget it, eh?'

Russell just sat there, his legs splayed, and his fingers tapping on the sofa. He was staring at the television but Skin could tell that his mind was elsewhere.

Chapter Thirty-One

Zaffir had been waiting beside the bus shelter for twenty minutes now. A pretty constant stream of Asian youth – sometimes even girls – came by this spot, most drifting idly up and down the pavement on their hooky mountain bikes with the fat offroad tyres that looked like squares of chocolate. Above him towered the town hall, a spartan sixties creation of sand-coloured concrete and black-tinted glass, ugly and inhuman enough to be a monument to Soviet space exploration.

Kids would come by at about this time to hang out, high five and catch the vibe, sporting their backward-facing baseball caps, sunglasses, Hilfiger threads and mobiles. Sometimes you saw a few white kids down here, sometimes black kids, but mostly it was an Asian thing, a place to escape the confines of the home, the sound of a nagging parent.

Zaffir kept checking his Swatch. Ranu should have been there twenty minutes ago. He had watched the coming and going around him, there were perhaps thirty or forty people hanging around the pedestrian zone now. Some of them would wait until it got really dark or too cold before returning home, some would head off to do homework before long, others to get into fights, do some thieving, maybe a little joy-riding. The rougher elements usually made a point of hanging round the KFC opposite doing their pimp shuffles, slapping skin loudly, sporting gold, eyeing each other's sportswear, ostentatiously checking their pagers. Wannabe gangstas.

He'd saved some of his stash to have a smoke before the two of them went into the cinema. It was there in his pocket, ready rolled, tidied and roached, premium Thai grass, none of that resin shit. Zaffir felt his head. It was a habit he'd adopted since hospital. The nurses had shaved it all off and now he couldn't stop stroking the sharp bristles that camouflaged his scars.

Fuck Ranu. Zaffir fired up the spliff, breathing in the hot, sweet smoke, holding it in his lungs as long as possible, releasing it in little short bursts. He pulled out his Sony headphones, cranked up the bass and closed his eyes to enjoy the buzz.

Zaffir was deep in the Todd Terry groove when he felt a sharp shove to his left shoulder.

Fucking Ranu. Zaffir kept his eyes closed to wind him up. Gave him the shoulder.

'Fuck off, dickhead.'

Next thing he knew his headphones had been torn off and he had been jerked to his feet. Before him stood two of London's finest, the boys in blue, square-shouldered in nylon waterproofs.

'Now that's not very nice, is it?' said one. The other was muttering into his shoulder-mounted radio. The one who spoke had short blond hair and a weasely little face. His cheeks bore the livid vestiges of a serious skin complaint. The other was tall and swarthy with a dull, stooped look to him. His trousers stopped an inch short of his shoes.

'Oh fuck,' said Zaffir to himself, his shoulders sagging inside his Stone Island jacket. The music continued to play through his headphones.

'We do have a filthy fucking mouth, don't we, sir?'

Zaffir shrugged, irritated by the gleeful attitude of the policemen, who were quite clearly excited at the prospect of making such an easy collar, another notch in their truncheons.

'Would you like to put the cigarette out carefully, sir, and pass it to me,' said the blond one. His colleague was still on the radio. Zaffir dripped saliva on his thumb and index finger before extinguishing the glowing tip of the Camberwell carrot. He handed it over to the cop who had already produced a clear evidence bag.

'Now, sir, I was wondering if you could tell my colleague and myself quite what you think you're up to?' The tall one was off the radio now and had his hands on his hips, making him look like an ungainly giant.

'I'm waiting for a mate,' said Zaffir. 'We're going to the pictures. We were going to get something to eat at the Kentucky first.'

'And while you were waiting you thought it might be a good idea to sit down and publicly indulge in smoking a class B drug? Because that was what you were doing, sir, wasn't it?'

Zaffir thought how good this policeman was at making the word 'Sir' sound like 'Paki'.

'I found it on the floor. I didn't know what it was.'

'Hang on a second, son,' said the cop. 'You're telling me that you found a joint lying there on the floor, so you picked it up and decided to smoke it. Oh look, up there, I see pink fucking piggies flying over the town hall.'

'I didn't know what it was,' said Zaffir, thinking how dismal the blonde one's attempt at sarcasm was. 'I found it lying on the bench . . .' The mood of the blonde one seemed to sour. Zaffir couldn't place his accent, he sounded like Paul Gascoigne, Newcastle or something.

'Look, don't fuck us about, son. We walked round the corner here and it smelled like there was half a dozen fucking Comanches smoking the pipes of peace. Now if you'd been a little more alert you might have realised that Plod had crept up behind you. But as it happens you were so spaced out and so engrossed in that fucking bollocks . . . Can you turn that shit off?' – Zaffir stabbed at the 'off' button on his Walkman – 'that you failed to notice us, the result being that you are nicked.'

'You're fucking joking, aren't you?' said Zaffir. 'You ain't nicking me.' The tall one turned ninety degrees to look behind him. Beyond him Zaffir could see a crowd was beginning to gather. Any street disturbance round here and the old bill knew they were working against the clock. They didn't like an audience. The tall one nudged the blond one who nodded that he understood. The crowd – mostly Asian youths, with a smattering of older, bearded men wearing small white pill-box hats – was edging in to take a closer look.

Zaffir spoke louder than before. 'You can't nick me, I haven't done nothing wrong.' There was murmuring in the crowd.

'Where the fuck are they?' the blond one said to the tall one. 'It's getting like a fucking tribal gathering here.'

Zaffir turned up the volume even further. 'I've not done nothing wrong. I was just waiting for my brother. We're going up the hospital to see my aunt.' The crowd pressed in tighter like storm clouds invading the sky.

'Fucking pigs,' shouted one youth, tracing circles on his mountain bike. His words gave another courage. He approached the two policemen who had edged closer to Zaffir, perhaps fearful that he might make a run for it.

'What are you doing?' he asked the policemen. He was young, intense, looked like he might be religious, the kind of kid that Zaffir found intimidating at school. The blond one now turned to face the crowd.

'There's nothing to see. Please move along. You're obstructing the pavement.' Not a soul moved. Zaffir could hear lots of discussion and cursing, most of it in Urdu. 'Please move along,' shouted the policeman. 'Under the Criminal Justice Act of 1994 this kind of crowd now constitutes an illegal gathering.'

'Bollocks', 'Fuck off', 'Kill the bill', came back. Zaffir looked at the tall one who now had his hand on his shoulder. He was sure that he could feel him trembling. The copper's face brightened slightly when he heard the oncoming siren. Zaffir couldn't believe it. He was going to be blued in, and all this fuss ensured that he was going to get a good kicking as soon as he was out of the public gaze.

The white van fish-tailed round the corner, its offside rear tyre bouncing off a pedestrian island. The driver was honking his horn madly and flashing his lights as he mounted the red herring-boned brickwork of the pedestrian zone. Suddenly it stopped. No matter how much the driver revved the engine and honked his horn the crowd was not shifting. Maybe ten youths had initially refused to move, but more were standing behind them. There were perhaps nearly a hundred people hanging around the vicinity, with more coming out of the shops and restaurants. The police van edged forward slowly, nudging bystanders out of the way.

Zaffir felt his arm being grabbed as the tall one started to frogmarch him briskly to the van. He heard a loud smashing noise and the tinkling of glass as it skidded along the pavement. Someone had thrown a bottle at the tall one. The two policemen were trying to push their way through the crowd to the van when the side door opened up and three cops, one of them with a huge bouncing Alsatian, jumped out. Zaffir watched as one of them flinched and grabbed the side of his face. Someone had thrown an object at him. The dog handler moved forward a little, trying to clear a corridor for his colleagues to get into the van.

Zaffir was suddenly pulled in another direction. The tall cop tugged harder, hurting his shoulder, but the force pulling the other way remained firm. The tall cop turned to look at him and tried to strike the two men who were now hanging on to Zaffir. After letting go a couple of blows he looked round to see that his colleague had reached the sanctuary of the van which was now coming under a hail of bottles and stones. It occurred to Zaffir that Asians were good at throwing stones. Pakistan weren't the dog's bollocks at cricket for nothing. One of the windows on the driver's side had a huge spider's web crack in it. The cop landed a punch flush on Zaffir's chin.

As he lay on the floor with the metallic taste of blood fresh in his mouth Zaffir heard the squeal of tyres and a roar of triumph punctuated by the hollow pitter-patter of objects bouncing off the van. A couple of people asked him if he was all right. Their mood was concerned but celebratory, buoyed by the electricity of victory passing through the crowd. Zaffir had pretty much been forgotten now. He realised this wasn't about him. From over the road came the noise of plate glass being smashed. The crowd turned to see that the window of the Kentucky had been put through. Several young men were dancing on the pavement outside, whooping and laughing. It seemed that there was shouting coming from every side.

And he'd thought the only trouble he'd have tonight was getting to the cinema on time.

Chapter Thirty-Two

There would be no note.

This was what Sonia had said. She had made up her mind. She was going. She and Russell had spent the following week fine-tuning the arrangements, privately acquainting them-selves with the deception. She'd wondered how she would feel when it was too late to change course, but when Ron had bellowed his farewell up the stairs that morning, before heading off to the races again, Sonia did not think it wrong that, as he slid down the M4 in a Lexus with the smell of leather upholstery in his nose, she would pack just a single Gucci suitcase and disappear from his life. Sonia told Russell that she had an idea that she might even leave some dinner for him in the microwave. Soften the blow a little.

Chances are he might not even come back tonight anyway. Might get a couple of girls and a suite at the Intercontinental. Once the Jacuzzi was switched on and the champagne had been ordered it would seem a pity to rush home.

This is what it came down to: Russell had asked her to book another seat on BA 59 flying south towards the sun over a vast continent he only knew from *Tarzan*, *Daktari* and pictures of emaciated children, their eyes infested with bluebottles. It all seemed too far away to imagine that you could get there by popping into a travel agent's on Barnet High Street and handing over a fistful of shekels.

South Africa. He knew about apartheid and Mandela and the birth of a new nation. Even knew a geezer, Clifton Swain, a rasta, who'd gone down there to import hair products for the new, consumer-driven liberated black majority. 'What white people don't understand,' said Clifton, 'is that black people spend far more of their income than whites.' He'd banged on about that for a while, like a broken record. And then he'd disappeared. Got some kind of import deal with a company called Hair Max in Brooklyn. Russell loved the idea of that: a Jamaican from Wood Green flogging a New York hair pomade called African Roots to black Africans. Coals to Newcastle. Maybe he'd try and look up Clifton.

He didn't even own a suitcase. He'd just stuffed as much as he could in his gym bag, hoped Sonia didn't mind him running out of pants in a few days. He thought she wouldn't, but he didn't know. After all, she was a very different woman to the one he'd known in the past. This time round they had been together for little more than eight weeks, had slept together no more than half a dozen times, knew little about each other's lives except for what could be gleaned over a few meals and many cups of tea.

It was enough, though, thought Russell. It was enough for him. The promise of a new beginning, the chance of a new life, the charge of such a relationship. And, although it seemed rushed and they were ill-prepared, he realised that if he thought back over the previous years he had trusted that it might happen like this. His hope had grown furtively at first, but now it basked in the sunlight, content and fulfilled as a recently fed dog. Maybe this was the first time he had ever felt he could clearly see his own future, maybe even a sense of destiny, down there in a vast continent which he knew only from the box. A mist had lifted from his vision and, like never before, he felt he was changing his life utterly and completely for the better.

It was five o'clock. The sun was setting in an ice blue sky. Large lumps of cloud had turned marshmallow pink, flushed by the sun's dying rays. He would wake up in the sky tomorrow. It was his last evening in London, but he didn't really fancy going down the Black Prince to say farewell to Steve and Curtis and Mick. No time, anyway.

Could just about squeeze it to get his stuff together. Might feel a bit odd going down there. He couldn't say nothing anyway. Ron had big ears. Russell knew that if he fell from grace he would fall at the speed of light. Flight left at quarter past nine. That only gave him just over four hours. He thought about his parents, how his mother would retreat further to the bathroom cabinet and his father see it as ultimate proof of his son's selfish unreliability.

Fuck it. It was too much agg. He'd send them a postcard when he got there, let them know he was all right. Later on he could even send them an address, but they'd never come and visit him, would think it too far away, too foreign, too expensive.

What he really fancied was getting a take-away Chinky – sweet and sour pork, beef in oyster sauce, spring roll, egg fried rice – and putting his feet up for an hour; maybe getting a bottle of Scotch to numb his mind a little, stop it from running so fast.

Matters had all fallen into place rather easily. Sonia had explained it to him: she had a step-sister who had moved out to South Africa in her late teens. Fifteen years and two divorces down the road she had amassed a nice little pile and had a couple of properties that supplemented her income as an estate agent. She was willing to let them stay in one of these places gratis for a couple of months and could maybe even help Russell get a job at a local gym that a friend of hers owned.

He had volunteered the five grand he'd stashed away since he started working for Ron, but Sonia had told him not to worry about money. It would be taken care of: she would be leaving Moore House wearing over a hundred grand's worth of ice and would have nearly seventy-three grand in cash stashed inside tampon boxes in her hand luggage, the result of some fancy footwork with her allowance, housekeeping and insider knowledge of the place in the garage where Ron ferreted his float.

Sonia claimed that Ron's anger would soon dissipate in a stream of champagne, coke and teenage girls and that within a month a slimmer, blonder version of her would be trawling through her closet in search of a D&G outfit to wear on a Saturday night out. Russell was doubtful Ron would leave it at that, but felt better when Sonia swore blind that she was certain that Ron had no knowledge of her South African connection. As both her parents were dead and she had no close relatives she was leaving a cold trail. And anyway, they were talking South Africa, not southern Spain where Ron might know people who owed him a favour.

It sounded good to Russell. Having a job and a home and a life. Living like normal people lived, going out to the pictures, going out to eat, having barbecues and friends. It sounded good and it sounded foreign and if he closed his eyes he could almost feel the sun on his back. Somehow he'd always known it would happen this way.

He thought it right to visit Skin before he left. Poor old sod. Once Russell was gone he'd have few visitors. Russell made a bet with himself that the old man's door would be unlocked and, sure enough, it was. He pushed it open.

'Oi, oi,' he shouted.

There was no answer. Russell waited for a moment and shouted again.

'Oi, Skin, those showers are on the bleedin' blink again.'

Some kids' cartoon played itself out on the TV in the corner. A couple of blue rabbits were being chased by something that looked like an animator's idea of an alien. He must be having a kip, thought Russell. Or having a dump. The immobility of Skin's bowels was notorious, mainly because it was a topic Skin liked to elaborate on at length.

Russell moved through the living room. The ashtray was brimming, there were some empty Hofmeister cans by the armchair and three plates smothered with dried food so thick that it could be excavated. The brown carpet with beige swirls was an inspired piece of design, managing to camouflage the detritus that had been ground into it by reeky footsteps.

Russell pushed open the door to the bathroom and turned the light on. The smell of damp tumbled over him. The far wall was almost entirely covered by a swathe of emerald fungus and, for some reason, the floor had been covered with old copies of the *Sun*. It was unlike any other bathroom that Russell had seen in that there was no soap, no towel and no mirror. The white ceramic sink was slicked with a black residue, as if someone had smeared oil from their hands on to the basin.

He must be asleep, thought Russell. Turning off the light he closed the door and turned towards the bedroom. He froze for a moment as he heard a low moan from within, the kind of absent-minded noise emitted during slumber. So that was where he was, sneaking a crafty kip before the regulars started banging on his door wanting the key to the gym for their post-work sessions. Russell thought he'd leave Skin to his own devices, but couldn't resist a little peek through the crack between the door and the frame.

What he saw turned his stomach.

As he pushed open the door and strode over the discarded newspapers and empty cigarette packets Russell wondered whether Skin could still be alive. The right side of his head, his shoulder and arm were thick with blood, his cardigan was glued to his skin. Russell pushed the old man gently to see if there were any signs of life. Skin's sides spilled over the edges of the single bed. There were no sheets on the mattress and a tangled blanket rested in a heap on the floor.

Examining the wound Russell saw that Skin's right ear had been almost entirely severed; all that connected it to the flesh of his skull was a ragged piece of cartilage that had proved too tough for a blade. The pillow had absorbed much of the blood, leaving it wet to the touch. It was clear that Skin had also been beaten severely around his face, head and shoulders. Even if the old man had tried to open his eyes he would barely have been able to see as his bruised forehead had moved down to meet his cheek, masking his eyes.

Russell tried calling his name, softly at first, but then more urgently. He saw the man's mouth move in recognition.

'Who's that?' Skin's voice was weak and asthmatic.

'It's Russell, Skin. Russell.' The old man said nothing. 'How many fucking times have I told you not to leave that front door open?' said Russell. 'How many? I mean look at you, you're a fucking mess, we'd . . .'

'Trevor . . .' said Skin faintly. Russell waited for the old man to continue, his voice still thin.

'It was Trevor,' whispered Skin. Russell's heart sank.

'What happened, Skin? Tell me what happened.'

'Russell came, wanted money.' Skin ran out of breath and paused.

'You mean Trevor came?'

'Yeah, Trevor came. I was asleep. He wanted money.' He halted. 'Didn't have none.'

'I'm going to call an ambulance, you hang on.'

'Wait, Russell,' said Skin. His voice was suddenly more urgent, had lost its weak breathlessness.

'You hang in there. I'm going to call for help, all right?' Russell pulled out his mobile.

'Bad news, Russell.'

''Course it's bad news. Wait one minute while I call the ambulance.' Skin reached over and grabbed Russell's hand.

'Russell, he knows.'

'What do you mean?'

'He knows. About you and Sonia.'

'You what?'

'I had to, Russell, he was going to kill me.' Russell looked skyward, trying to focus. This was too much information. 'Couldn't stand the pain, Russell, had to give him something.'

'When, Skin? When was Trevor here?'

'Dunno, Russ . . .'

'When, Skin? It's fucking important.'

''Bout an hour ago. Maybe three-quarters.'

A tear fell out of Skin's swollen right eye, rolled down his lined face and was absorbed into the blood on the pillow

'All right, Skin, all right,' said Russell, trying to calm himself as well as the old man. 'I'll call you an ambulance in a minute.' He punched the keys on the mobile. 'First I've got to make another call.'

Chapter Thirty-Three

He tried to think clearly, tried to haul in his frayed, racing senses. Everything had gone out of focus, adrenaline thundering, pursuing composure from his frame. His memory blurred as his mind accelerated, feeling like it might race away, chasing nothing. He knew that he had to get hold of Sonia. He focused on his mobile and flicked through to her number. His fingers felt heavy, as if the task was too momentous for them.

'Hello.'

'Sonia, where are you?' He realised that he sounded out of breath.

'Just pulling in the driveway. I needed to pick up my passport. Get the money and that.'

'Listen. Don't go in. We're in big fucking trouble. Ron's found out. He knows. He knows about us.'

'You're not serious . . .'

'Trevor. Trevor got it out of Skin.'

'What? That bloke down the gym? You told . . . Russell, for . . .'

'Look, we can't get into that now,' said Russell. 'I fucked up, OK?'

'Oh, fucking hell . . .' said Sonia. 'What should I do? I mean I'm here now, in the driveway. Shit.'

'Just go,' said Russell. 'Don't go in the house. Ron is bound to come back. He found out nearly an hour ago. He'll be looking for you.'

'I've got to,' said Sonia. 'All the money, all the jewellery, I've got to get the tickets, they're indoors.'

'Sonia. Do *not* go in the house. Do you hear me?'

'I can get my case out of the loft quickly and be gone . . .'

'Sonia, believe me. Don't even think about it. If Ron comes back . . .'

'I can be quick . . . Fuck it, Russell, you know I haven't really got a choice,' said Sonia. She sounded scared. Putting a brave face on. 'I'll meet you at the check-in desk, all right? Be there, OK? Just be there.'

'Sonia, listen to me. Are you listening? This ain't a joke . . .'

'I'm not laughing, Russell. If you're not there I'll leave the ticket at the desk. You know the flight number, right?'

'Sonia, don't go in there.'

'I don't have a choice, Russell. We need the money. Just get on that plane,' she said. 'I love you.'

And then the line went dead.

Sonia shook her head trying to clear her thoughts. Suitcase. Cash. Jewellery. Get the fuck out. She left her handbag containing the tickets and credit cards by the front door so she wouldn't forget it.

She took the stairs two at a time, something she'd never done before, feeling her quads working against her Joseph moleskin trousers. Maybe all that time on the Stairmaster was going to pay off. She could be quick. She knew she could. Everything hinged upon it. She had no choice.

The case was in the loft. She retrieved a long cane that was kept behind one of the bedroom doors and prodded the loft door. The latch clicked off and the heavy door swung down violently, forcing the cane away. An aluminium ladder dropped down and Sonia rattled up its light metal steps. Once inside the woody smelling loft she picked up the torch Ron left by the door and waved the beam through the darkness searching for the suitcase, which she hadn't used since their trip to Portugal over four months ago. She'd left it up there on top of an old trunk.

She switched off the torch and stood silent for a moment, straining her ears. She was sure she'd heard something. Every inch of her body combed the stillness of the house.

There it was again. The noise. Unmistakable: a car on gravel. Ron was back. Sonia dropped the suitcase and pressed her hands to her head, as if trying to squeeze a solution out of her skull – she didn't know whether to climb down and try to make a getaway or hide where she was. If he caught her in the house she wouldn't stand a chance. Her heart raced, her mouth was dry. She could see the avalanche approaching but didn't know which way to run. There was still silence in the house. She heard footsteps on the drive outside. Ron's shoes grinding the stones.

She grabbed the ladder and hauled it inside the loft, dragging the door up with it until she heard it fasten. Then she waited, alone in the gloom. There was a gap between the door and the frame through which she could see the hallway. She kneeled down and peered through, trying to control her breathing, stop the frantic rush of blood around her system.

The keys rustled inside the lock and the front door opened. She heard feet wipe on the mat and the door close; the sounds of normality, each tiny noise louder than she could have ever imagined it. Ron lingered by the front door for half a minute before walking through to the kitchen. He had not announced his entrance as he normally did when he stepped over the threshold.

She couldn't remember the last time she had squatted. But that was what she was doing now. Breathing fibreglass and dust in a cramped, dark space. She knew that he would beat her senseless if he caught her. She tried to focus on the airport. Tried to think of Heathrow, Terminal Four.

Ron was stalking around the living room. He didn't zap the telly to life. Unusual for him; he had other things on his mind. He was drawing curtains, opening cupboards, searching corners, closing in on her. He mounted the stairs, his footsteps heavy all the way up. Like someone banging out seconds on a drum. He pushed the door of the bedroom back so it touched the wall, the hinge whining where it needed oil.

She heard the bedroom closet open, the scrape of hangers on the rail as Ron rummaged among her clothes, the clobber soaked by her perfumes and lotions. He passed into the bathroom, swinging open the shower curtain, opening the airing cupboard. No joy. He passed beneath her to check the spare bedrooms. Above the thump of her heart she could hear him breathing heavily through his nose.

The bedroom investigated, he reappeared on the landing. Then he doubled back on himself as if remembering something. There was such a din in her head that she was sure he could hear it. Her eye was watering from not blinking, but she saw the stick. Ron was holding it in front of himself, like a blind man carries a cane. He positioned himself beneath the trap door and looked upwards. He looked her directly in the eye.

She snapped the trap door open. Before Ron had a chance to raise a hand to protect himself it struck him on the forehead, knocking him over. She heard an initial thud followed by a heavy collapse. Sticking her head from the loft she saw his crumpled body lying skewed on the landing. She sat there for a moment, unsure of what to do.

Flee. She had no other option. She grabbed the case and climbed down the ladder, the loft's dusty fragments dropping on to the carpet beneath her. Stepping over Ron to get to the bedroom she noticed something sticking out of his breast pocket. She reached down and removed the envelope containing the two tickets to Cape Town. It was unopened. He'd been through her bag but he didn't know where she was heading.

Sonia grabbed the tickets and went to her closet, pulled up a corner of carpet and grabbed her jewellery from its underfloor hiding place. She shoved the jewellery box in the case, snatched some clothes and ran downstairs and into the kitchen. Bending down she reached behind the washing machine – a place Ron was never likely to explore – and pulled out a ragged manilla envelope which, over the years, she had filled with cash. Her nest-egg stored up for a rainy day. Everyone needs a little insurance.

She went to the front door. Looked in her bag. Her purse was gone. Ron. She needed the credit cards. She had to go back. She raced up the stairs. He was still sprawled across the landing like some basking bull seal, a large red welt forming across his forehead. Cautiously, as if approaching a creature that spat poison, she opened up his jacket with a dipper's velvet touch and pulled her purse out.

'Bye, Ron,' she said and headed back downstairs. She went through a mental inventory: tickets, passport, purse, money, jewellery. All present and correct. Reaching for the front door she quickly cast a last eye over the inside of her home. It was all over. She was gone.

But there was another noise. She looked towards the stairs. Her husband was still unconscious on the landing. It was gravel. More fucking tyres. She looked out of the window and there, scowling out of his Golf, was Trevor. Sonia rushed into the kitchen and stuck a three-inch vegetable knife in her jacket pocket. It was no good. She couldn't stab him in the street. She couldn't stab him. Think. Think . . . Ron's mobile. It would have Trevor's number on it. Keep him outside.

She leaped up the stairs and reached into Ron's jacket pocket. She went through the list of numbers. The doorbell rang.

'Come on, come on . . .' she said to herself.

She hit the number and heard Trevor's phone chirrup outside.

'Yeah.'

'Trevor, itsh Sonia.' She slurred her words as if her mouth was swollen. She tried to sound weak, broken, humiliated. 'We can't answer the door. Come round the back, all right? Itsh open.'

'Yeah, erm, all right,' said Trevor, wanting to do things right.

Sonia suddenly felt a hand grab her ankle. She gasped and looked down to see that it was Ron, his fat fingers clasped around her right leg. She kicked him in the stomach. He grunted as if asleep but his grip remained firm. Trevor was going round the back. He'd find out that the door was locked. She slammed Ron's phone against his forehead. His grip loosened. She did it a second time and his eyes closed and his hands slipped from her leg.

She didn't look back. She flew down the stairs and out of the front door, suitcase bumping her body behind her. Hitting the cold air she realised that her clothes were drenched with sweat. There were three cars in the driveway. She had to stop them coming after her – bag a bit of breathing space. The knife. She pulled it from her jacket and drove it into two of Ron's tyres, hearing the satisfying gasp of fish-smelling air. She was just about to start on the second on Trevor's car when she heard a voice behind her.

'That's enough.' She stood up to face Trevor. She smiled weakly. '*Areyoushaw?*' hissed Trevor. 'You stupid bitch.'

She put the suitcase down and hung her head, offering the knife to Trevor. As he reached to take it from her she plunged the blade through his palm, feeling the tendons momentarily impede the blade before they were severed. Collapsing on to his knees he screamed in short bursts, pulling at the knife, dragging it back through his own flesh.

'Need a hand, Trev?' she asked, but didn't wait for an answer. She flung her bag on the passenger seat and peppered Trevor with gravel as her tyres screeched from the driveway of Moore House. As she floored the accelerator she could still feel Ron's fingers slipping from her leg.

Chapter Thirty-Four

The words kept ringing in his ears. The last words she'd said to him, coming through the effervescent maze of the Orange network: I love you. It was not the first time he had been told as much, but it was the first time he had believed it, the first time he'd wanted to believe it.

Russell tried to think clearly, be practical. It was later than he'd thought. He'd got lucky, a friend of a friend had once asked him for first refusal if he ever decided to sell his motor. He'd called him up to see if the offer still stood. It did, and after a spot of tut-tutting and shaking of the head and some cursory haggling the geezer – who was the kind who could lay his hands on a mountain of cash at short notice – passed him five freshly counted grand bundles and called Russell a mini-cab. It went through Russell's mind that the money might be moody, but he had no time to get into a cross-examination.

He'd tried Sonia's number a couple of times in the hour and a half since they parted, but the line was down. He'd have to assume that she was all right. He figured that he was still marginally ahead of the game. Ron and Trevor would be looking for him now, but he should still have enough time to get home and pick up his stuff. He'd get a black cab to Heathrow.

The mini-cab came quickly and Russell stomped out into the night, his breath freezing in the cold air, the bundles of notes pressed tightly to his chest. He got in the A reg Volvo and locked the door behind him.

'Falkland Road, mate.' The driver, a balding black geezer with scars down his cheeks, dressed in an old red Puffa jacket, barely nodded. His two-way radio was turned down low, as if he was more interested in listening to what was happening in his car. Although he could barely hear it, Russell could tell that there was heavy frequency on the radio.

'I cannot take you all the way,' said the driver, his voice sing-song West African.

'Why not?' asked Russell.

'It is not just me. No one can take you.'

'What are you talking about?'

'There is a riot. They are demolishing Illingford,' said the man taking both hands off the steering wheel in a gesture of exclamation. 'The roads are closed. You can't get in or out. They are burning it.'

'Just get me as close as you can,' said Russell.

They crawled on to Shadwell Road; the traffic had virtually slowed to a standstill. Every so often they budged over to let an ambulance or fire engine hurtle past. When a police van came by it had a metal grate pulled over the windshield, making it look like a huge, mobile American football helmet.

Russell looked at the coppers inside the van. The driver focused on the road in front, the one riding shotgun talking impassively into a radio microphone perched on his lapel. In the back a dozen or so helmetted, visored and fully armoured officers sat in silence, aware that they were being watched, frightened but secretly savouring the chance of being let off the leash.

The traffic inched along, car exhausts thickening the night air with acrid smoke. Engines began to overheat, despite the cold. Passengers peered out of windows in the hope of getting a glimpse of something juicy. Groups of drinkers stood outside pubs. The circus had come to town and they were enjoying the show. Once in a while an opportunist would crash a beer glass on top of a speeding police van, its lights momentarily turning the drinkers' cheering faces blue.

'Just drop me here, mate,' said Russell. 'I'll take me chances.' He passed over a fiver and wished the driver luck. The noise of engines, sirens and shouting was occasionally punctured by the throbbing of a helicopter which hovered somewhere over his house, a mile away, beaming a searchlight down into the streets, a torrential cascade of light.

Russell continued up the road, where the traffic sat stationary, drivers fiddling with radios and tapping their steering wheels nervously. Some suit stuck in the back of a black cab yanked down the window and peered along the road, fretting over the ever-ticking meter. Hurrying under a railway bridge he clocked a horde of uniforms. Some were traffic cops, bald-tyre bandits funnelling traffic into a diversion round Illingford. Further back, manning a metal barrier erected across Station Road, were a dozen riot police tapping their plastic shields, like ewes and lambs bleating, letting each other know that they have a friend out there in the night.

A few ordinary uniformed officers were standing around trying to disperse the rubberneckers who were disrupting the flow of the traffic. Russell recognised some of the pavement princesses, whose pitch this normally was, talking among themselves, livid at missing their regular johns and champagne tricks on their way back from the City. A further gaggle of nosey-parkers stood around waiting for something to happen, seemingly hypnotised by what was beyond the riot cops. There was nothing to see but smoke, which hung dreamily in the night air. Russell approached some deputy do-right.

'Excuse me, mate, I live in Falkland Road. I need to get home.'

The copper was young, probably no more than twenty-three.

'Ah'm sorry, sir,' he said in a Glaswegian accent. 'We're not allowed to let anyone through. We're awaiting further instructions regarding local residents.'

'How am I supposed to get home then?'

'We should know soon, sir.'

'Look, I just want to get home.'

'My instructions are not to let anyone through. As I'm sure you're aware there are other matters of greater importance than residents having access to their homes.'

'So I can't come through, even though I live here.'

'Right.'

'This is unbelievable.'

'Can you move away from the barrier, sir?'

'*Yeravinalaugharentcha?*' said Russell, dumbfounded. This was serious. He looked at his watch. He had to get his stuff, had to get his passport. He only had two hours to get on the plane. 'I've got to get to Falkland Lane, I ain't got time to waste, mate . . .'

Fear gave the young copper courage. 'Sir, I've already told you. You can't go up there . . .'

'For fuck's sake . . .' said Russell. A rustle of nylon signified the presence of another cop.

'You got trouble here, Gordon?'

'Nothing I can't handle, Sarge.' The other one gave Russell a once-over, flexing his gloved hands before walking away. 'Now if you don't fuck off I'll nick you for affray. Got that?'

Fuck.

Gotta get home.

Russell headed back down Shadwell Road. He checked his watch again. Half nine. More than enough time for both Trevor and Ron to be down here looking for him. Better stay off the main streets. He ducked into a side road and realised what some of the noise he had been hearing was: every car alarm in the street was going off. With the old bill stretched more ways than Joan Collins' boat, every opportunist tea leaf in London would be out tonight on a car-thieving, shop-trashing, burglary bonanza. Any citizens with sense would be staying indoors looking out neglected gardening tools, rummaging through cutlery drawers or removing the tyre iron from the car boot. Just a bit of insurance.

Russell, on the other hand, had no fucking insurance, just over two hours to get to the airport and two psychotic career criminals, plus associated cronies, flapping at his heels. He wished he were a good burgher of Illingford settling in for a long night on guard duty cradling a garden spade in front of *Brookside*.

It looked like there was no way of getting home by road. He'd have to go cross-country – if he got behind one of the houses he could get down Station Road by working his way through the gardens. Then he'd only have a few streets to get down. After crossing the high street he'd be home and dry.

He trotted up to the end of the street where he would be less noticeable. Even with all the noise he was overpoweringly aware of the sound of his own movement. In the distance he could still hear shouting and screaming and the constant rhythm of the riot cops beating on their shields. But for the whirring of the helicopter it sounded as if he could be heading towards some kind of carnival, albeit one featuring a lot of bullyragged blues ready to rough-house anyone who danced towards them. There would be two kinds of cops. The whooping insolents who inched forward behind long shields that covered their whole bodies, and the mobile bunch with small, round shields and truncheons who appeared from behind their colleagues in little packs, tearing forth and manhandling wrongdoers.

When he reached the end of the street Russell climbed over the wooden fence that bordered the last uniform semi. The blue light of a television played through the net curtains and aluminium window. Probably watching the riot on the tube, thought Russell. Walking across the springy turf of the garden he wiped his nose and smelled creosote on his hands. By the time he'd gone over half a dozen fences he'd worked up a sweat, licking the salty moisture from above his upper lip and breathing heavily. He looked at his watch. Quarter to nine. He was definitely out of time. If they could get through the cordon then Ron and Trevor could catch him at any moment. He had to be wary, cast an eye around every corner.

He stopped for a moment and sniffed the air. It was thick with smoke, not the kind you get from a bonfire, more an acrid kind; there was a bitterness to it that hurt his lungs and lodged in his palate. He kept hopping over the fences, each the same height, some rickety, some stable, until the noise began to grow again. Momentarily he wondered how the riot had begun and was surprised that the whole thing didn't seem more strange to him, that he wasn't more shocked that the streets where he lived had become film crew fodder, broken glass shining on the pavement like glitter. But the afternoon's events and the current scenario had blurred into one, the level of fear and desperation hurtling around his system like coolant round an engine. He had to keep focused, had to slide through a white-knuckle night.

He came to the final fence and peered over. His face was warmed and bathed in an orange glow from a burning launderette. For a moment he wondered how the hell they'd set fire to a launderette. What is there to burn? He looked up and down the street. Nothing. No one to be seen. It was like the end of the world, like someone had dropped a bomb that removed human beings but left buildings intact.

He was tired from the effort of hauling himself over so many fences, but he had to do it one more time. He jumped up, locked his arms and swung his right leg up so that it was hooked over the fence. He made to spring over the fence but caught his trailing left leg on the edge of the wood and landed on the pavement.

Jesus Christ. It was his right knee that hurt. He sprang up, balancing on his left leg, trying to shake off the pain. It was too much, as if someone had removed the knee cap, and he sat down, his face red and contorted from the pain. Fuck! Shit! Bollocks! He rubbed his thigh, having once been told that the sensation of touch travels to the brain that much faster than pain. Better than that, the thigh was closer to the brain than the knee.

He didn't have time to waste and hobbled on to his feet. He had started for home when he heard the sound of fast-moving footsteps coming towards him. Russell threw himself into a doorway just as two riot cops hurtled round the corner. Flattening himself against the door he closed his eyes and listened to the panting men pass him by. He caught a snatch of the radio: '3.5, 3.5 need everyone you can spare over on Middleton Road. We've had to withdraw until we get reinforcements. They've got petrol bombs. Unconfirmed, repeat, *unconfirmed* report of handgun fire.'

Jesus. That's all he needed. Just trying to pull a bunk from the country and the place turns into Bosnia. They'd have tactical firearms squads on every corner before you knew it. Cops with equalisers and the full backing of the popular press.

Just two more roads and he'd be there. He passed a shoe

shop with scores of high-street casuals haemorrhaging from its broken windows. Next to it clouds of black smoke billowed from a Sierra that had been turned on its roof. Up the street a gang of kids, probably no more than ten or eleven years old, were trying to smash Woolworth's windows with bits of paving stone that they'd clawed from the road. The plate glass bowed every time it was struck, but wouldn't break.

He was home. Russell felt for his keys, but his hand passed through his jacket pocket. Christ almighty. The keys were gone, lost during his calamitous vault over the fence. He checked for the wedge. Thank fuck. It was still there. Don't panic. Russell pressed the bell for Mr Oza's flat, although he was rarely there, had got his family out to a nice semi in Chingford. He tried Mr Abache on the top floor, but remembered that he worked nights.

Russell stepped back from the door a few paces and, shoulder lowered, charged at it. He could feel that the Yale had loosened, but the mortice was still solid. Raising his left leg he hammered at the mortice until it began to give way, the red paint of the door frame jumping off to reveal green beneath. Fuck knows what this was doing to his knee.

It would probably only need one more kick . . .

He hadn't seen them coming. Without warning he found himself manhandled against the wall, his face pressed up against the brickwork so that he could feel the pigmentation of the mortice against his skin.

'You all right, George?' came a voice.

'Yeah, got 'im.'

'Hands against the wall, spread your legs and don't move a fucking inch.'

He'd been pinched. Russell tried being polite.

'Look, I know this is hard to believe, but I actually live here and I've lost my keys . . .'

'Zip it, you fucking comedian.'

'Got any 'cuffs, Rog?' asked one.

'Used mine on some Paki kid down the road.'

'Me 'n'all. Ain't they brought up none of them plastic ones yet?'

'What'dyou think? It's a fucking shambles.'

'It's true, I lost me keys,' butted in Russell.

'Don't waste your time, son.'

'For real. Believe me. I can tell you what's indoors in the flat.'

Russell peered behind him and snatched a view of two sets of blue trousers before he was told to keep his eyes in front of him.

'4.2 to Control,' one of them said into his radio. 'We've got another here we're going to have to lay down. Looter, corner of High Street and Falkland Road, over.'

'Roger 4.5,' came over the radio. 'Someone will be over to collect suspect soon.'

The policemen were both tired and edgy. For a few moments they stood listening to the frantic activity on their radios. 'You hear about Roy?' said one to the other distractedly. 'Fractured fucking skull. Brick in the 'ead after his helmet got knocked off over on Scottsdale Road. Big fucking cheer went up from those toerags when they saw him being carried off. Dancing round like a bunch of fucking savages. I tell you . . .'

The other suddenly raised his hand, having heard his call-sign. 'Roger,' he said, pressing the receiver on his lapel. 'They want us back on Lyonsdown Road. Re-grouping.'

'Well you shoot off, I'll wait for someone to pick this one up.'

'Sure?'

'Yeah, they'll have someone over soon.'

'Radio if you get any agg.'

'No worries, mate.'

One of the cops made off towards Lyonsdown Road, weaving snappily in between the debris scattered across the high street. In the distance a cheer went up, followed by a loud explosion echoing throughout the neighbourhood.

'It's a fucking crying shame,' said the policeman, fingering his truncheon. He removed his helmet and mopped his brow.

It was what Trevor had been waiting for. Walking swiftly from the shadows he struck the policeman a blow across the shoulder blades with his blue Louisville Slugger. The man crumpled to the floor face forwards, his helmet skidding across the street, scattering some ash into the air.

'Evening, Russell. Going somewhere?'

Russell turned to face Trevor and Ron, both of them perspiring heavily, boiling with the heat of exertion and rage in equal measure. The policeman's knife- and bullet-proof armour stuffed beneath his nylon jacket made him look ungainly, like some badly stitched and discarded soft toy. He moved slightly, trying to get to his feet, toppled and crashed to the floor again.

'I think you know what this is about,' said Ron.

Before Russell could form any kind of answer Trevor was at him, swinging the baseball bat around his head. Russell kept ducking and moving, trying to keep his balance while avoiding the blows and keeping an eye on Ron who stood behind his brother, encouraging him. Russell noticed there was a big black bruise on Ron's forehead and a cut that looked like it needed stitches.

'Get him, Trev. Kill the bastard,' Ron slurred. 'You're dead, Russell.'

Trevor gripped the Slugger in his left hand – his right was heavily bandaged – and traced long arcs with the bat that Russell found it easy to predict. He knew that if he could contain the conflict like this then Trevor, with only one good hand, would play himself out. Confident that he could out-run Ron, he could get away. Somehow he'd have to get back here to pick up his passport and money and . . . the bat lashed down inches from Russell's head. He could worry about his passport later.

The blows were coming less frequently. Trevor was tiring. Russell could sense an opportunity. He tried to stoop down to pick up a half-brick from the gutter but slipped, splaying his legs on the floor. It was the chance that Trevor needed. Russell twisted his body to avoid the bat, inadvertently dragging his leg into the blow. It was the right knee again. Christ. This time it felt like it had exploded.

Trevor had stopped momentarily, catching his breath and savouring Russell's pain. Knowing that he had to keep moving Russell hoisted himself on to his left leg and hobbled slightly, trying to buy time for his right to recover. After a few moments there was a minor improvement: it started to feel like he'd had a red-hot needle inserted through the knee-cap. He noticed Ron pulling away from Trevor on to his flank and knew that unless he got away from this place they would beat him to death. They would kill him outside his own front door.

He had to get to the noise, had to get where there were people. With his leg in this state he knew that he would not be able to outpace Ron and Trevor for long. Trying to shut off the nervous system in the bottom half of his body Russell turned on his heels and fled towards the noise. He was sure that he could feel bone rubbing bone and was thankful that he didn't have any time to think about the damage.

Picking his way among the glass and rubble that had transformed the high street into a kind of lunar landscape he tried to separate the noise inside his head from what was going on nearby. Small groups of kids furtively looted ransacked shops, grabbing as much as they could carry before disappearing up side streets. Satisfied that the three white men haring up the road were not old bill the kids paid them no attention, going about their job deafened by the cacophony of intruder alarms.

Russell thought that the action was probably occurring somewhere along Station Road, near the bus depot. He didn't want to look behind him, couldn't face the images of his pursuers. His attention was attracted to an odd shape that lay in the road. He had no time to waste but, just as his foot was about to land, he realised that – Christ, no – he was about to press down upon a face. There was no avoiding it. His Reebok pushed down, but the visage didn't give and Russell saw that this was not what he had feared but a mannequin dragged from Top Shop, stripped bare of its clothes and left sprawled in the street with the other looted wreckage.

Russell kept going, forcing himself not to think of the pain. And briefly the whole thing seemed so absurd that he couldn't help a smirk passing across his face. Everything was out of control – Trevor, Ron, the rioters – like being on a crazed, high-speed motorway with no off-ramp and no traffic cops. It didn't seem possible but, tonight, the streets were theirs.

Chapter Thirty-Five

Like an exhausted, hunted animal Russell knew he was going to have to go to ground soon. The pain was unbearable; at every step he feared that he might feel his leg buckle and collapse beneath him. He must find people. Although Ron was trailing a good hundred yards behind him he could feel Trevor's hot, toxic breath on his collar. Russell feared a trip from behind and a miserly end on the pavement.

The volume of noise was gradually increasing and he sensed the buzz of people. He chanced a quick glace over his shoulder. Ron was nowhere to be seen and Trevor was losing ground, his weaselly face purple with fatigue. Russell was almost there, if only he could . . .

There was no way of knowing why it happened where it did. His knee gave up and he was on the floor, not knowing whether to try to lie still and hope Trevor didn't see him, or just to start crawling. The pavement was freezing to his touch as he tried to put more distance between himself and his pursuer. He looked round to see that Trevor had stopped running. Hands on hips, head bowed, chest rising and falling rapidly trying to catch his breath, he knew that the chase was over. His prey had been run to ground. Now it was time for the kill.

The air was so raw it stuck in Russell's throat as he tried to gather himself for what was to come. Trevor was almost upon him and a smile had risen on his face. Momentarily he stopped and scoured the street. He'd dumped the slugger during the chase, but found a metre-long piece of two-by-four which he tapped on the outside of his leg as he advanced towards Russell.

'You've had this coming,' said Trevor. 'This ain't just for

Ron.' Russell was lying on his back waiting for the beating to begin, vainly searching for an equaliser. He watched the piece of wood swing behind Trevor's head and come down towards him. He raised his heel towards Trevor's striking arm and caught him on the middle of his forearm. Trevor dropped the wood and pursed his lips in pain.

'Bad mistake, cunt,' said Trevor, picking up the wood again. Russell realised that if he could rotate on his backside he could slide round and keep a distance between Trevor and his head and upper body. It wasn't much of a chance but it was something. Trevor approached and Russell slid forward and kicked him in the shin before he had a chance to strike a blow. Then he wished that he hadn't, wincing in pain as his bad leg dragged lamely beneath him.

Taken aback by the assault, Trevor stepped forward with the stick – the first blow missed but the second caught Russell flush in the abdomen, making him gasp. Trevor followed this up with a couple of body blows. Russell vainly tried to protect himself with his arms. He didn't feel the kick, but it caught him right in the temple, causing him briefly to go limp. The pain was of the explosive type, not feeling too bad at first before flowering seconds later in a sickening sourness. Trevor whooped with delight as his victim keeled to one side, and brought down the stick on Russell's shoulder.

'You're a dead man, Russell,' brayed Trevor.

'No, Trevor. You've made a mistake,' said a voice that Russell didn't recognise. 'You're the dead man.'

In his groggy state Russell raised his head to see a group of five Asian youths. All of them were dressed for the street, Hilfigered up and armed with bits of wood, bottles and bricks. All had handkerchiefs or bandanas wrapped around their faces. One of them, smaller than the rest and wearing a tight blue Stussy baseball cap, pulled down his mask to show Trevor his face.

'Remember me?' he asked Trevor. 'Well, I've got news for you. It's payback time – and I ain't talking money.'

Trevor had a strange expression on his face, somewhere between disbelief and astonishment. Like someone who'd arrived home to discover a surprise party in his honour when it wasn't even his birthday. He made no effort to defend himself as Zaffir Khan strode forward and drove a blade into his belly, just stood there for a couple of seconds fingering the handle of the sticker before toppling over into a couple of black rubbish sacks, doubled up around his wound.

It was then that Russell realised that Ron had come upon the scene. He was carrying his jacket and his face was crimson. Zaffir pulled his mask up about his face and looked at the man.

'I know who you are,' said Zaffir. 'Fuck off or you'll get the same.'

Ron raised both hands and pressed them to his head as if trying to contain an exploding skull.

'I said fuck off,' said Zaffir. Ron just pointed at him, his eyes ablaze, gently nodding his head. He pointed at each of the youths then raised his forefinger to his neck very slowly and passed it across his throat. He looked once again at Trevor who lay motionless, a huge pool of purple blood forming by his side. The front of his grey sweatshirt was stained claret and his skin had taken on a waxy quality as colour drained from his face. His feet twitched as if mimicking some fleet-footed dance.

Ron made to leave but turned as if remembering something minor. He looked at Russell. The two men regarded each other with an intimacy that Russell would always remember.

'I'll be back for you,' said Ron, his voice flat and bitter. 'Never close your eyes.' As he walked slowly up the empty street a helicopter buzzed low overhead and trained its searchlight upon him. Refuse and debris was whipped up by the hot gusts of the engine and rotor blades, and a tornado of filth scoured the street like some raging mythological creature. Embers fell from the sky, as if bearing messages. Ron Chisholm disappeared from Russell's view with a revelatory beam upon him that made it look for all the world like he was being transported into an alien craft.

The helicopter disappeared into the night, buzzing over to monitor events near the besieged police station. There were no clouds tonight and the April sky was a deep, deep blue, the colour of Indian ink. A plane traversed the sky above Russell, its nose pointed upwards as it gained altitude. He'd lost track of time. Maybe that was his plane heading towards the southern hemisphere at hundreds of miles an hour with Sonia peering from the window, an empty seat by her side.

She was gone and so was his chance of escape. He tried not to think about it, taking a look at his leg. There was no blood showing through his jeans but the pain was increasing by the second as the adrenaline subsided. The youths had gone and he was alone, breathing the blood in his nose and the burning buildings around him. He raised his body from the icy pavement and looked for someone to rescue him.

Chapter Thirty-Six

They had closed the doors. That, they said, was that. The luggage was stowed and the last of the children and old people were now seated and asking the stewardesses how to work their in-flight entertainment systems and fussing with their small acrylic pillows.

A perma-tanned steward announced that the flight was full and that the slight delay was on account of a passenger failing to check-in. The seat, he said, had been re-allocated to someone waiting on standby.

One passenger missing, thought Sonia, trying to relax into her seat. One passenger missing. She watched the standby passenger, a tall, dishevelled man of about forty, stumble on to the plane before the door hissed shut. He squinted when a stewardess pointed him towards the back of the plane. He had too much hand luggage and apologised to those seated in the aisle seats whom he bumped with his over-stuffed rucksack. When he passed Sonia's row of seats she smelled that he needed a wash. His clothes reeked of tobacco smoke and his hair was stringy and matted.

They were moving, lurching towards the runway on legs so thin they looked like they should snap. The stewardesses put on a video, the usual charade of safety information, models miming away with uninflated lifejackets and oxygen masks. Sonia set her eyes on the gesticulating women, but her pupils were dead and her mind was elsewhere. She'd waited for three hours by the check-in desk. Watched the rest of the passengers arrive with hope and anxiety on their faces, at every moment forcing herself to think that maybe, in a minute, she'd see a familiar face working his way through the crowd, casting his eyes from stranger to stranger, visually sifting the swarming mass of people and luggage until he plucked her from her vigil.

As time passed the crowd thinned and Sonia was accompanied by a bored-looking cleaner and a couple of check-in staff who smiled understandingly as she explained for the umpteenth time that she intended to check in for the flight but could they possibly hang on, just for a few minutes, because her companion had mysteriously been delayed?

The airline staff had smiled and found her a seat in smoking and asked her if she was going to be all right. And after she'd wiped a small tear from her eye with the back of a shaky hand she'd nodded yes, she would be all right. She ghosted through security checks and passport control like a sleep walker surprised when anyone spoke to her, fretfully running through every possible reason for Russell's absence.

Gazing out of the window of the 747 into the black night she took her last look at London as they banked to the west before swinging to the south. She watched the patterns extending beneath her, the firmament at the centre of town and the strings of fairy lights that played out into the suburban wilderness. And though she felt a little sad and a little strange, there was an odd pleasure to being cocooned in the safety of the aircraft. She was tired from the tension of the day, exhausted by her escape from her husband and his terrible brother and waiting for Russell in an airport where it seemed that only she had been alone.

The no-smoking light went off as the plane began to level. Sonia reached for her Silk Cut and lighter which were wedged in the pocket by her knees that was stuffed with crumbs and duty-free brochures. As smoke curled from her lips she took another look at London as it slipped from view. Russell was there beneath her, somewhere within the light and shade. Sonia always thought the flight would signify something tangible about her and Russell, that they could soar above the ties that bound them to lives they had never planned. In her mind it wasn't meant to be like this, they were supposed to be riding high, propelled forward by Rolls-Royce engines and their faith in each other.

But life with Ron had done nothing if not make Sonia a

pragmatist. When the engines stilled and her feet touched sun-baked ground she would find Russell. She didn't doubt that she could make a new life for herself, could reinvent Sonia Chisholm and paint her anew, and it was in this spirit of renaissance that she would reclaim Russell from the fall-out of her former self. During the frugal, plasticised meal, the duty-free parade and the out-of-sync movie her mind was still churning with anticipation and anxiety, but Sonia took comfort from the knowledge that, even in her weakest moments, it had never occurred to her, not even for a second, not to get on the plane. And it was with this thought uppermost in her mind that she shut down her mind and fell into a profoundly contented sleep.

Chapter Thirty-Seven

It was all over the papers. Skin had brought them to the hospital. Pictures of Russell, bloody and broken, lying on a stretcher wearing a neck brace with a baffled, slightly dreamy look on his mug. Beneath the picture the caption ran: 'Hero Russell: pal Trevor wasn't so lucky'. Jesus.

Pal Trevor. According to the reports he and Trevor had left his flat to go to the aid of an injured policeman who had been attacked by 'race hate thugs'.

Unbelievable.

The police had come by to ask a few questions, but understood Russell's hazy recollection. He had, after all, been knocked unconscious by an unseen assailant who must have killed Trevor. All he could tell them was that the killer had definitely been white.

Skin knew that this might not be the whole truth, but he didn't ask what had really happened. Best not to. He'd shuffled in, head bowed, unsure whether he was welcome. His face was still puffed up and sore-looking and his hair sprouted out of the top of a thick bandage that was wrapped around his head, like a carrot top.

They'd exchanged a few words before Skin pulled the papers out of an old sports bag and spread them over the bedcovers for Russell to read, the old man's swollen, arthritic hands making the paper rattle. He didn't say that he was glad that Trevor was dead, but Russell knew that he was. In a low voice he told Russell that he'd heard that Ron had put a contract out on Russell. That he was already a dead man. That he should be making plans. That he could no longer call Illingford home. That he should be gone. And he wasn't just talking the manor, he was talking London.

'Make yourself scarce,' said Skin. 'Do a bunk. Up north. Scotland or something. Somewhere your boat ain't known. Make new friends. Build a life.'

And then he stood up and Russell thought for a moment that the old man might have had to look away for a moment to compose himself. But when he looked back there was nothing but dread in his eyes, hard stones set in the heavy fullness of his face.

'Be lucky, son,' he said. 'Don't expect we'll see each other again. Send me a card wherever you get to.' He made to go, but looked over his shoulder, turned again and scratched his neck absently.

'Look, I'm sorry about what happened, all right?' he said. Before Russell could nod, the old man had made tracks across the linoleum. A nurse waited patiently, holding the swinging door as he made his way off the ward. And even though the old man had chosen not to say it, Russell knew what he knew – that either one of them could be dead soon.

The time had passed slowly. The doctor had told him he'd be all right. A couple of bruised ribs and a fractured knee cap wouldn't have warranted a stay normally, but he'd twisted his neck badly, would need physio, and he'd been unconscious when they'd blued him in.

There was nothing they could do for him otherwise, they said. Just wanted to keep him under observation. He'd have to wait it out, go through the motions of healthcare with the NHS ghosts who traipsed around in their threadbare dressing-gowns trading small talk about their prognoses and what they were likely to get for lunch and wasn't the system a shambles these days what with the cuts.

Russell was doing his own observation – keeping watch for some ex-squaddie with shards of ice in his heart and a sawn-off inside his jacket. He kept his eyes on the door. He didn't know why, there was nothing he could do beyond throwing his bedpan at the assassin. Force of habit he supposed. He found himself sitting for hours focusing on the same spot. He didn't want to, but he couldn't help looking. He told himself not to. He didn't want to see death approaching

But he did. The doors swung open and a tall man in bicycle leathers strode into the room scoping the patients. With his helmet on and his heavy biker boots he looked like some footsoldier from *Terminator 2*. Ron would have liked that. Russell opened his eyes wide, suddenly angry that this was how it was going to be, that he was just going to lie there and wait for someone to pump holes in him.

Their eyes met and Russell set his teeth awkwardly, jutting his jaw slightly forward. Fuck this. If he was going to die he was going to look this fucker right in his face. Make the bastard live with it.

The man approached as if drawn towards him, his footsteps slow and purposeful. Russell maintained his stare, he saw that beneath the visor the assassin's eyes were grey. For a moment he thought of Trevor's cold-fish stare. Those eyes that gave nothing back.

The man reached into his leather jacket. So this was how it was going to be.

'Russell Fisher?'

For a moment he thought about saying no, just playing dumb.

'Yeah.'

The man pulled his arm out of his jacket decisively. Russell braced himself.

'Courier. Got a delivery for you. Letter. Sign here,' he said, pointing a greasy finger at a soiled docket sheet he produced from inside a plastic folder.

Russell stared blankly at him. He managed to sign his name, even with his cast on, but he was too surprised to say thank you.

'I thought you were here to kill me,' he said to the courier, who laughed the way people do when they don't understand what the hell you're saying, but think that you're trying to make a joke. 'Do me a favour. Just open it and leave it on the bed.'

When the man had gone Russell reached into the unevenly torn envelope. With one hand he pulled out a plane ticket. He held it up to his face for further examination. It was for that evening, one way, to Cape Town.

He closed his eyes and laid his head back on the pillow.

Chapter Thirty-Eight

Former Council Leader Malcolm Goodge had cause for celebration last Thursday when he was elected MP for Hampton Green South in a by-election caused by the death of veteran Labour MP Dame Brenda Smith. Goodge, who had led the local Labour Party for eight years and been Council Leader for six, sent a special message to the people of Illingford.

'Without the encouragement and commitment of my friends and supporters in the borough I would never have been able to stand for Parliament,' Goodge commented from his house in Hampton Green. 'Although I am no longer representing the people of Illingford I thank them for all they have given me and everything I have learned while serving them. I wish the Borough every success in the future.'

All Fourth Estate books are available at your local bookshop or newsagent, or can be ordered direct from the publisher.

Indicate the number of copies required and quote the author and title.

Send cheque/eurocheque/postal order (Sterling only), made payable to Book Service by Post, to:

> Fourth Estate Books
> Book Service By Post
> PO Box 29, Douglas
> I-O-M, IM99 1BQ.

Or phone: 01624 675137

Or fax: 01624 670923

Or e-mail: bookshop@enterprise.net

Alternatively pay by Access, Visa or Mastercard

Card number:

Expiry date ....

Signature ....

Post and packing is free in the UK. Overseas customers please allow £1.00 per book for post and packing.

Name ....

Address ....

....

....

Please allow 28 days for delivery. Please tick the box if you do not wish to receive any additional information. ☐

Prices and availability subject to change without notice.